WORLD SAVING
— AND —
OTHER DISASTERS

WORLD SAVING
AND
OTHER DISASTERS

Bethany Meyer

World Saving and Other Disasters

Copyright © 2022 by Bethany Meyer.

All rights reserved. Printed in the United States of America. No part of this book may be used or reproduced in any manner whatsoever except in the case of brief quotations embodied in critical articles or reviews. This book is a work of fiction. Names, characters, businesses, organizations, places, events and incidents either are the product of the author's imagination or are used fictitiously. Any resemblance to actual persons, living or dead, events, or locales is entirely coincidental.

For information contact :

5935 Talbot Road, Lothian MD 20711

Edited by Angela Watts Cover design by MiblArt

Paperback: 978-1-7375984-2-8 Ebook : 978-1-7375984-3-5

Library of Congress Control Number: 2022919754

First Edition: December 2022

To the friend who read this in a coffee shop and almost cried. I still feel kind of bad about that, but also maliciously happy.

GLOSSARY AND TERM GUIDE

Ambrack (AM-brak) — A satyr of some small importance in satyr territory.

Aro (AIR-oh) — The country where Wick and Archer live, a coastal country wherein eight different sentient species live in harmony.

Caihu (KYE-hoo) — A prophetic centaur, now considered mad and irrelevant. Deceased.

Cohn (CONN)—A centaur known for her strategy and cunning.

Crowned Head — The ruler and king of the manghar.

Dana (DANN-ah)—A human woman and a friend of Archer.

Door in the Wall — A magical door that one of the long-past human sorcerers created, allowing one to pass through walls.

Eland (ELL-and) — A young centaur with red hair, still in apprentice training.

Eri (AIR-ee) — One of the biggest cities in seraph territory, well-known for its riches and beauty.

Fair Folk (FAYR FOHK) — A race of small, nomadic agricultural people. About three apples tall.

Farris (FAIR-iss)—A scholar and a centaur friend of Cohn.

Frutelken (froo-TELK-ehn)—A common household drink of the seraphs, with a fruity, spicy taste.

Heather Stone — A magical stone used to cast spells for the protection of Aro, currently split into eight pieces and given to each race in Aro for safekeeping.

Hessen (HESS-ehn)—An important family in the seraph city of Tor.

Hirim (HEER-imm)—a red-haired centaur of some small importance in the centaur valley, and Eland's father.

Isleberg (IZZLE-berg)—A small family of Fair Folk living in Tor.

Kanri (KAHN-ree)—A satyr girl tasked with protecting the Heather Stone.

Leshy (LESH-ee) — A race of people with the appearance of trees on legs, with glowing yellow eyes. The protectors of the forest.

Lif (LEEF) — The younger sister of Wick, also known as Reesa.

Manghar (MANG-harr) — An aggressive and terrifying race with the appearance of giant bats on two legs.

Nixies (NICKS-ees) — A race of pale green people with many teeth, dressed in armor and sea findings.

Oak Leaf — The formal name for the leshy piece of the Heather Stone, named for its ornate setting, which is shaped like the leaf of an oak tree.

Oman (OH-mahn)—A centaur man known for his diplomacy and his soft voice.

Ongel (ON-gehl) — A centaur with dark skin and hair, commonly a mentor figure to centaur apprentices and to messengers.

Ryga (RYE-gah)—A mysterious creature Wick and Archer encounter.

Seraphs (SAER-affs) — The winged people.

Sker (SKARE)—A seraph colony in the Northern mountains.

Skorffv (SKOR-fah-veh)—An old seraph word meaning -1. The moment between flying and falling. -2. A moment where failure is imminent but anything is possible as the inevitable has yet to happen.

The Scorch — An unknown outside force bent on destroying Aro, only seen once every few hundred years.

Tinor (TEE-norr) — A centaur with grey hair, a mentor among the centaurs.

Tor (TOHR)—One of seraph territory's richest and most important cities.

Transmogrification (Trans-mohg-riff-ih-CAY-shuhn) — A leshy's ability to change his or her appearance into something different, usually used as a defense mechanism. Irreversible and normally discouraged by the leshy.

CHAPTER ONE:

Two Idiots and an Unfillable Bag

IT WAS MIDNIGHT, and Archer and Wick were in prison for trying to save the world.

But they wouldn't be stuck for much longer.

Wick pressed his face between the bars and checked left and right. Nothing moved in the prison's silent hallway.

A mysterious note had arrived earlier with their lunches: *Be ready to leave tonight.* They both searched their plates at dinner time but found no further directions.

"Maybe no one's coming after all," Archer muttered in the next cell. "Could've been a trap of some sort."

"Strange trap," Wick answered in a low voice. "There were no instructions, nothing that could be trying to trick us into acting rashly. All the note said was that we're getting out tonight."

"Could still be a trap."

Wick ignored Archer and watched for movement

through the windows facing his cell. No shadows broke the slats of light on the stone floor, and outside nothing made any unusual noise. Slowly the night eased into the dark hours of early morning. Could Archer be right? Was no one coming after all?

A soft click echoed from the opposite end of the jail. Wick slid closer to the bars and squinted down the single narrow row of cells. Not a breeze stirred the straw bedding in the other cells. The sound of hooves crept closer across the cobblestone floor, and at last moonlight glinted on bright red hair.

"Eland!" Wick said. His fingers prickled with nerves. "We're getting out after all?"

"You are." Eland approached Wick's cell, a sack clenched in his hands. "I've been talking to the centaurs, and I convinced a few of them to let you out. . . But because of Tinor and his group, we're going to release you as quietly as possible. Tinor still adamantly opposes you, and his group would make a spectacle if he knew about this. I'm here to get you out of the valley quickly, and once you're gone you can start making new plans."

Sprawled dramatically across the straw in his cell, Archer said, "Good. If no one had released us by then, I was going to spring us free tomorrow night."

Eland's brow crinkled. "I don't think you could have. People move around in the valley all night, so someone would have noticed if you escaped. And you couldn't unlock the cells on your own."

Archer sat up, making the straw crackle. "I've gotten out of much better jails than this. I already had my plan ready to go."

Wick shot Archer a warning glance, and Archer stopped talking with a raise of his eyebrows.

With an echoing *clank*, Wick's cell door swung open. Eland inserted the key into the lock of Archer's cell. "We'll need to move quickly. I don't know if anyone will try to stop us."

Archer frowned. "Are the centaurs letting us go or aren't they?"

"They are, but again, not everyone agrees on that. Everyone's just a jumble of conflicting opinions," Eland said. "We've still seen nothing in our visions that could prove you right. So a few of us have made an executive decision to release you before anyone can stop us." He swung the second door open. "Right now, I doubt anyone will hunt you down if you leave, but the centaurs also can't protect you once you're gone. That's the situation."

Wick nodded.

Stepping back, Eland pulled a strap off his shoulder. "Here," he said to Archer. "I thought you'd be happy to see this."

Archer's eyes lit up. "Ecs*tat*ic." He snatched the unfillable bag from Eland's hand and squeezed it tight like a long-lost friend.

"I was able to retrieve most of your things, but not all," Eland said. "There were some odd rocks they threw out, sorry."

Archer scowled. "That was rude of them." He flipped the bag open and stuck his nose inside. "Sasha?"

The bag snorted softly.

Eland jerked his head for them to follow him. "We need to move. Come on."

Wick and Archer followed him without another word.

With the tiny size of the prison, only a few steps took them to the exit. Wick stopped in the prison's doorway and glanced around the valley, wondering when someone would notice them and sound the alarm. Although according to Eland, the odds were as much in their favor as against. They hurried across the open space and into the shadow of a gold pavilion. Scattered across the valley, Wick spotted the movements of other people, either early risers or night owls or those involved in late-night studies.

"The best way out will be the tunnel," Eland said, turning to them. "But we'll have to cross the whole valley to reach it. It would be faster to take the mountain path behind the prison, but that would take you through a residential area, and lots of people might see you. So we're taking the tunnel. We just have to make it safely across the valley, that way." He pointed.

The valley had never seemed so broad and so. . . exposed. They would be walking out in the open for quite a ways. And the moonlight was bright tonight, too, like daylight.

What if someone caught them?

Eland looked back at Wick. "Walk fast."

Wick nudged Archer's arm. "Let's go before I run out of nerve."

Resolve took over Archer's face. "Right."

The three of them started across the open space.

Dry grass and fallen leaves crunched under their feet, too loudly for comfort. Their shadows flitted across the grass, first centaur, then human, then seraph. Temporarily, they passed by a group of boulders that cast them in shadow, and Wick felt safe from any prying eyes. But all too quickly, they left the cover behind.

A few months ago, Wick never would have needed to sneak out of the valley under the cover of darkness.

If I could ever get anything right, maybe I wouldn't have to now, either.

Wick put his head down and walked faster.

In the middle of the valley, they passed by a centaur woman studying a book by moonlight. Wick's mind screamed with alarm bells. The centaur woman glanced up at the passersby, then went back to her studies.

Still, the muscles of Wick's shoulders tensed, and his fingers prickled with nerves. Maybe one centaur woman wouldn't care that they were leaving, but what about the rest of the valley? How long until someone noticed them and gave chase? Surely it wouldn't be long.

Noticing Wick's unease, Archer nudged Wick's shoulder. "Remember, we have a backup plan."

In case anyone saw them that might try to stop them, Archer's backup plan was for Wick to make himself look really big while Archer crouched down behind him. From a distance, Archer claimed, they would look something like a centaur.

Wick didn't like that backup plan.

Eland beckoned for them to hurry. A full run would draw too much attention, but they walked as quickly as they could. Wick's heart tried to beat out of his chest.

Wick's eyes darted as they went. When they had covered nearly three-quarters of the distance, something darted in the corner of his eye.

Any trace of the backup plan disappeared from his memory.

"Get down, get down!" he whispered.

Archer's head turned as he spotted the same thing, and he lunged for some tall grass with Wick close on his heels. Wick's foot caught on something, and he fell directly on top of Archer. The sweet-smelling stalks of grass nearly stabbed him in the eye.

The pair of centaurs were closing in fast. There

wasn't time to get more comfortable, so Wick did his best to lie still. Then he realized Eland wasn't hiding.

As Wick watched between stalks of grass, Eland straightened his sleeves and began strolling away from the grass where Wick and Archer hid. As he did he took a small book out of his robe and flipped through it as though he was looking for something.

The pair of centaurs in Wick's peripheral vision closed in. They approached Eland.

"Eland," one of them called, "did you hear something?"

Eland looked up from his book. "Like what?"

"I heard something," the other centaur said. "A crash or something of the like."

"Ah, that was me," Eland responded. He pointed to the tall grass, and Wick stiffened. "There was a fallen branch, so I threw it into the grass. I'm sorry if it scared you."

The centaurs exchanged some other small talk and kept walking. On his back, half sprawled across Archer in the grass, Wick tried to stay still until they were gone. After a few seconds, Archer squirmed and shoved at Wick's legs.

"Get off me!"

"Sorry, sorry," Wick whispered, rolling off Archer's back. Archer sucked in a huge breath.

"You're huge!" Archer hissed. "Suffocate someone else next time."

"Sorry!" Wick scrubbed at his elbow where it had landed on some sharp stalks. "Come on, we have to go."

This time they did run. Eland couldn't fully run, not without leaving them behind, but Wick and Archer raced, limbs pumping, clothes flapping, mouths open. Wick could taste the dew in the air.

The edge of the valley drew nearer. Wick spotted the shadowy hollow where the tunnel led out of the valley. It was only a few yards away now. He picked up his pace.

They ran into the musty darkness of the tunnel, and Wick skidded to a stop, listening. No sounds of alarm came from the valley. For now, no one had realized they were gone. If they were lucky, no one would realize before morning.

"I think we're safe," he murmured to Archer. "Let's keep going."

"I need to stay here," Eland said. "I want to talk more of the centaurs over to your side if I can."

Wick stopped a few yards further on and looked back. "Thank you."

"And Wick? Don't leave me out this time. I don't want to wake up one morning and find out you staged a coup."

Wick tried for a reassuring smile. "I'll try to get our plans to you as they happen."

"Good luck," Eland said.

"Thank you," Wick answered. "And to you, too. I know talking your way out of this won't be easy."

Eland nodded. "I hope I'll see you soon." Then he disappeared.

Already halfway down the tunnel, Archer turned and shouted, "Come on, Wick!"

Wick left centaur territory behind and raced down the tunnel after Archer.

CHAPTER TWO:

Why I Don't Regret A Single Thing I Stole

AFTER LEAVING THE TUNNEL, they ran again, trying to put as much distance as possible between themselves and the valley. After about ten minutes, Wick waved for Archer to stop and collapsed against a tree.

When he could speak again, Wick gasped, "My chest feels like it's going to explode."

Archer leaned against the other side of the tree and took a few deep breaths. "That's normal."

"I know it is. It still hurts."

Archer dug through the unfillable bag and made a harrumphing noise. "He said they threw out my rocks, he didn't say they also stole my pots and pans. What am I supposed to cook with?"

When Wick didn't answer, Archer circled around the tree and sat against a nearby stump. "Where are we headed?"

Wick shrugged. "I don't know. One thing is for sure,

if we're going to try this again, we'll have to go about it differently. Stealing isn't going to work a second time; they'll have put everything under heavier security now."

"I thought you were going to say 'stealing is wrong'."

"That too."

"Yeah, that's what I figured. What do you suggest, then, O Diplomat?"

Wick tilted his head back against the tree bark. "I'm not sure yet. But it can't be stealing. We've made an impact, we've made our point, now we have to carry it through to the end." He paused. "It would be good to have a base of operations. Someplace where no one can surprise us and put us under arrest, where we can formulate some real plans."

Archer looked up at the sky, and the moonlight reflected harshly off his face. "Pretty sure there aren't a lot of places like that. Just finding a place where no one wants to arrest *me* is hard enough."

In the woods behind them, something stirred. Wick sat up straight and looked around. "Did you hear that? I think they might be sending out searches already. We should get moving again."

Archer dragged himself upright. "Why do they have to be so efficient? We couldn't sit down and catch our breath for five minutes?"

Together they hurried into the trees. An advantage to leaving at midnight was the promise of hours of darkness to travel in, hidden. With any luck, by first light, they would be miles away from the valley.

As they walked, Wick considered their options. It certainly helped to have Eland on their side, and maybe with time, Eland could convince more centaurs over to their side.

Still, they needed more allies, but the last few weeks had only proven how few their allies were. Even Ongel, one of Wick's mentors and closest friends in centaur territory, had refused to believe what Wick said. As for Archer... Well, Archer couldn't have many allies.

The moon sank toward the western end of the brightening sky as Wick and Archer traveled away from centaur territory. Wick didn't know yet where they were going, but no one had come after them yet, so for that he could be grateful.

The sky was just starting to turn a weak shade of greyish pink when they first heard a sound.

Archer stopped mid-stride and turned his head into the breeze. "Did you hear that?"

"I did." There had been a faint sound from their right, somewhere past the line of trees. Almost like a sniff or a sneeze, gone so fast it would have been drowned out by a large enough wind.

There was someone else nearby.

Archer retrieved a hefty rock from the forest floor. Wick picked up a small tree branch and held it by his side. Then, as one, they moved quickly and silently toward the other side of the clearing.

The forest was still quiet. Perhaps the noise had only been an animal.

As they reached the trees, something came soaring out of the shadows and struck Wick on the shoulder.

The moment Wick hit the ground, the forest exploded. Five nixie men leaped out of the trees, their hair and nails long and unkempt, screaming bloody murder. Two of them were covered in the grey-blue clay of nixie war paint. All of them were armed. With a war cry, the sea people charged at Archer and Wick.

Archer hurled his rock, missing the biggest of the nixie men. One of the other men slammed into Archer, knocking him into a bush. They both vanished from sight, followed by two other nixies. The last few came after Wick.

Even as he had fallen, Wick managed to hold on to his branch. It was smaller and flimsier than he would have liked, but it was the only weapon he had. He let go of his injured shoulder and swung the stick, using all the force he had to whack it against the side of a nixie's head. The nixie tumbled sideways, giving Wick enough time to scramble up before the other one reached him. The second nixie swung his club, but Wick ducked it and slammed his shoulder into his attacker, throwing him back. The club flew into the trees. Wick's eyes followed the falling club, but the first nixie man scrambled up, his hand going for a knife at his belt.

Somewhere past the bushes, Archer cried out.

Just as the dagger appeared from the nixie man's sheath, hooves sthundered into the clearing, and a great voice shouted, "Peace!"

The two nixies in front of Wick both stopped in their tracks. But something in the bushes continued thudding, and the voice thundered, "I am Ongel of the centaurs, and I demand you cease immediately!"

As the scuffle in the bushes stopped, Wick turned around and faced his old mentor.

CHAPTER THREE:

Making Choices, All of Them Bad

WICK HAD NEVER SEEN Ongel's expression so dark. But then, until recently he had never seen him in armor, either, and they'd never before been at odds the way that they were over the Heather Stones. Ever since the ordeal with the Heather Stones began, it seemed that Wick saw a new side of Ongel every day.

Ongel towered over the group, his eyes alight and brow furrowed. Pawing the dirt with a hoof, Ongel demanded, "What is happening here?"

The nixie who had gone for the knife did his best to stand tall and look Ongel in the eye, but Ongel's stormy gaze never wavered. The confidence on the nixie's face flickered. "We caught these two escaping from your valley. Perhaps your prisons aren't as secure as you say."

Ongel's tail whipped. "They are secure enough. But they were never meant to be used."

The note of disappointment in his tone cut into Wick

like a shard of ice.

"Then how did these two escape?" the nixie insisted. "They were—"

"The question I have for you," Ongel interrupted, "is why you and your friends were lurking in these woods, waiting to ambush them, when all military forces were supposed to be withdrawn to reinforce the peace."

The nixie spluttered, and Ongel's deep brown face softened slightly.

"Of course," Ongel went on, "I understand that you may have only been passing through, peacefully, and thought you were the ones being attacked when these two appeared. You couldn't have known that we let them run to test our security."

Wick's blood ran cold. They had only been set free as a test?

Across from Wick, the nixie's mouth moved without a sound, as though he wanted to speak but couldn't find the words. He looked utterly disarmed by Ongel's news.

"Now, I'll thank you for your help and take our prisoners back to the valley." Ongel spread his hands. "I won't keep you from the rest of your journey."

The other nixies deposited Archer next to Wick. Archer's hands were bound behind his back, his left cheek already darkening into a bruise.

The nixies banded together and left the way they came, casting bewildered glances over their shoulders as they went.

The forest returned to silence.

Wick worked up the courage to speak. "Ongel—"

"Quickly," Ongel whispered, still watching the way the nixies had gone, "untie your friend."

Wick blinked. "Untie—"

"Yes, quickly, and follow me. Eland is waiting for us in a valley not far from here. We'll be hidden there."

Now as mystified as the nixies had been, Wick started on the knot that bound Archer's arms together. Wick's wounded shoulder blazed with pain, and he hissed between his teeth.

Ongel heard. "Did they injure you?"

The knot finally gave, and Wick unwound the ropes. "I think they only grazed me with the spear. It doesn't feel very bad." But how could he tell? He had never been *grazed* by anything before.

Whisking his arms free, Archer inspected his wrists for chafing. "They didn't have to tie it that tight. It's like they wanted to take my arms off."

"Maybe they did. Now come on," Wick urged.

They hurried after Ongel, going deeper into the woods and further away from the nixies.

"What do you think he's up to?" Archer whispered.

"I'm not sure," Wick responded. His shoulder still stung horribly. "It doesn't feel like a trap."

Archer made a faint, ambiguous noise.

Wick walked a little faster to catch up with Ongel. The first rays of the sun started to peek over the horizon, shining into their eyes. "Did we really only escape to test the valley's security?"

Ongel glanced back at him with a look of surprise. "No," he said gently. "It's unfortunate that we even had to use those prison cells; they were only built as a warning. The fact is that there *is* no security in the valley."

"Then why did you say so?"

"Because, my dear Wick, I had to say something that would make them leave. If they hadn't thought that everything was completely under control, they would have wanted to take you back to the prison themselves."

Relief filled Wick's heart. "So when Eland came, he really was letting us go?"

Ongel smiled and nodded. They approached the edge of a deep ravine and started down the side. Wick and Archer grabbed onto rocks and tree roots to let themselves down, but Ongel came rushing down all at once in a clatter of hoof beats and a shower of gravel. At the bottom, shielded by a shelf of overhanging rock, was Eland.

Eland rushed out to embrace Wick. "Thank goodness," he said with a breathy laugh as he released his friend. "When we heard the nixies, we thought all was lost already. But without the nixies, we probably wouldn't have found you again."

The four of them shifted to stand under the shelf of rock, where they would be hidden from anyone who looked down. The woods smelled damp.

"But why are you here?" Wick asked.

"Yeah," Archer agreed. "We had already gotten away."

"Because I was finally able to procure this for you." Ongel reached into one of the bags at his side and produced a familiar leather cord with a small pouch at the end.

Wick's mouth dropped open. "You're letting us have the centaur stone?"

Ongel's hand wrapped around the pouch. "Only so long as you let us help you with your plans this time."

Ongel deposited the necklace in Wick's palm. The weight of the bag and the crunch of the leather were so comforting and familiar that Wick's stomach clenched. He slid the cord of the pouch over his head and hung it around his neck.

"Hold up," Archer said. He squinted at Ongel. "You weren't on our side before. Wick said you tried to stop us. What changed?"

"I talked to him." Eland looked at Wick. "While you were in prison, I took him to see the trees, just like you said, and I told him everything you told me."

"It worked?" Wick's heart soared.

"It did. That's what convinced the others, too," Eland said.

"This is wonderful." Wick put a hand to his head, reeling. "With the help of the valley, we could—"

"Wick," Eland said, suddenly somber. He adjusted his hooves. "Ongel believed me because he already suspected he didn't have the whole picture. He was ready to listen, and he trusted you completely. Not all the centaurs feel that way. I told plenty of the others the same things that I told Ongel, but they still didn't believe me because their visions showed no danger. They just assumed that the trees were diseased."

Wick's heart dropped again. Even Archer's face fell.

"But," Ongel said kindly, "you have Eland, you have me, and a few of our friends as well. Already you have quite a bit more than before."

But also quite a bit less, Wick thought. Now they had no element of surprise, no allies, no stones save the centaur piece. Even with extra help, their next attempt would be no easier than the last.

"What will you do now?" Ongel asked. "What are your plans?"

"We don't have any yet," Wick admitted. "All I know is this time, we won't steal. I don't want to go through that again. Maybe we could talk some of the leaders into lending us their stones."

"But where will you go?" Eland asked.

"We were thinking about that, too." Wick rubbed a hand across his cheek as he thought. "I think we need some kind of diplomatic immunity. Someplace where no one can capture us because of the consequences."

"I wish I could offer you the shelter of the valley," Ongel lamented, rubbing the palm of his hand across his brow. "But as we said, you don't have nearly enough supporters there for it to be safe for you, and for that I'm sorry."

"We can't stay with the leshy," Wick said. "I hope they would take us in, but my people have so little weight in the political world, and I don't think we would be safe from enemies there either." He mused some more. "The satyrs' safe houses would be a good place, but they aren't meant for long-term residency, and the satyrs are too hostile toward Archer for that to work."

Archer shifted uncomfortably. "I might know a place."

Wick turned to him. "I thought you said there wasn't a place in the world where no one wanted you arrested."

"And that's still true," Archer protested. "There probably isn't one. But I'm pretty sure I know of a place where the people who want to arrest me. . ." he spread his hands, ". . . *can't* arrest me."

Wick was silent for a moment, processing what Archer had said. Then he took a quick breath. "Archer?"

"What."

"Don't take this the wrong way, but—Who *likes* you enough to give you diplomatic immunity?"

Archer made a face. "Is there a way *not* to take that the wrong way?"

"Just answer the question."

"Well, Wick," Archer said with an air of arrogance and disdain, "it may come as a surprise to you, but I come from a decently important family—in seraph territory. So what I'm saying is no matter what might or what kind of people come to arrest me, my family wouldn't let it happen."

Past Ongel, Eland was frowning. "What family?"

Wick turned to Archer. "Yes, what family?"

"The Hessens."

"Really?" Eland squinted at Archer's face. "I suppose I can see the resemblance."

"Of course you can, they're my parents," Archer said. "But I don't want to go to them. If we're going to the seraphs, we're going to Eri to stay with my grandfather. Oak Hessen."

Oak Hessen. An iron window frame imprinted with a leaf emblem flashed across Wick's memory. "The house we stole the seraph heather stone from?"

"Yes. But as it happens, my grandfather actually likes me, and I think we would be safe if we stayed with him."

Wick wasn't sure what to say about that, so he moved on. "Well, if we have that figured out, we have the *where* in order. Now we have to figure out the *what*. What is our plan? What are we going to do?"

"I think your best chance this time is to try banding everyone together," Eland said. "If you could get them all to unite for the cause, you wouldn't need to worry about being caught anymore."

Ongel nodded. "I agree."

"I don't work well with others," Archer said.

"I'm not so concerned about that as trying to unite everyone at all," Wick said. "The last time everyone in this nation united for a cause was the alliance two hundred years ago when they first used the magic of the Heather Stones to cast the barrier spell and keep the Scorch at bay. And think of how long that took. On top of that, if Eland couldn't convince any of the centaurs, think of how hard it would be to talk the manghar into this. Or the nixies. It just can't be done."

"I may have thought of something else, though," Archer said.

Everyone looked at him.

Archer pointed at Wick. "You told me that a while ago, some bandits got most of the stones and nearly wrecked the whole country. The stones are supposed to be that powerful, yes? I know the idea is to get all eight stones from each of the eight territories, but if some bandits could do all that with only some of the stones, we could probably put up your fancy barrier with only some of them."

"It. . . *could* work," Wick mused. He brightened. "And we would only have to convince a few people! This could work!"

"I don't think it's ever been tried," Ongel said, "but if that's what you want to do, we'll help you wherever it's needed."

"Thank you." Wick and Archer gathered their things, and Wick said goodbye to his friends. With that, all four of them climbed out of the ravine and went their separate ways: Ongel and Eland walking back toward the valley, Wick and Archer now heading north for seraph territory.

Once again, Wick and Archer were on a journey to gather the Heather Stones, and once again, they seemed to be at odds with the rest of the world. Many things felt like a repeat of before.

Still, Wick knew that nothing was really the same. His changed body proved that. He missed the weight of his messenger's bag on his now human shoulder, but what did he need that bag for now? He wouldn't be carrying any messages, maybe ever again, and anything they needed to carry could go in the unfillable bag. The clothes he wasn't used to needing moved around his limbs with jarring unpredictability, and the boots weighed on his feet.

The sun poured over the horizon now in wide beams, bathing everything in lemon yellow light. He lifted his face to it, and suddenly remembered that he could no longer drink the sun's rays. The sun was warm, and it was bright. But it stayed on the surface of his skin without providing that familiar blast of pleasant energy. His heart twinged with sadness. The sun was still good and comfortable, but it no longer held the same meaning that it used to. It used to mean life and energy and wakefulness, now it was only a nice feeling on the skin and a glaring brightness in the eyes.

Some things would never be the same.

But Wick had chosen to change his form willingly, and now that he had changed, he could never go back.

If Archer noticed Wick's sadness, he said nothing. They walked in silence for hours. Occasionally they had to take cover to avoid some other travelers or change direction when they heard the sound of voices. The last thing they wanted was to be caught again, especially somewhere that Ongel couldn't rescue them.

Toward noon, they both found they were hungry. The gnawing in Wick's stomach was a new and unpleasant feeling, and he wondered how all the other creatures could stand feeling so hollowed out every time they needed food.

He turned to Archer. "How can anyone stand being hungry?"

"I don't know, I guess we get used to it early on.

When we're babies, and we're allowed to cry about it." Archer dug through the bag as they walked. "But you had better not start crying about it, or I'll pretend I don't know you."

"I'm not an infant, I won't be crying," Wick said icily.

"That's what I thought. Now, did those centaurs leave my food in here or not?" Archer dug deeper. "Oh, they restocked it. With *fruit*. And nothing else."

"They live in a valley full of fruit trees and only eat meat on special occasions." Wick caught the two apples Archer threw to him and sank his teeth into one. Teeth. Another strange thing that came with his new body, and another thing he hadn't thought of before changing.

"It's a shame we can't work from the valley," Wick said once he had swallowed. "It would be a lot easier to recruit the other races if we had the centaurs to support us. But with Tinor's group against us, it just isn't possible."

Archer frowned at the pear in his hand. "That Tinor guy is a real jerk. I think we're better off without him."

"He was one of the ones who trained me once my messenger job took off," Wick said, and Archer clamped his mouth shut. "He took me under his wing ages before I even met Ongel or Eland, and he taught me everything about the various territories and how they interact with one another. But," he went on, "he's always had a strong moral compass. I guess that's what turned him against us; he can't agree with our methods."

"*You* didn't agree with our methods, either," Archer pointed out. "At least you used your eyes in the end. Doesn't seem to me like he's doing that."

"Hmm." Wick then asked the question that had been nagging at his mind since the ravine. "You said you come from a family of some importance. I've been inside and out of seraph territory and I know almost everything about the culture. Seraphs have a democratic government where heads of households make decisions. There is no nobility."

"Yeah, I know that."

"So how is your family important?"

Archer rolled an orange from one hand to the other, trying to avoid looking at Wick. "First of all, I said 'a decently important family', not 'a family of some importance'. You got the wording all wrong. Secondly," he went on bitterly, "I know seraphs don't have nobility, and so do they. But that doesn't stop them from letting some people climb the ladder. There aren't a lot of them that try it, just a handful who think they're lords and ladies, but they exist. And they're sneaky, too. You wanna know why you don't know about them? Because they don't want you to."

Wick's brow furrowed.

"They stay under the radar of the centaurs, and they stay under the radar of diplomats. To you, they would have slightly nicer houses, and that's all. But they control the cities, and they influence the people. Seraph territory might not have nobles, but they have some sneaks that are close enough. And my *father* is one of them."

"Then what kind of influence does your grandfather have? Since he isn't one of the nobles," Wick guessed, taking another bite of the apple.

"My father has influence because he takes it. My grandfather has influence because he deserves it. He didn't climb the ladder like my father did. He's a good person, and people like him. They listen to him because they respect him." Archer paused. "And he actually cares about me, so I'd rather go to him than stay with my family."

Wick thought of the disappointment he expected from

his family when he saw them next. "I can understand that. Not all of it, but a little."

Archer made a noise that sounded like a laugh and dug at the skin of his orange with his fingertips. "I can guess. You didn't even want to see your family."

"It's not like that." Wick thought about what he wanted to say before he continued. "I love them, because they're my family, and they care about me. But I don't feel like I know them very well. It's normal for my people's children to be sent away to school at a young age, and then come back when they're older and they're done their education. It's normal. And it seems like everyone else is fine with it. For them, the bond doesn't weaken, but I've felt distant from my family for a long time. I never see them, I never spend time with them, and I don't understand them. But at the same time. . . I don't want to let any of them down."

Archer watched him without speaking.

"First I had to get my education, and then I did well as a messenger and needed training for that." Wick stepped over a log. "Then my route expanded, and I was gone for more time and home for less. And now that the messenger thing is probably over, I feel like I have to succeed with the Heather Stones or I'll have let them down again. If I can do this I can still do something for my people."

"I don't see why you should feel obligated to people you don't know," Archer said. "I don't see the point. If you don't know them, either get to know them better or don't. Obligation doesn't work in place of actual love, that's just how it is."

"I know. But it's all I've got." With that, Wick decided to give up on the conversation and inhaled. "How long do you think it will take us to get to Eri? About two days?"

Archer squinted at the sun, then the woods in front of them, as though he could scope the distance. "Give or take. If we don't take any pit stops in anyone's jail cells."

"We only have a few months to get the stones together and stop the Scorch. And we already lost a few weeks in jail."

"I know. But it'll be fine."

CHAPTER FOUR:

Traveling Companions

MID-AFTERNOON, dark clouds gathered overhead, then, toward evening, they let loose, pouring down rain in torrents. If this were casual travel, they probably would have found some shelter and waited it out. But Wick didn't want to stop, and Archer said he didn't care if it was raining. They kept walking with the rain pouring down their faces in rivers and their hair sticking to their foreheads.

Twice again they heard other travelers in the forest and had to take cover until the danger passed. Wick found himself missing the days when another traveler had been a surprise or at worst a vague nuisance. Now they were dangerous.

The second time, as they hid in the mud behind a clump of bushes, Wick hissed, "Please tell me your grandfather can write us some kind of papers so this doesn't keep happening."

"I'm hoping that too," Archer whispered back. "Now shut up or they'll hear you."

Once the sound of footsteps faded, they got up and

continued their journey. The rain had stopped, and the crickets were starting to sing, something that was clearly getting on Archer's nerves.

"Being wet would be bad enough without having to listen to insects shrieking, too," Archer muttered, trying to stomp on a particularly loud cricket that sat too close to the path.

"Leave it alone, Archer," Wick said, already tired of the crickets himself but more tired of Archer's grumbling. "We need to keep moving."

Archer stomped at the cricket one more time and missed. The cricket escaped into the underbrush.

"What *was* your plan to get out of the valley?" Wick asked, remembering.

"Running really, really fast," Archer replied. "Plus I was counting on you knowing some secret ways to get around the valley without being seen. You always know something like that."

"I see. And how did you plan to get out of the locked cells? Picking the locks?"

"I'm not very good at picking locks, actually." Archer clasped his hands and swung them up over his head, stretching his back. "But there was an aeration vent in the back of my cell. A little too small, though. So I originally planned to dislocate both of my shoulders—"

"In your plan, we wouldn't have escaped at all, is what you're saying," Wick said.

"What? No. We were getting out."

"I didn't think I could possibly be more grateful to Eland for getting us out, but apparently today is a day for miracles. Maybe you'll stop talking sometime today too."

Archer frowned.

"What do you know, I was right."

"Hey!"

A moment later, Archer asked, "But was I right? You know some sort of secret way to get around the valley."

Wick squinted into the distance. "Sort of. There are lots of tunnels in the valley linking the surface to the caverns beneath, and they connect most of the valley."

"Knew it."

"But it wouldn't have gotten us out of the valley. None of them let out outside the mountains."

"I was still right."

Come midnight, they couldn't walk anymore and did their best to find dry ground to sleep on. There wasn't much to be had. In the end, even the 'dry' ground they found turned out to have a massive damp spot under Wick's back, and the moisture seeped into his shirt along with the chill.

In his sleep, he heard voices. There were two things in the trees, watching him and Archer.

"Soon," one said.

"Not soon enough," said the other.

The second creature was larger than the first.

"What strange things."

"They think their rocks can save them."

"Their rocks couldn't save them before, why would they try again so soon?"

"These creatures have no grasp on the impossible. They are foolish and they are small. They can't fight the fire."

"It's coming for them all."

"They had their days in the sun, now it's our turn."

"I want this place to burn."

Wick's eyes snapped open. He jerked upright. His eyes raced across the branches where the two things had crouched, but nothing was there. Not even a bird.

He thought about waking Archer and asking him if he had heard it too, but he knew waking Archer would have more consequences than reward, so he decided not to and laid back down.

The dreams that followed were not worth going back to sleep for. He dreamed that they had failed, and he was forced to stand in the ruins of his home, watching the fences and gardens slowly burn into nothing.

He was woken in the morning by a stick poking his side. Seeing he was awake, Archer sat back down next to the smoking fire. "Took you long enough. I thought you'd never wake up." He jabbed at something he was cooking with the stick he had just used to poke Wick in the side.

Wick sat up and ground the heels of his palms into his eyes. "How late is it?"

"Not very. I found some mushrooms. Hopefully, they'll be edible and we can eat something other than fruit today. I was hoping a bird would fall from the sky or something so we could have some meat, but I never have any luck."

Wick edged closer to the embers, hoping the warmth would dry the dampness in his clothes. "Did you hear anything last night?"

"Other than you snoring? No." Archer lifted the edge of a mushroom to check the underside.

"I thought there was something in the trees. It was talking."

"It might have just been a dream. Dreams are still new to you." Archer shrugged. "Some feel more real than others."

"I know how dreams work." Wick sighed. "Maybe it was a dream, I don't know. Maybe it wasn't real after all."

But he still wondered about it.

It was roughly noon when Wick noticed. Something had been eating at him all day, a nagging sensation that something was wrong, that something was different that shouldn't be.

It was almost midday before he realized what was wrong.

"Archer."

Archer didn't even look around. "What?"

"It's quiet."

This time Archer did look back at him, his brow furrowed. "So what? Can't it be quiet?"

"It's too quiet." Wick stopped and turned slowly, listening. "Listen. Normally the birds don't mind us, but they're not making a sound."

Archer stood still for a moment, head cocked as he listened. "You're right," he said finally. "It's not usually this quiet."

For a moment neither of them said anything. Not a twig snapped. Not a wing fluttered. The animals seemed to be hiding.

Or maybe they were holding their breath.

"If it isn't us," Wick said quietly to Archer, "what's making the forest so quiet?"

Archer's eyes darted through the trees, his posture tense. "I don't know, but let's get moving."

They started walking, faster this time. Wick kept an eye out behind them. If something was out to get them, he didn't want it sneaking up on them. As his feet thudded through the leaves, he couldn't help but think of the two shadows from his dream. It was silly, but what if they were what had scared the birds? What if the shadows were hunting them down?

They cannot fight the fire.
It's coming for them all.

A cold breeze blew down his collar.

He walked faster.

For three miles, they walked at top speed, glancing over their shoulders and listening carefully for any sound.

Starting into mile three, Archer said, "Wick."

Wick looked up. "What is it?"

"The birds. They were in those signs you were talking about. The signs of the Scorch coming back. Right?"

"Well yes," Wick said. "First the plants die, then the black rain, then the trees start going, then the earthquakes, and then the Scorch. But they're not supposed to go completely silent until it's almost too late. And that's supposed to be months away."

Neither of them pointed out the obvious. The speed of the Scorch's approaching had accelerated before. If it had accelerated before, nothing was stopping it from coming still faster. Nothing at all.

Wick started walking again, passing Archer and ducking a tree branch. "Let's hope that's not it. I never thought I'd say this, but if we're lucky, it's just someone chasing us."

It was then that, not far off, a bird started singing.

Wick's shoulders relaxed. "See, there's a bird. We don't have anything to worry about."

"Because all the birds were obviously sleeping in," Archer said with disdain.

"They were late, but at least they haven't gone completely." Now light with relief, Wick could breathe a little easier. "I think at this point we can safely assume no one is following us."

"Well, hello!"

Archer slowly turned to Wick with an expression of murder on his face as a fair folk couple strolled out of the bushes.

"We were traveling in this direction and chanced to hear your voices," the woman said.

"Care to travel together?" the man asked.

Wick could already see Archer sizing up the tiny couple. Only shin-high, the fair folk couple were both leaning toward their later years, with greying hair and the beginnings of wrinkles on their brows. The woman's hair had been red at one point, but now it was nearer the color of the grey shawl that wrapped her shoulders. Her mossy green dress was made for traveling, long enough to keep her warm but short enough that it wouldn't tangle with her delicate brown boots.

The man was also warmly dressed. A brown cap came down over his ears and covered most of his hair. The matching brown coat looked worn but was lovingly patched at the elbows, probably by the wife. Unlike many fair folk, he didn't have a beard, but rather a nicely trimmed handlebar mustache that bounced comically when he spoke.

Archer and Wick exchanged glances. As much as Wick didn't want to travel with anyone (and Archer certainly wouldn't), refusing the offer would seem suspicious. His messenger's training resurfaced. "Some company would be welcome."

Archer's eyes bugged out.

But the fair folk resumed walking, and so did they. "We seem to be headed in the same direction," the man said. "Where are you bound?"

"To Eri," Wick said amiably.

"What for?"

"Visiting a family friend." Or a friend's family. What difference did it make? "Where are you traveling to?"

"Emilda's niece is getting married," the man said, patting his wife's hand on the crook of his elbow. "They live in a village outside of the seraph borders."

"My daughter will be the maid of honor," the woman said with a smile. She looked at Archer. "Have you ever been to a wedding?"

Archer squirmed. "I haven't."

The woman clucked her tongue. "A tragedy. Weddings are an excellent place to meet eligible young ladies."

Archer's squirming intensified.

"I've never been to one either," Wick said. "Not yet, anyway."

"I'm sure you will one day, dear," the wife said encouragingly. "They're quite unavoidable."

"I'm sure you're right." If the world didn't end, anyway.

"Hey Wick," Archer called from the back of the group. "Can I talk to you for a minute?"

Wick fell back a bit, and he and Archer walked together several steps behind the fair folk couple. "Why are we doing this?" Archer whispered. "I thought we were trying to shake off anyone who was following us."

Wick was skeptical. "I'm not sure now that anyone was following us."

Archer gestured indignantly to the tiny fair folk couple, who were walking ahead of them chatting together in pleasant tones. "Then what do you call that?"

"Some travelers," Wick explained. "Nothing more. Fair folk aren't dangerous, and they aren't hostile, I'll have you know. I couldn't tell them not to travel with us, or they would be suspicious. What we need to do is travel with them, be forgettable, and then part ways once they get to where they need to go. They only want us with them for company and protection. It'll be fine."

"This doesn't feel *fine*," Archer hissed.

"Or maybe you just don't like traveling when you're not traveling alone," Wick pointed out.

Archer spluttered but could provide no argument.

"I don't think they have any hostile intent," Wick repeated. "As I said, all we have to do is be forgettable, and everything will be fine."

With that, Wick moved further up to talk to the fair folk. Archer, determined to have the last word, whispered, "They're so short! They'll slow us down!"

"Discussing travel plans." Wick apologized as he reached where the fair folk were walking again.

"We were discussing our contribution to the wedding," the woman said. "If we were to bring a wedding present, it would be too heavy and slow down our travel."

"I want to build something for their new home," the husband said.

"But I think it would be better for them to build things for themselves," the wife finished. "You never know where they may be living, Fergus. I wouldn't want to provide them with furniture that doesn't fit."

"I can imagine that would be a problem," Wick mused. "Especially in a village where things might be more cramped."

"See, he understands, Fergus," the wife said. "I stand by my opinion that we should provide some kind of food for the wedding feast and contribute that way."

The husband made a protesting noise, and the two of them fell to whispered bickering in the fair folk language.

Wick did his best to stay quiet and not interfere.

After several minutes, the wife pressed a finger to her husband's lips and said, "That's enough, Fergus. We don't need to argue in front of our traveling companions." She turned her head and called to Archer. "Come closer, my dear boy, there's no need to walk so far behind us. Conversation has room for everyone."

Archer sidled up a little closer. The wife waved him to walk beside her. Since they were now too wide to still fit through the trees, Wick moved back to walk behind the others.

"Now, child, there's something about you that's familiar," the wife said.

Archer stiffened.

"Do I know your parents?" she asked. "My daughter used to live in Sker, in the mountains of seraph territory. Maybe you lived there at the time?"

"No," Archer managed at last. "I never lived near Sker."

"Do you have any relatives near there?" she asked.

Archer shook his head.

"Stop bothering the boy, Emilda," the husband chided gently. "You're flustering him. But I must say, my boy, that bag of yours is beautiful craftsmanship. Did you do it yourself?"

"Uh, no," Archer said quietly. "I didn't make it. It was given to me."

"It looks quite a bit like a bag I saw in a book once," the husband noted lightly. "But that bag was historic, and missing. No one has seen it in a long time."

Wick found himself hoping these fair folk were enough out of the loop that it wouldn't matter if they recognized the bag. Maybe they didn't know about the thefts. Maybe they didn't know him, or Archer. He hoped.

When Archer didn't say anything, the man continued, "I heard a rumor that it had resurfaced lately, that it had been stolen again by some thief. But that can't be. That bag must be long gone by now."

"Yeah." Wick could see how tense Archer's shoulders were in front of him. In his mind, he scrambled for some sort of way to divert the conversation.

"It was quite the story, that rumor," the man said. "Thieves and prophecies and impossible escapes. It's the escapes that make it a lie, you see. No one could escape from the manghar the way that they say the thieves did."

"No, probably not," Wick said. "I know the manghar, they don't let people escape."

"But what I found truly odd," here the man scratched his mustache, "is that when we left on this trip to go to the wedding, we didn't expect to see anyone on the road. The world is dangerous these days. Traveling is a risk. But for the wedding we thought, why not go anyway, stay with the family for a while. And when we came across you two in the forest, I thought to myself, how odd."

He glanced at first Wick, and then Archer.

"How odd, that the travelers we met look exactly like those two treasonous thieves."

Then Archer said, "Run."

The two of them broke into a mad dash. They hadn't made it down the path ten steps before the wife threw back her head and loosed a piercing, familiar bird call.

Fair folk exploded from the trees.

Armed with ropes, pickaxes, and assorted pointy objects, they charged from the trees, sprang from the bushes, and even dropped from the branches. Slingshots pelted them with rocks. Pain exploded in Wick's ear as one rock struck him, but he covered his head and kept running.

The fair folk kept coming. Every time Wick thought that it had to be the end of them, more appeared. And the longer they ran to get away, the larger the mob behind them grew. The fair folk kept throwing rocks and sticks, even slicing with knives when they were lucky enough to get close, and Wick suddenly remembered that the fair folk had greater endurance. They would still be running long after he and Archer tired out. Already Wick was starting to get a deep stitch in his side that dug with every step.

Even worse, the fair folk had a plan.

Not fifty yards later, a rope sprang up ahead of them on the path, yanked taut by two fair folk. Already tired and distracted, both Wick and Archer tripped over it and went sprawling. Archer landed on his bad wing and yelped like a wounded dog. Wick's injured shoulder pulsed.

Then the fair folk were upon them. They swarmed over Wick and Archer like rats—rats with a vengeance and armed to the teeth.

Something stabbed Wick's side. He yelped and swatted at the offending spear. He scrubbed his hands up and down his body, trying to shake off all the fair folk, but they kept swarming up. He struggled first to his knees, then his feet. The fair folk were small, but they weighed more than he ever could have expected. Still they kept climbing his legs.

Only a few yards away, Archer made a sudden loud sound. But not like he had been hurt. More like. . . a cry of discovery? Of realization?

Archer got to his feet with great difficulty, clinging to a tree with both hands. As soon as he was up, he flared out his wings, throwing most of the fair folk to the ground. "Hey!" he yelled. He shook off the rest of the fair folk and leaped into the tree.

Now abandoned, Wick was dragged back down to the ground under a mound of fair folk.

"*Hey!*" Archer yelled again. "Look over there!"

Most of the fair folk looked. Even Fergus, standing on top of Wick's chest with a stout staff, looked the way Archer was pointing.

From the ground, Wick could hardly see anything. Was it a roof? Up in the treetops?

"Now tell me," Archer said firmly. "What is that?"

"A seraph house?" one of the fair folk women peeped.

"And what would that tell you?" Archer prompted.

The fair folk mumbled among themselves. One of them faltered, "It means there's a tall house nearby?"

"It means," Archer said slowly, "we just crossed the border. You're in seraph territory now." He crouched on the branch, hanging on to the trunk with one hand as he gazed down on the fair folk. "Any of you know Ochre Hessen? He's my father. And Oak Hessen is my grandfather. Which means that now that I'm in seraph territory, I am untouchable!"

As he crowed, the fair folk stirred uncomfortably.

"And so is my friend," Archer continued. "Now let him go, and I won't mention any of you to my father when I see him."

The mob of fair folk hesitated. Fergus shifted. "What if you're bluffing?"

Archer raised his eyebrows. "You think I would bluff? I'm a thief and a vagabond, and recently it looks like I've committed treason. If I was going to lie, I wouldn't push it this far. Now, do you want my father to know that you tried to kill me or not?"

Fergus thought a moment, clearly trying to find an

excuse. Finally, he heaved a sigh and threw his staff to the ground. "Bad luck to shed blood before a wedding anyway. Come, Emilda, let's go."

Emilda appeared from the crowd, her dismal face painted with dirt and a long knitting needle in each hand. She took Fergus's hand, and they trudged off into the forest. Little by little, the rest of the crowd followed them. As the last of them left, Wick scrambled up from the ground and checked himself for injuries. His hurt shoulder had begun to bleed again, but that was the worst of the damage. Maybe he would be bruised later, but it seemed the fair folk hadn't managed to cause any serious harm.

Archer jumped down from the trees and landed awkwardly on one leg. "Come on, let's go," he said. "Before any of them have second thoughts."

They started off into the forest at a quick clip.

"So much for the fair folk not being hostile, like you said," Archer said as they went.

"They aren't hostile, not usually." Wick watched the ground as he walked. "They're normally peaceful. I suppose the times must be changing."

"You're telling me."

"You aren't really safe as soon as you step over the seraph border, are you?" Wick asked. "I didn't think it worked like that."

"It doesn't." Archer checked over his shoulder. "I only have immunity inside of Tor, and not even then if someone could drag me out of the city without being caught. But they don't know that, so let's keep moving in case any of them realizes. The city isn't far from here."

An hour later, they entered the city of Eri.

Much like the last time, they didn't stop to see the sights. But this time, they walked in the middle of the street instead of hiding in the shadows. That was Archer's choice. Archer seemed a little more comfortable this time, his step a little lighter and his head held a little higher. He almost seemed happy to be here.

Now that he thought of it, Wick wasn't sure if he had ever seen Archer happy to be anywhere before.

In the time they had been gone, fall had come to the city. The air smelled crisp and slightly damp from the piles of leaves on the ground. What leaves remained on the trees were vivid orange and red and in places, even a hint of gold. The seraphs were dressed a little more warmly this time as well, garments of light wool and velvet flapping around them as they leaped into the air and swooped through the trees.

"Do you smell that?" Archer said suddenly, tilting his head up for a better whiff.

Wick smelled the air as well. A waft of cinnamon and fruit, mixed with something sweeter, hit him full in the face. It was a warm, comforting smell. "What is that?"

Archer grinned. "Someone's making frutelken somewhere." He took another deep breath of the smell. "It's the best thing in the whole world. I'd sell my soul to be able to make it."

Wick's brow creased. "Is the recipe secret?"

"No, it's not a secret," Archer said with a quick shake of his head. The smile still lingered. "But reading a recipe would take all the fun out of it. I want to figure it out for myself. Besides," he added, "it's a household drink. Everyone's recipe would be different."

Wick thought about this and loved it. The way that people could have their own recipe that was different than their neighbor's recipe, the same way that their preferences in food or the way they greeted one another in the streets, was all unique, and that was beautiful. It was the little intricacies like that which had made his time as a messenger so special.

"There it is," Archer said, nodding up ahead.

In daylight, Oak Hessen's house was even larger and more impressive than it had been at night. The darkness of the night had swallowed most of it and made it seem like a tall beam of floating lights and laughter. But in broad daylight, it was massive. The tree stretched up to the sky, the canopy of orange leaves providing an elegant dappled shade across the street before it. The house itself, wrapping around the tree in broad coils, some of it nested among the branches, was beautifully designed so that it almost looked like it had grown there. Wick could spot the fine ironwork on the upper floors and around the windows, the same ironwork they had climbed on their way to take the seraph stone. And unlike most of the other houses, this one had a staircase leading up to the house.

"Archer," Wick said, interrupting Archer as he began to speak. "Sorry. But if your grandfather doesn't dislike you, why did we steal the seraph stone from his house rather than ask him for it? Wouldn't he have given it to you?"

"He would have," Archer said. "But I wasn't so worried about him. It was everyone else. I knew he was having his big birthday party that week, and I knew there would be a lot of people there. I didn't know if any of them would try to stop us, like how Eland tried to stop you when your paths crossed. Plus I didn't trust you, so I didn't want you to know who my family was."

Wick could tell he was missing a piece of the picture. There was a glaring hole in the middle of the excuse, thinly veiled under all of Archer's bluster. But he didn't want to pry, so Wick let it go.

"Hey, Tree," Archer said slowly.

"What is it?"

Archer took a breath to speak, then let it out again. "Never mind. It probably won't matter. Come on, let's see if he's home."

They climbed up the winding staircase, and Wick found that it wasn't as hard of a climb as he had expected. Perhaps it was built for walking, or perhaps the stairs in manghar territory had left him expecting the worst. The higher they climbed, the smaller everything on the ground shrank. As they came level with the door and the deck hugging the trunk around it, Wick took another glance outward and a smile split his face.

So that was the secret. Seraph territory was never meant to be viewed from the ground. Their cities were meant to be viewed from up in the air.

From here he could see through the tall windows into the front rooms of other houses and across dozens of shining porches. Winged couples swooped by arm in arm, children laughed in the treetops. Swings swayed gently from branches. One dark-haired girl peered over the side of a branch a few trees over, sitting in some kind of nest she had built for herself.

Archer glanced over as well, and he smiled faintly. "Come on, let's go." He pushed the door open, and they stepped inside.

The wooden floor of the entry hall creaked faintly under their feet as the door swung shut behind them. The air chilled their skin, and Wick smelled a faint mustiness.

"Hello, I'm here!" Archer shouted, walking deeper into the house. No one answered. The house felt very still.

"Hello?" Archer called again. His brow furrowed.

"Maybe he isn't home?" Wick suggested.

They left the entry hall and moved into the large sitting room beyond it. It was as bare and quiet as the entry hall had been. Wick found it a little too bare.

Archer strode to the opposite doorway and bellowed through it. "*Hello?*"

A soft sound came from the space beyond the doorway, and a seraph with a long black ponytail dropped down into the room. He landed next to Archer and folded his soft beige wings behind his back.

"Archer?" he asked with surprise, squinting at Archer's face.

"Yes, it's me," Archer said impatiently. "I'm home again. Is my grandfather here right now?"

A strange look flickered across the seraph's face.

Archer's face went blank. "What?"

The seraph looked at Archer, then at Wick, then back at Archer. "No one told you," he said softly.

Archer seemed a little put off, but he licked his lips and demanded, "What? No one told me what?"

"I'm sorry," the seraph said, "your grandfather died three weeks ago."

CHAPTER FIVE:

How the Seraph Fell

"MOST OF THE FURNITURE has been sold," the seraph said in the same soft, astonished tone. "Your family is trying to sell the house in the next few weeks."

"But that's. . ." Archer blinked. "We were here three weeks ago. He was fine then. Wasn't he?"

The seraph nodded. "He was old and tired, but he was healthy. I was his caregiver. I made sure he was in good health and eating the way he was supposed to every day. He was perfectly cheerful and lively the week of his birthday party, and even when you took the stone out of his attic and I caught you, he laughed about it."

Archer said nothing. His expression remained the same, of fear and anger and disbelief.

"He died in his sleep." The seraph struggled for something else to say. "It was a surprise to everyone. I didn't know how to react. He wasn't in pain, ever. He was just gone."

Archer looked down at the ground. His wings fluttered behind his back. Then he said, "I see."

He turned and walked out without saying anything else.

Not knowing where Archer was going or whether he would even wait for him to catch up, Wick knew he had to give chase. But he couldn't leave the poor caretaker so suddenly. He turned to the seraph and placed a hand on his shoulder. "I don't know if you remember me, but my name is Wick. I used to stay here sometimes when I was passing through the territory. I didn't know Oak Hessen personally, but I'm sorry to hear he's gone now. Truly. Thank you for looking after him."

The seraph's face crumpled. "Thank you. We were good friends."

"I'm sure. I'm sorry that it's over now."

The door slammed. Archer was gone.

"I'll make sure he doesn't burn anything down," Wick added. "If you're struggling to find work after this, go to the centaurs. They'll help you."

"Thank you."

Wick stepped out onto the porch. Archer was nowhere in sight. He started toward the stairs.

"Over here," said Archer's tired voice.

Wick followed the voice around the curve of the porch to where Archer sat against the side of the house, defeated.

"If I let you wander off, I'll never find you again," Archer said, without looking up. Curled up against the side of the house, wings tucked around his body and head down, he didn't look like the intimidating, overpowering seraph Wick knew, full of bravado and energy. He just looked small. Small and mortal and hollow.

Wick leaned against the wall beside him. Unsure if Archer would accept or even want help, he said nothing.

Instead, it was Archer who filled the silence. "We missed him. Not even by a lot."

Wick was about to point out that three weeks was a lot, but Archer went on.

"He was here when we came to get the stone. I should have swallowed my stupid pride and gone to see him." Archer picked up a leaf off the deck and peeled it apart, piece by piece. "But I didn't know if he'd believe me either, you know? No one else believed me. And he was the only one that really cared about me around here. . ." He trailed off. "I don't know."

"You didn't want him to be disappointed in you," Wick said.

"I guess." Archer stripped the rest of the leaf off the stem and threw it off to the side. He leaned his head back against the slats of the house. "Something like that."

Wick reached for something to say. "Maybe he wouldn't have been disappointed."

"The *maybe* helps, thanks."

"Sorry."

"He's not here. He can't protect us. And on top of everything, they're trying to sell his house," Archer said flatly. "We couldn't stay here even if we wanted to."

"What do you want to do, then?" Wick asked. A wind blew by, ruffling their hair and their clothes.

"At this point, it doesn't look like we have another choice." Archer got up and stood at the edge of the deck. The bright light from the sun made the bruises on his face look much darker. "We'll have to go to my parents."

"I thought you didn't want to go to them."

"Well, it's not looking like I have another choice now, is it?" Archer demanded. "I'm not planning to stay there, not if I can help it. I just have to convince my father to extend my immunity beyond Tor's outskirts, and then we'll come back here. They can't sell the house if I'm still sitting in it."

For a moment, Archer paused.

"I used to be here all the time, you know?" he said. "Me and my family, we don't. . . I didn't like being with them if I could help it. I'd spend hours walking from Tor to here and back again. I always got in trouble for it. But my grandparents, they always looked after me. I don't know if my father ever even hugged me, but they did. They always had food and a spot on their sofa and there were toys down in my grandfather's study so I could be with him while he worked on trade agreements. They probably sold the study, too."

With sudden clarity, Wick remembered the strange abandoned study they hid in the last time they were in Eri. It had been on the ground, not in the treetops, perfect for an elderly seraph who tired of flying everywhere. . . or for a boy with weak wings.

Archer glanced back at Wick, his black eye looking much more accentuated in this light. "You know what? Come on. Let's go now."

"This soon?" Wick asked in surprise.

"Yeah." Archer hitched his bag on his shoulder. "I don't feel like processing my grief right now anyway, and the Scorch won't give us more time just because someone died."

They left the city without another look back.

Tor was Eri's sister city, and the two were only a few miles apart. The cities made rules about the expansion of borders and outskirts to make sure they would never overlap. By comparison to the cities, the forest between them seemed oddly still and small. The trees didn't grow nearly as large, and the forest life didn't even seem to register that they lived sandwiched between two huge civilizations. Or maybe they did know, and they knew their way of life would never be interrupted.

As the first large trees began to silhouette themselves against the skyline, Archer declared a rest for lunch. He dug some more fruit out of the bag, and they sat on the ground to eat.

Once all the food was gone, Archer said, "Wick?"

Wick looked up.

Archer squirmed uncomfortably. "I was hoping to keep this to myself, but you're probably going to hear a lot of twisted versions of the story once we get into Tor, and I think even if we stay in Eri there might be some rumors darting around, so I just want to make sure you know the real version first. Because lots of people have got it wrong, and lots of them don't tell the whole story. So." He cleared his throat and extended his wings. With them side by side, the mangled shape of his bad wing was even more obvious. The patches of missing feathers, the huge bow in his wing, shaped like the dip between two mountains, the bent shape near the tip—all stood in stark contrast to the soft grey of the other wing. Being new to a more human variety of pain, Wick couldn't even imagine the agony.

"This is broken. And it broke a long time ago," Archer said. "It still hurts sometimes, when the weather goes weird or when I take a bad fall." He cleared his throat. "I don't know how to put any of this. I've never had to tell anyone before."

"Take your time," Wick said. "I'm listening."

"Thanks." Archer took a deep breath and blew it out, ruffling his shark fin of hair.

After a long moment of silence, he started again. "I

was born with weak bones. If you care, it's something that only appears in a family every six generations or so, and it's supposed to be bad luck. Seraphs are very superstitious. Anyway. If I tripped on the stairs, I could fracture something, or if I played too hard with the other kids, I could get injured. I remember there was a playground accident when I was a toddler, and I fractured my arm and broke I think three fingers. So they wouldn't let me fly." Archer swallowed. "All the doctors said that the pressure of catching the wind would snap my wings. The theory was that with time and enough disgusting medicine all my bones would get stronger, and I would be able to 'live normally' eventually. But I got older, and nothing happened. I had to walk everywhere, and use stairs and things, and everyone looked at me like I was a. . . a tiny hapless *thing*. I hated it."

He looked up at Wick and got more animated. "And I could tell that it wasn't about me anymore. It wasn't about helping me or getting me better. I was just something that helped my father, and his campaign to get the whole city under his thumb. They'd drag me with them everywhere, and it was always 'oh the poor Hessens, how strong they are', 'oh Willow your patience is admirable, your son's condition must be so hard on you', 'oh Fowl, you're such a good older brother'. They turned themselves into these pillars of good grace and strength, and I was the weak thing that made them look strong. Once I saw what they were doing, I couldn't unsee it again, and it only got worse. I couldn't stand it."

"I became a teenager and I got hardheaded enough to decide that I was going to fly, whether they wanted me to or not. If everyone else could do it, so could I." Archer's eyes wandered up to the treetops. "I climbed as high as I could, and I jumped, and in the end, they were right. I couldn't fly. I just fell." He looked down again and picked at the skin of his thumb. "My wings caught the wind, but like everyone said, they couldn't take the strain. I hit a faster wind and changed direction too fast. The wing broke, and I fell." The movement of his hands stopped. "I think the doctor said the full damage was a shattered wing, a sprained wrist and shoulder, and internal bruising up one of my legs. He said I was lucky it wasn't worse. I didn't feel lucky."

"So that's what happened," Wick murmured.

"And it's worse than that, too. Getting injured didn't take any pressure off me, even when the doctor told me to rest. They didn't comfort me, they just babied me. It was all for looks, you know? My broken wing was only helping them more. Once I thought I could walk comfortably enough to travel on my own, I took what I needed and I left." He smiled dryly. "It's funny, because I'm glad I left when I did. If I hadn't, I don't know what I would have done. Because I left, though, the wing never healed properly, and now it's stuck like that. I don't mind it anymore. It makes me unique. It's something that's mine and no one else's. But that quack doctor was right about one thing. My bones don't break now when I fall, or at least not most of the time, so they did get stronger. Just not fast enough." Archer's fingers tapped on his leg. "I think that's everything."

Wick couldn't think of what to say. The story was much longer and more complicated than he had ever imagined.

Archer laughed. "Tell me you didn't believe me before when I said I broke it on purpose."

"No," Wick said. "I knew that was a lie. You're not a

very convincing liar."

Archer looked offended for the briefest moment, then his expression sobered again. His knee bounced nervously. "Yeah, maybe not. I'm better at covering things up than lying."

"You broke it much younger than I thought," Wick said, still mulling over the story. He gazed off into the trees. "I always thought maybe you broke it in a fight somewhere."

"That does sound like me."

"You have a better reason to feel distant from your family than I do," Wick said. "From the sounds of it, things were tense between you for a long time. I don't have any excuse like that."

Archer shrugged. "Not everyone's the same. I'm sure a lot of people would feel the same way you do if they were in your situation. Just because your friends have it different from you doesn't make you the weird one. Maybe all of them are the weird ones."

"Probably not," Wick said.

Archer shrugged again and threw his apple core into the forest. "Just a thought. You don't have to agree with me."

Wick brushed apple peels off his lap. "Should we go?"

"Yeah. Let's get this over with fast so I can go back to Eri and take the house hostage."

"First stealing priceless artifacts," Wick mused, "now kidnapping a house. What will we do next?"

"Start a peaceful uprising, maybe," Archer said. "You'd like it if it was peaceful."

"I don't know, I'm starting to like punching."

"And I couldn't be prouder."

With that, they walked into the city. Wick felt for the cord around his neck and was comforted to feel the centaur piece of the heather stone still there.

Tor's contrast to Eri was obvious as soon as they entered. Eri transformed gradually from a peaceful forest into outskirts into a bustling, open city. On the other hand, Tor's limits were defined with a wide ring of posts stuck between the trees, lit with lanterns at the top. While the architecture in Eri was all swooping ironwork and beautiful wood varnished and polished to a glow, Tor was a citadel of shining glass and brass and gold. Pots and troughs full of flowers covered almost every surface and ringed every balcony. Beautiful gardens flourished at the bases of many trees, their leaves stretching toward the filtered sunlight.

To Wick's eyes, the people of the city looked about the same in their dress and posture, but it was obvious that the city itself thought it was the most beautiful and most important thing in the world.

Archer's discomfort became obvious as they went further into the city, and no wonder. In Eri, they had somehow remained anonymous, but here, everyone stared. Whether it was because they hadn't seen Archer in a long time or whether they were unaccustomed to outsiders, Wick couldn't tell, but it seemed that every other head turned as they passed. A glance up proved that at least a dozen seraphs had landed on their balconies or branches of trees to stare at the two of them as they passed under.

In many ways, it reminded Wick of their reception in manghar territory, although the manghar had been courteous enough to make their hostile intent clear. Visibly, the faces of the watching seraphs only held mild interest, but Wick had seen enough to recognize a practiced blank mask. Only the children didn't seem to care about the visitors. They raced through the treetops at top speed, screaming and chasing one another, tumbling over branches and nearly falling in their pursuit of going higher, higher, faster, faster.

After a million years, Archer said, "That's their house over there."

The Hessen house was a tall, impressive tower of arching glass windows, high ceilings, and overlapping balconies. On an upper level, at least five sets of glass doors were thrown open to let in the autumn air. On one of the lower levels, curtains made of some light, airy fabric flowed in the breeze. The garden at the base of the tree—a perfect circle of delicate blooms, wiry fruit trees, and gently guided tendril vines—had been lovingly curated to perfection, and while most of the plants had passed peak bloom for the season, the yellows and greens were no less elegant for the change of weather.

It seemed no one was coming out to meet the pair of them, so they took the pebble path through the garden and started up the stairway that wound around the tree trunk. Wick grasped for the railing and found only a thin golden chain strung between the newel posts.

"Something tells me this staircase was built for fashion, not function," he commented.

Archer glanced back. "Yeah, a lot of the staircases are. Hang on to the tree bark and you should be fine."

Wick clung to the bark and kept climbing. Somehow the insult of a railing felt more dangerous than no railing at all.

Miraculously, they reached the top alive. Archer reached the top first and leaned against the side of the house as he waited for Wick.

Wick climbed the last of the stairs and rushed across the porch, trying to put as much room as possible between himself and the edge. His breath came in quick bursts. "I hope I never have to do that again as long as I live."

"Don't be such a baby. The staircase at my grandfather's was taller."

"But that was a real staircase," Wick said. "With a real railing. The rail on that one was a joke."

"Not really," Archer said. "Jokes are usually funny."

Tired and slightly unsettled as he was, that made Wick laugh.

"Archer?" a woman's voice called. "Is that you I hear?"

In an instant, Archer's face changed from laughing to a blank, carefully empty slate, like the seraphs in the city. "Yes, Mother, it's me."

A woman raced around the side of the house and enveloped Archer in a huge hug.

Archer's mother was much shorter than he was, barely past Archer's shoulder. She had the face of someone who had managed to carry her beautiful looks well into motherhood but was now starting to take signs of wear. Her long, dark curls had light streaks of grey, and her eyes and mouth bore the first indentation of wrinkles and lines. She wore folds of white linen and a shawl knit from deep orange wool. Like Archer, she wore no shoes, but on one leg glinted a silver anklet.

Releasing Archer, she said, "How we missed you. We never know how long you'll be gone, and you never write." As Archer floundered for something to say, she spotted Wick standing behind them both. "And you brought a friend! How wonderful." She squeezed Archer's arm. "You must come inside, and I'll track down your father and your brother. You were lucky to come at a time when they're both home. I never know where Fowler goes these days, so if he wasn't home I wouldn't even begin to know where to find him."

"Not that I'd want to find him," Archer muttered.

"Shh," his mother said softly but firmly. "I know you don't mean that. And you shouldn't say things like that in front of your guest, especially when I don't even know his name."

"I'm Wick," Wick said, trying to soothe the tension any way he could.

"Wonderful to meet you," Archer's mother said. "Please come in, Wick, and I'll try to find the rest of the family. I've just finished preparing the supper for tonight, so I hope you'll be able to stay and enjoy it with us."

"Yeah, we will," Archer said.

"Good."

They entered the house through a tall, peaked door. The house was just as bright and huge on the inside as it had looked on the outside. Wick wondered at the mathematical impossibility of how one tree could hold all this weight and still grow healthily as Archer's mother flew off into the house to find where the rest of the family had gone.

The moment she was gone, Archer found a chair and sat down heavily. "Enjoy your last few minutes of peace," he told Wick, rubbing his eyes with his knuckles. "The rest of the ride won't be as nice."

"How long has it been since you've visited?" Wick asked.

Archer looked up at the ceiling. "A year, maybe. I try not to stay long when I'm here."

Wick nodded. "I see."

Archer's mother returned in a gust of wings and announced that she had found the others, and they should all proceed to the dining room. They followed her into a long, high room with chestnut sideboards and a wonderful view of the setting sun through the high windows. Archer's father and brother, who looked quite similar, entered from the other doorway. Everyone arranged themselves around the long oval dining table with Archer's parents at either end and Wick and Archer sitting opposite Archer's brother.

Wick studied the faces of the Hessen family as Archer's mother chattered and brought in silver plates heaped with steaming, salivating food. He saw the vague resemblance that Eland had mentioned. Archer's mother's face resembled Archer's, but hers was an older, more rounded out version, with wider eyes and an easier but more practiced smile.

Archer's father was exactly the opposite. He was so grim and haggard that he was almost frightening to look at. He looked like Archer, but in a very different way. His face had rough edges where Archer's was smooth, flat planes where the bones of Archer's cheeks were. A sleek silver ponytail hung down his back, tied in place at the nape of his neck with a cord. His clothes were made up of a flowing cream-colored shirt and long black pants, wrapped in a wine-colored robe.

The brother was the one that resembled Archer the most. He looked slightly older and his face had seen less of the sun and the elements, but they were two halves of the same coin, two variations of the same genes. The same piercing eyes, the same angular face, the same dark hair, though the brother's hair was long and loose where Archer's was clipped close to his head. Wick came to realize that he had never noticed how crooked Archer's broken nose had looked until now.

The brother had brought a book with him, and he hardly looked up from it for a second as his mother prepared the table.

"Well," Archer's mother said after the table had been set and prayers had been offered. "I think some introductions would be in order now. Archer?"

Archer set down the platter of fish. "Everyone, this is my friend Wick. If you've seen any kind of news recently, you probably know the name. Wick, this is my father Ochre, my mother Willow, and my older brother Fowler. Fowler who won't talk to any of us, I guess. How ya doing, Fowl?"

Fowl closed his book and set it down beside his plate. "As well as life will allow. I take it this is the friend who went to jail with you?"

"I've been to jail more than once, thanks, but yes, the most recent time he was there, too," Archer said. "We had a good time, didn't we, Wick?"

Wick wanted to say that the best part was leaving, but he felt that it would be inappropriate in this setting, so he kept his mouth shut. A few months ago he would have never thought of saying anything like that. Archer was making an impression on him, and he wasn't sure what he thought of it.

The rest of the family also moved on from that comment.

"Unless I'm mistaken," Ochre said, turning to Wick, "you're a messenger of some kind, but I don't think I've seen you in the city before. Could this be your first visit?"

As soon as he spoke, Wick saw Ochre's face change from that dark, severe expression to a jovial, sociable expression. It was like watching a change in personality, or a demonic possession in reverse. Wick knew that face all too well. It was the politics face, the socializing face.

The false face.

He knew it well.

Nonetheless, he played along. "You're right, this is my first visit," Wick said, putting on his own sociable false face. "My messenger's route was all over, but Tor was on most everyone else's routes and they didn't need me for this city as well. Usually, when I needed to take something to seraph territory, it was to one of the smaller settlements or to Eri. I believe I stayed with a relative of yours there several times in my travels. Oak Hessen."

"Ah," Ochre said, becoming serious. "Oak Hessen was my father. He recently passed away. The funeral was only a few weeks ago."

"I was sorry to hear about it as I was passing through Eri," Wick said.

"Speaking of which," Archer said, twirling his fork through the scattered vegetables on his plate, "when we were there, I heard that there was an estate sale. All the furniture was gone. The caretaker said you were trying to sell the house, too."

Wick realized too late that the topic of Oak Hessen's house was one he probably should have avoided. He scrambled for a way to redirect the conversation, but the talk was already stampeding toward the inevitable.

"Yes, I'm indeed trying to sell the house," Ochre said. "I wish we could keep it, but it would be far too expensive since none of us would be living there or ever really be near enough to use it."

"I would use it," Archer said. "I'd take care of it."

"You're hardly ever here," Fowl pointed out, stabbing

another forkful of his salad, "let alone Eri. You would never get any use out of it either."

Archer bristled. "I would if I wanted to. And what's more, it's your own family's home. You shouldn't be selling it like this. Doesn't it make you feel any guilt?"

"We can discuss this another time," Willow said, swooping up the conversation and tucking it on a high shelf. "I'm sure your guest doesn't want to hear about things like this, and we shouldn't fight when we're dining as a family."

Archer shot Wick a look full of venom.

Wick knew the look wasn't for him, and yet he found himself thankful that he no longer received looks like that in earnest.

"Well then, Archer," Archer's father said, setting down his goblet and resting his chin on his steepled fingers. "What brought you this time? What do you want?"

"What makes you think I want something?" Archer challenged.

"Don't play games. We all know well enough that you don't enjoy our company, and you only appear in this city when you have no other choice, so what brought you here? What do you want this time?"

"*Nothing*," Archer insisted. "For crying out loud, I can come and go as I please, I can do whatever I want. Can we eat some food without attacking me for once? Just because I'm not your precious little pawn anymore, does that count as a reason to start a fight every time I turn around?"

Ochre Hessen sat very still and quiet for several breaths. Then he adjusted his positioning in his chair and said, "I'm glad to see you think of me so fondly when you're gone, my son."

"Good to know that you assume the worst of me when I show up, too," Archer snapped back. "So forget about it." He set down his goblet, then said more softly, to his mother, "Thank you for the meal. Everything was very good."

"I agree," Wick said, grateful to have a safe topic again. "It was a wonderful meal."

"Thank you," Willow said, her soft face brightening a bit. "Though I can't take any credit. It's my mother's recipe." She looked around the table. "Is everyone through eating? We can move to the drawing room if you like. I'll make some tea."

"I don't think we'll need tea, darling," Ochre said, rising from his seat in a swish of robes. "I'll thank you for the meal as well." He held out his arm to her, and the two of them led the way to the connected drawing room, which was painted a dark green and hung with long linen drapes. Everyone situated themselves onto the padded chairs that surrounded the merry, crackling fire. Though the fire may have been the only merry one in the room.

Wick grasped for a topic that wouldn't lead back to more tension or any mention of the thefts but came up empty.

Far too much time passed before Willow finally said, "I don't know if you saw, Archer, but those flowers I planted so long ago are finally blooming."

Archer shook his head. "I didn't pay a lot of attention to the garden, sorry."

Across the room, Fowl sighed deeply.

"It's all right, son." Willow gave Archer a reassuring smile. "I thought they might be in the ground forever. They were well worth the wait, in my opinion. They're some of the finest blossoms in the garden now."

"I'll have to take a look when I walk through the garden next," Wick said. "It looked wonderful as a whole, and I'd love to see it in more detail."

Willow beamed.

"That garden is her pride and joy," Ochre said. His false face was back, more aggressive than ever. "I gave her full permission to do whatever she wanted with it when we got this house. At first, I thought I would never see her out of that garden again. It seemed like she worked on it nonstop."

"It was prime planting season," Willow explained. "I had to get all my bushes and bulbs in the ground so they would all bloom at the right time. I couldn't be happier with the result."

"I know exactly what you mean," Wick said. "My mother has a huge garden next to our dwelling. When she says it's time to plant, we won't see her but for a few hours every day. But it always looks so beautiful in the spring."

"It sounds lovely." Willow smiled. She raised a finger as if she remembered something. "I meant to ask Archer. How long do you think you'll stay? Overnight, at least?"

"At least overnight," Archer said. "I don't know exactly how long we'll be here." His eyes darted toward where his father sat. "I'll figure it out soon."

"Are you waiting for the heat to die down?" Fowl asked.

The question took Wick off guard. He looked up and saw Fowl's eyes glittering slyly in the firelight.

Fowl *had* been listening.

"Now, Fowler, that's not fair," Willow chided.

"It's fair enough," Ochre said. "They've both been trying to hide it since the moment they arrived. We've all been avoiding the topic. But it's there all the same: we received word not long ago that you had been imprisoned. I can't think of a reason anyone would let you go so soon. Your friend they could pardon, perhaps. But not you, Archer. So you must have escaped like you've escaped everywhere else."

Archer smiled. "At least I'm reliable. It's one of my many virtues."

"Is that why you came?" Ochre asked sharply. "You're here to hide in the shadow of my good graces until enough people have given up the chase. Is that it?"

Archer leaned forward. "Look, if you don't want me here, I can understand that. But if you want, I don't have to stay here. Let me keep the house in Eri. We're not safe there, but if you extend my safe zone to Eri and send some people to keep an eye on things, we wouldn't have to see any more of each other again for a long time, just the way you want it."

His mother's face fell.

"That's what you're after," Ochre said with a nod. "I knew it would come out in the end, it always does. You're after diplomatic immunity. I imagine it was Wick's idea. I can't see you coming up with something quite that clever."

"So what if it was Wick's idea?" Archer demanded. "It's a good idea and I'm standing by it. It could work. Are you going to let us get out of your hair and go to Eri, or not?"

"No." Ochre settled back in his chair with an expression of empty satisfaction. "I won't give you any kind of immunity, and I won't give you the house. I won't be pushed around so easily. Your only choices are to stay here in Tor, or to leave the city and get arrested somewhere else."

CHAPTER SIX:

Splitting Up

"HEY!" ARCHER LEAPED to his feet. "You can't do that!"

"I can do whatever I want, Archer," Ochre said. "I'm your father, and I'll decide what's best for you. If we're going to discuss what either of us can or can't do, you can't waltz in with demands like this. It's been eighteen months since we've seen you, and you sail back into the house with less respect than ever before. You track in a reputation of thievery and recklessness like mud, you're covered with the marks of your most recent fist fight, and you ask for the freedom to gallivant off and cause more trouble."

Wick immediately saw that this wouldn't get any better by more talking, not tonight. He tried to pick up the pieces. "I think—"

"Fine, do whatever you like," Archer snapped at Ochre. "But you can't stop me. I'll find a way." He spun on his heel and raced out of the room, and the sound of feet pounded up the stairs.

Wick didn't expect they'd see any more of Archer for the evening.

AFTER WILLOW had settled Wick into a guest room on an upper level of the house, apologizing for the conflict all the way up the stairs, Wick sat down on the edge of the bed and buried his face in his hands.

Everything had already fallen apart. He should have expected no less from Archer, who fought with everyone he saw. Now they had no assets, and they weren't likely to get any, not from Ochre.

They were going to need a different plan.

*

A LEVEL ABOVE HIM, Archer hit his head against the wall and rested his forehead there. "You dummy."

He'd gone and messed it all up. When everything was riding on him getting this one thing right, he'd gone and ruined everything.

He thought back through the conversation but found he couldn't imagine himself saying anything differently. He couldn't picture himself taking any of that lying down. It just wasn't in him.

He sat beside his bed and leaned against the side of it.

Everyone was probably embarrassed now. Wick, his parents. . . Well, probably not Fowl. He couldn't picture any of that embarrassing Fowl. He couldn't picture much of anything embarrassing Fowl. Fowl seemed to take everything in stride and make it work, the way Wick did.

Archer wasn't like that.

They hadn't gotten diplomatic immunity, not for Eri, and certainly not for the rest of the country. And he didn't know how long he would have to wait before it was safe to ask again.

They were going to need a different plan.

He stared out at the room. There was barely anything in it, these days. He only had three pieces of furniture in the whole room—his bed, a dresser against the wall opposite the footboard, and a small chest to the left of the bed, beside the window. The high ceilings stared him down the way they always did. The beautifully high ceiling in this room had always felt like a mockery of his useless wings. Or maybe a challenge to grow stronger.

Everything he had, everything from his childhood, was all either in the dresser or in the chest. Maybe there were a few things kicked under the bed from years ago, but the chances of those remaining after so many years of spring cleanings were slim to none. All his baby clothes were probably still in the dresser's bottom drawer, waiting for who knew what. Whenever he was home, it always struck him that the room probably needed more furnishing, but adding to it would imply that he intended to stay in the room more often.

Moonlight from the window suddenly shone in his eyes as the curtain shifted, and he realized he hadn't been thinking about possible plans for a long time. He cursed his brain for being so useless and climbed into bed. The blanket smelled the same way it always had, like baking and soft soap. It was the only comforting thing in the house. He slid further under the blanket so he was covered head to toe and tried to run the race to dreamland.

Come morning, things looked a little brighter, but not very. Archer dreaded coming out of the room, but he desperately wanted to talk to Wick about new plans. He left the blankets in a heap at the bottom of the bed and stuck his head out into the hallway.

It seemed like he was the only one up. Going on a gamble that Wick was probably already awake or at least willing to be, Archer stepped out into the hallway and started for the stairs.

Heading down the stairs, he tried to guess which guest room his mother would have put Wick in. She normally started with the one that had the best view, didn't she? The one with all those big windows. Which one was that?

Reaching the hallway, he poked randomly at a door, and it swung open. Inside Wick was trying and failing to make the bed. Behind him were the big windows. Archer made a face. He had forgotten how ugly those curtains were in here. And was that a painting of their family hanging over the dresser? He'd thought his mother was supposed to have good taste or something like that.

Wick surveyed the crooked bedspread. "You know, it looks a lot easier when someone else does it."

"Forget about it." Archer beckoned, and Wick followed him out into the hallway with only one more reluctant glance back at the unmade bed. "We need to make a new plan," Archer said.

"I know," Wick answered. "I've been trying to think of something all night."

Archer briefly wondered if he should apologize for messing up the night before, but what did it matter? He'd already ruined it, apologizing wouldn't fix it.

"All I can think of is getting more of the messengers on board, and then we could build our own messenger system." Wick rubbed his eyes with his fingertips. "I don't know if it can be done, and negotiations would take much longer since we wouldn't be there in person, but it might be our only option."

Archer nodded. "I guess if all else fails, we could get the Door in the Wall back and try to get everything together fast."

"No," Wick said. "We can't do that. We aren't stealing this time. I'm set on that."

"Fine." Archer studied the dappled light patterns on the floor. "I guess sending messages could work. It's not like we need all the stones, anyway. We just need a few."

"Yeah." Wick nodded slowly at the floor. "What happened last night?"

"Not talking about it," Archer said firmly. "I don't want to."

"Understood." Wick thought for a moment. "I suppose I could at least go to my people."

"What?"

"Maybe the leshy would be willing to provide me with some kind of immunity," Wick said. "Or they'll lock me up the first chance they get. But I'm hoping they'll be forgiving. If I'm lucky, maybe they'll even let me have the Oak Leaf again. The most I can hope for is their protection, for what it's worth."

"I'll see if I can ask again this morning," Archer offered. "I'll try to leave the fighting out of it."

"And if that doesn't work, then I'll try to travel to my people and ask for their help," Wick continued. "For better or for worse, that's what it'll have to be."

"Yeah."

Over breakfast, Archer worked hard to keep his mouth shut. He ate quickly and didn't interject anywhere in the conversation about the city and how politics were doing and the outcome of the harvest, not even to agree. He didn't make a single noise.

So when Ochre asked what their travel plans were

going forward, Archer finally seized his only opportunity to speak. "Well, Wick is going back out today to visit his people and see his family—" a slight fib but who would know— "so if you wanted to maybe reconsider what happened last night, it might be nice."

Ochre looked ready to get up at arms again.

"Not that I'm saying you did anything wrong," Archer continued, hating every word he was saying, "but a lot of things went sideways yesterday, and Wick would be a lot safer traveling around if he wasn't constantly in danger of being attacked or something." Having said his piece, Archer clamped his mouth shut again.

"And he can go," Ochre said, taking Archer by surprise. "Wick is not my son, and he seems far more responsible than you are, Archer. If he wants to leave or see his family, I can't and won't stop him. Should anyone try to arrest him on the road, I can vouch for his character, and I'm willing to give him papers that say so. He can go wherever he likes." Ochre dabbed at his lips with a napkin. "Could someone pass me the fruit juice."

Only Archer was trapped, then. This was good news, and it meant that Wick could travel practically anywhere. But everything was still in danger, and until who knew when, Archer would be stuck here because no one would vouch for his character.

He didn't know if he could even vouch for his own.

But at least Wick could go.

Later in the morning, Wick had gathered everything he needed for his journey—as well as some things that he didn't that Archer's mother insisted on sending anyway—and he was ready to start his journey. It irked Archer deeply that this time they weren't going together, but for the time being there was nothing he could do about it.

"Can I at least walk with my friend to the edge of the city?" Archer asked his father. A sarcastic note slipped into his voice before he could catch it.

"Of course, Archer." Ochre flipped through a series of papers in his hands. "I'm not a jail keeper. You're welcome to go wherever you want in the city. It's outside of the city where I won't be your willing guardian anymore. Wander if you like, but leave me in peace."

Oh, well thank you very much, Archer thought, turning away and starting back down the stairs to meet Wick outside. *So generous*.

The air was much colder than he had expected it to be, chilly even for an autumn morning.

"It's freezing," Wick commented, even though he was wrapped in a cloak that Willow had given him. "I hope it's not a bad sign."

"With our luck, it's probably a bad sign," Archer said.

"I'd rather not think that." Wick looked around for his bearings and pointed a finger toward the south. "That way, then."

They started down the wide road between the trees. The city was less active this morning, either because of the cold or the earliness of the hour. Archer didn't care which. But it was quiet enough that the leaves crunching under their feet sounded unnecessarily loud.

"Do you really think they'll help you out?" Archer asked. "You saw how well it went here. And out there with everyone else. You'd think we stole all the most valuable things in the whole country or something with the way they're acting."

Wick didn't crack a smile at the joke. "I hope so. If they can't help us, I don't know what we'll do."

The trees suddenly felt oppressive. "Saving people

shouldn't be this hard," Archer complained. "This was supposed to be a quick side trip to get my bag working again so I could go back to normal. Why am I even here?"

Wick gave him a dry look. "I was hoping it was because you thought it was the right thing to do."

"No, that's not it." Archer scratched his head. "I'm probably still hoping there will be money in it somewhere."

"Probably."

"But really, why does everyone seem so set on not saving their country from a horrible death? It's almost like they *want* to die. Maybe we should let them."

Wick rolled his eyes. "If they die, so do we."

"Oh." Archer thought. "Well, there is that."

"Everything's so much more complicated now than when we started," Wick said. "And it already looked complicated then. If only I could have foreseen all this then. Maybe I would have acted differently. Just knowing that the human stone was fake would have been plenty. If we had known that, we might have avoided this part of the adventure altogether."

"And avoid the adventure of meeting my lovely family?" Archer asked. "Why would you ever want to miss out on that?"

Wick smiled but said nothing.

"What?" Archer said.

"Nothing," Wick said. "I have no comment on anyone else's family. I learned a long time ago to avoid commenting on that topic if I want to keep certain friends."

"Wow, how many broken families do you know?"

"None. A lot of them are a little bent is all." Wick smiled. "But they don't like being told that, and they don't want help straightening the problems. It's best if I keep my mouth shut when I notice those sorts of things."

They reached the edge of the city a few minutes later. "Wish me luck," Wick said.

Archer thought about it, then said. "No thanks. Just run and you won't get caught. That doesn't take too much luck. And don't forget to hit them if they come too close."

"Remind me never to come to you for advice." Wick hitched his bag higher on his shoulder. "Don't kill anyone while I'm gone."

"Never mind, you're not a good advice giver either." Archer gave Wick a little wave.

"I'll see you soon," Wick said. Then he turned and walked into the woods.

Watching his friend walk away reminded Archer horribly of when they had fought after escaping the manghar, when he thought they had parted ways for good. It made him feel something strange.

What a talent he had for feeling so alone in a city full of people.

You're pathetic, Archer, he told himself, and wandered back into the city.

They had estimated that Wick would be gone for about five days for travel alone, maybe six if convincing the leshy took some time. Which meant that Archer only had to survive on his own in that house for five or six days.

The task sounded easy enough.

He wondered where Fowl was. Probably hiding out with his friends. Fowl seemed to hate when Archer was home almost as much as Archer hated *being* home. Both of them usually avoided being in the house as much as possible and only showed up for meals or a few times in between when they guessed the other wouldn't be home. It was always awkward when they ran into each other despite their best efforts.

He found himself wondering what to do while Wick was gone, but as it turned out, he wouldn't have to wonder for long. When he stepped back inside the house, his mother met him with a piece of paper in her hand. "I think your friend left this for you."

Sure enough, the paper was neatly folded in thirds, and on the top fold of the paper was Archer's name, written in steady, even handwriting.

Archer took the paper and cracked open the top flap.

"And your father said that he wants you at an event today with the rest of the family," his mother said.

Already? "Tell him I can't today." He read the top line of the note and found his excuse there. "Tell him I have stuff Wick wants me to do."

His mother smiled faintly and drifted away, and Archer leaned against the wall to read his note.

While I'm gone, here are a few things I need you to do. They'll help you keep busy so you can't cause trouble.

Already he was sounding like Archer's father.

Get some nice stationery and write to a few of the leaders in the other territories: Queen Frey of the nixies and Crowned Head Theodore of the manghar. Present them (humbly) with an offer to join us in our endeavor, apologize for any misunderstandings or offenses in the past, and make sure to tell them that you also wrote to the other party and are awaiting their response. The nixies and the manghar have one of the strongest alliances in our country, and they'll be more likely to join us if they both think the other party is already in our favor.

It was a clever plan. Very clever, in fact. Archer cocked his head. He'd never known Wick was this tricksy.

Send those out with the next messenger who comes through Tor. Keep an eye out, you don't want to miss him.

If you have time, you could also write to the following representatives from human territory and any of the fair folk listed below. The fair folk are a democracy and only gather twice a year. Their next assembly is coming up in a few weeks, and I want us to attend if we can, so we can address all of them at once and present the vote. The fair folk I've listed are members of large families, and having their foreknowledge of what we're trying to do might give a larger number of the fair folk time to consider before the meeting. Make sure to tell the fair folk that we'd like to attend their assembly with all respect possible, and that we'd be grateful for their consideration. When you write to the humans, make sure to write as to a peer and not to a king or a queen. The human representatives are important, but they're only elected officials and the people like to see them as one of their own. Try to appeal to their better nature if you can.

If the situation in your people's territory is the way you say it is, maybe finding some other authority figures and convincing them to our side would be beneficial. See who you can talk to in Tor who might have some sway on the people's opinion, even if it's only your parents.

I know this is a lot to ask, and if you can't do it all, I won't blame you. Do what you can, and hang on until I'm back. Don't fight with anyone.

P.S. Make sure to mention that all letters are from both of us, but don't sign for me, and when you sign use your full name.

Below was a lengthy list of fair folk and human names, each list organized by territory and then family. At the bottom of the page was Wick's tidy signature.

Wick wanted him to do all this.

Even though Archer's head was still spinning with the sheer volume of names and instructions, he read through everything again. It now occurred to him that he had never been responsible for anything in his life. He had been the younger son and the pity child, and then he had been a feckless vagabond. Now he wasn't sure what he was. He didn't even know where to start with all this.

He squinted at the paragraph about the nixies and the manghar. How was he supposed to write a letter 'humbly'? Wasn't making a request all about confidence? Wasn't that the core of politics? Assuming that you'd get what you wanted before you even asked about it?

He shrugged. Wick knew more about this than he did.

But at least Archer could start with the stationary.

CHAPTER SEVEN:

Under Pressure

THREE HOURS LATER, he still struggled with the first of the letters.

Finding the stationary and the pen had been easy enough. His father's office had enough paper to cut a hole in the forest. The next step had seemed simple as well. He had decided to write the manghar letter and the nixie letter at the same time since they were supposed to be similar in format.

But it turned out that writing two letters exactly the same wasn't as easy when you didn't even know how you wanted to start even one of them.

He had all his 'respected sirs' and 'honorable so and sos' written at the tops of the pages, but he didn't even begin to know how to start them. Several pieces of paper had already been balled up and tossed on the floor, chucked at the wall, or catapulted out the window. And now the ink had spilled on the page.

Archer ripped up another piece of paper with a growl and threw it down next to his makeshift desk. He had dragged a chair in from another room and leaned on the top of the toy chest to write. It wasn't comfortable, but at least no one else had to witness his humiliation.

What did you write before you got to the point of the letter? Did you ask about the weather, the grass, the price of tea? And why did it matter?

Finally, an idea crept into his head. He could steal some of the letters from his father's desk and use them as a cheat sheet to write his own letters. He snuck out of the room and up the stairs to the study. This was a room he had seldom visited as a child. When his father was at work, no one wanted to bother him, and Ochre made visits as inconvenient as possible by putting his study on the highest level of the house. The spiraling stairs leading up to it creaked with every step, and Archer winced with each squeal of the wood.

As he reached the top of the stairs, he realized he was too late. His father was already in the study, and the door was closed. Archer listened, just as he had as a child, and could hear his father pacing. His father always paced when he was trying to solve a problem.

Archer didn't like realizing that he did the same thing when he needed a way out of a problem.

The door was closed, but the expedition wasn't a total loss. Someone—probably his mother—had left a tray outside the door with a jug of frutelken and a dish of peaches. Archer took the whole tray. His father wouldn't notice for a few hours at least. Since he couldn't get into the study, at least not yet, he took the tray back down the shrieking stairs to his bedroom and shut the door behind him.

He had yet to quite figure out the secret to frutelken. He'd tried to make it over the years, usually when he was bored and had enough supplies, and some of them had even turned out as tasty drinks. But none of them had ever tasted like real frutelken. His mother's fruit drink was the best he had ever had, better than any others inside or outside of seraph territory, and for the life of him he couldn't figure out the recipe. But he would.

He dug inside the top drawer of his old dresser and felt for the familiar crinkle of well-loved paper: his guesses at the ingredients for frutelken. They probably weren't good guesses. In fact, he knew they weren't good guesses since none of them had turned out to be right, but he had worked on it too long to give up now.

He took another sip of the drink and wrote down *cloves*. The other guesses on the list had been the same over the years, *cinnamon, nutmeg, peach, strawberry, raspberry*, but he couldn't get the amounts right. Had he guessed cloves before? He couldn't remember.

Archer reached for the jug to pour himself another glass and laughed.

Tucked under the jug were two envelopes. His mother must have gathered the mail and sent the letters for his father up with the drink. Instead of taking them from the study, Archer had gotten two letters by accident.

But it also meant he had missed the messenger.

Send the letters with the next messenger. You don't want to miss him.

Archer hissed and raced to the window. Was the messenger still on the street? He couldn't see anyone. Throwing the door open, he hurried down the stairs. "Mother!" he shouted. "Is the messenger still here?"

Through the doorway to the kitchen, his mother looked up with startled eyes. "No, he came an hour ago. Why?"

Archer sighed. "No reason. I was hoping to catch him before he left is all. He's probably long gone."

So what if he'd missed the messenger, he told himself as he climbed back up the stairs. He didn't even have a finished letter yet to send. The letters from outside the office would help, but his writing was slower than the movement of the sun. Something in the back of his mind told him that if he wasn't so stupid, he wouldn't have missed the messenger in the first place, but he pushed the thought out of his mind and told it that it was crazy.

Archer cracked the seals on his father's letters and read them through, and then through again. It seemed you did start with pleasantries, after all, maybe even a bit about what you were doing recently, and then went on to the real point of the letter. And after that, you ended with unimportant things as well. A wholesome sandwich of importance and unimportance. Interesting. Archer mentally filed away the names of the people in the letters and the things they wanted to report to his father and set the papers aside. Now he could write his own letters.

Think like Wick, he told himself. *I know you don't want to, but think like Wick.*

His pen made scratching noises on the paper.

To the esteemed Queen Frey of the nixies,
Greetings.
Wick and I have been released by the centaurs and are now staying in Tor with the rest of the Hessen family. We are safe and want to extend hopes that you are as well.

He laughed at the stupidity of what he was writing.

Since we last saw one another (a phrase taken directly

from one of the stolen letters), *both Wick and I have come to see that our original approach to gathering the stones was dishonest, and we humbly beg for your pardon.*

Humbly with an underline, more like.

We now want to forge alliances with the territories if we can and especially want to ~~get cozy~~ make relations with yourself and Crowned Head Theodore of the manghar. We have already written to him and his advisers and are waiting for his approval.

He went on to explain the basics of what the problem was (the world was going to end), and their solution (to get the stones together to avoid such inconveniences). He finished the way he thought his father would, with an appropriate amount of oil.

We look forward to an alliance with you and hope that your piece of the heather stone will be the first we gather with this new strategy.
Best of wishes toward your harvest and spring.
Sincerely,
Archer Oak Hessen, son of Ochre Hessen, of the Hessen family tree

Curse his stupid handwriting.
But it was the best he could do, for now. He wrote out the letter addressed to Crowned Head Theodore of the manghar and slapped them both in envelopes. He even went to the effort of putting it in the outgoing basket by the door with all his father's mail.
With that he considered his work to be done for now.

The letter writing had been more than enough mental effort for one day, so he downed one more glass of the frutelken and raced down the spiraling stairs.

"Archer," a voice called behind him.

Archer nearly slipped trying to stop mid-run. Clinging to the tree bark for balance, he looked back.

His father stood at the edge of the porch with his silk shirt whipping in the wind, his features harder and sharper than ever. "I'll need you back later. There's an event this afternoon that requires the whole family."

"Political?" Archer asked.

"To show our support for the opening of a new establishment here in the city," Ochre responded.

Archer shook his head. "Then no thanks. Like I told Mother, maybe next time, but not today."

His father's features hardened. "You can't avoid your duties forever, Archer. You know that."

Archer cocked his head. "Do I? As far as I can see it, they're not my duties. They're yours." Turning, he started back down the stairs.

As he paced through the trees with his hands in his pockets, Archer spotted an old couple down the street. Not too weak to fly, but too tired to lift off. They would probably have stairs at their house soon. People weren't supposed to need stairs until that age.

The urge suddenly struck him to find a tall ledge and jump off, but he knew from many past mistakes how that would end: bruised ribs, broken hands, straining of his older injuries. It never went well. But every few years or so he always found himself plunging off some ledge or another. Like he thought eventually something would get better.

The old couple spotted him and waved at him, but all

he could manage was an awkward smile. He wondered if they knew who he was, or if he'd finally been forgotten.

Which would be better, to be forgotten entirely, or to be remembered as the skinny little invalid who could never do a thing for himself? The little thing who stood in the corner at events and never said a word because he didn't dare?

Would it be better if people forgot *that* Archer?

He tried to imagine a world where he was more than a prize people kept chasing after, or something other than a face that had meaning because of what it stood for. *Imagine if things had been different, but don't really because it's not worth the energy.*

There was a ledge under a nearby bridge where he could sit and hide from all the eyes. He hid there a lot when he was younger, thinking or drawing or singing quietly to himself. He would often fall asleep there while avoiding going to some event or another with his father.

He also remembered sitting there on a different occasion, with his wing wrapped up in bandages and splints in some doctor's attempt to set it straight.

Luckily he still knew how to climb down, and when he dug through the stones of the bridge, the lead pencil was still there. He wrote the date on the ceiling, under all the other dates he had written there sitting in this same place. It was damp under the bridge, but the numbers had somehow stuck to the stones, and the older ones were only a little smudged. Then he started sketching a picture above his head, trying to get the shapes right from his memory. First, a rough oval, then hair, then the features slowly took on a slightly askew but familiar look. The harsh angle made his shoulder start to burn after a few minutes.

A memory surfaced as he drew: one of the many

times he had chosen to spend time with his grandparents rather than another minute around his family.

"What did your parents think of your hair?" his grandfather asked. "Were they surprised?"

"Surprised is one way to put it." Archer scratched his head, and the bristles of his freshly cut hair scraped against his hand. The floor of his grandparents' sitting room was cold against his back. *"Father made a big deal out of it, something about the image of the family and tradition and all kinds of nonsense. Mother doesn't like it either, but she's making a huge show of not taking a side."*

"Willow was always a well-meaning girl," Oak said. *"Give her some credit."*

"I don't think meaning well is actually helping." Archer rocked his head back toward the ceiling. The beams of the roof looked so high and far away. Light from the windows danced merrily across the rafters. *"Honestly, I can't tell the difference anymore between what she thinks and what she wants everyone to think she thinks. I don't get it."*

Out of the corner of his eye, he saw his grandfather smile slightly. *"I have half a mind to cut my hair like yours in solidarity."*

"Nah, your hair is a lot nicer than mine was. All mine ever did was get tangled in things." Archer also knew that his grandfather's hair, wrapped in a knot at the nape of his neck, was one of the things his grandmother liked best. It wouldn't be worth it.

The secret he carried weighed on the tip of his tongue. I want to leave. I can't stand it here anymore. I can't stand the seraphs anymore. Archer turned to his grandfather.

Before he could speak, a woman's voice called from downstairs. "Who can help me carry these dishes to the dining room?"

"That will be your grandmother." Archer's grandfather got up from his seat on the sofa. "Come on, my boy, let's give her a hand."

Just like that, the opportunity flew away like a sparrow. Archer heaved himself up off the floor. "Yeah, let's go." As he trotted toward the stairs, one of his wings ached strangely. It felt like an injury, but even with all his falls and accidents, he had always managed to keep his wings from coming to any harm.

It felt oddly like an omen.

Archer shoved the memory back down where it belonged.

When he finished drawing his grandfather's face, he stuffed the pencil back into the crack between the stones and laid back on the rocky ledge. It was a little uneven, and very damp, but the trickling of the water made the space under the footbridge feel peaceful.

Maybe the peacefulness of this little space was what had always brought him back here. The peace under this bridge was what his grandfather's memory deserved.

With the water trickling next to his ear and the quiet cool to cover him, he fell asleep.

CHAPTER EIGHT:

A Few Fowl Words

"MOVE OVER, you're taking up all the space." Something nudged Archer's shoulder.

Groggy and a little cranky, Archer grunted and sat up, rubbing at his eyes. "What?"

Fowl sat down next to him, then moved back to lean his back against the bottom of the bridge. Looking down at his own legs pulled up against his chest, Archer realized that the way Fowl was sitting was a lot more comfortable. He'd never thought about it. He usually just tucked his legs up whichever way he could so they wouldn't dangle in the water up to the knee.

Then it occurred to him that Fowl wasn't supposed to be here. No one was supposed to know that Archer hid under the bridge.

Archer scrambled up the ledge and glared at Fowl from hands and knees. "What are you doing down here?"

"You disappeared and I guessed you'd come here," Fowl said casually. "This is where you always hid when you were younger, why would that change now?" His long hair was sticking to the dampness of the bridge, making it almost appear that he was fading into the bridge itself.

"You couldn't let me alone?" Archer demanded. "I can't get a moment alone if I want it?"

Fowl's lip curled. "I didn't realize I would offend you so deeply. I just wanted to see what you were doing."

"I was sleeping. Normally when someone's sleeping, you leave them alone, not bother them and nearly shove them off the ledge."

Fowl looked at him. "I didn't push you off the ledge. I gave you a nudge and that was all."

"I'm trying to give you the impression that I don't want you here. Is it working?"

"I got that impression," Fowl said. "But I'm not listening to you just because you say so." He looked up at the drawing on the ceiling. "The chin isn't right. You made it too square."

Archer immediately took offense. "So what? You could tell who it was, couldn't you? So it doesn't matter."

"I knew who it was because we only have one relative that died recently that you would draw on the ceiling." Fowl took a closer look. "Where's his second ear?"

"I don't know!" Archer cried, throwing his hands up. "Did you come down here just to criticize me, or do you have a reason to be here tormenting me?"

"No reason. It probably isn't important." Fowl settled further down the wall and crossed his arms over his chest. "I just wanted to see if you were all right. It's not like I don't care."

"No, really?" Archer's voice dripped with sarcasm. "And I thought you wanted to be a stone-faced statue. You have feelings?"

"Look, we grieved too. You missed it because you

weren't here," Fowl snapped.

"Did it last five minutes?" Archer demanded. "Because it hasn't even been a month, and you've sold nearly everything he had. I asked for one thing, and none of you wanted to give it to me."

"For all you've done to deserve it, I'm sure." Fowl rolled his eyes. "You're still such a child, Archer. You think everyone has it out for you. Everything that goes wrong has to be the end of the world."

"It's funny that you say that when the end of the world is actually on its way and none of you want to do anything about it. Or even to help us when we're trying to do something about it."

"Don't pretend you're being a hero." Fowl's eyes turned on Archer in a blaze of fury. His crossed arms snapped down to his sides. Archer knew he had finally pushed Fowl too far. "I never know whether to believe a single thing you say, because everything out of your mouth is a never-ending stream of lies and exaggeration. If even a crumb of what you say about your latest calamity is even *mildly* true, you aren't doing it to be a good person. There's something in it for you, there has to be. You've never done anything out of the goodness of your heart. And now you want us to give you whatever you want when you've never done enough to earn a thing from anyone. You take whatever you want, and when you want people to look at you, you scream so they have no other choice. Don't try to tell me you're doing something so great when I know you too well."

Archer knew he had already pushed Fowl far enough, but he couldn't let Fowl win. He couldn't be allowed to say things like that. He pushed him further. "That's rich, coming from you. Did you come up with all that yourself?

You do whatever Father says so often that I didn't guess you were capable of original thought."

Fowl's eyes blazed. He swung at Archer's head, knocking him into the stream. Archer got a mouthful as he hit the cold water. He was submerged for only a moment since, after all, the stream wasn't deep. He sat up quickly, gasping, wings dripping and soggy, hair falling in his eyes, but Fowl was already gone. The harsh flap of wings and a distant shout of anger at some unsuspecting passerby was enough to tell him that Fowl wouldn't be coming back.

But Fowl had also made sure that Archer couldn't stay in the cold under the bridge. Now soaked through and muttering under his breath in frustration, Archer sloshed out from under the bridge and struggled onto the bank of the stream. He drew a few gazes, but he slogged back across town, dripping and collecting small patches of grass the whole way. Everything he touched stuck to his wet legs and arms, and with his hair falling in his eyes, he could barely see a thing. He tried to shove the hair out of his eyes as well as he could, but only made the problem worse. Finally, he gave up on it.

The last straw came when he reached the bottom of the stairs. Three steps up, his foot slipped on all the sticking grass and his feet went flying. His chin hit a stair and his shoulder slammed against the railing. Groaning, he slid back down to the bottom stair, clutching his face. Had he bitten his tongue? Everything tasted burnt.

A dark hand was offered to him, and he reluctantly took it. Pulling himself up hurt almost more than the fall.

When he looked up, Ongel's face loomed over him, covered in the starts of kind wrinkles and full of concern.

"When did you get here?" Archer asked. His tongue still felt wrong. He must have bitten it when he fell.

"I arrived just now," Ongel said. "I wanted to see how I could help you and Wick collect the stones. I assume Wick would want to arrange some meetings to talk to the leaders. How is that going?"

"Wick isn't here," Archer said. "He's in leshy territory."

Ongel's eyes brightened. "Then I take it everything went well with getting the diplomatic immunity you were looking for."

No. They didn't have the diplomatic immunity, they didn't have a hideout, they didn't have much of anything, because Archer had messed up. Now Wick was gone, hopefully safe, and Archer was still failing at everything. He couldn't write the letters, he couldn't get along with his brother, and he had missed the messenger.

Archer sat down on the stairs. "No, it's not going well." Then he buried his face in his hands.

Ongel listened as Archer told him everything about the disasters of the last few days, about the fights and the failures, about how he was trying to do everything Wick wanted him to while he was gone but didn't know how to do any of it, about how everything was going wrong and he didn't know how to control a bit of it. Ongel listened without offering judgment or advice, then when Archer was finished talking, he suggested they go for a walk around the city. At this point, Archer wanted anything but to go back into the house, so he agreed.

As they walked through the trees, Ongel told Archer stories about how he had lit an important historic scroll on fire with a candle when he had first started as an apprentice in centaur territory, and how the burned part still hadn't been restored, and how he had argued with a few of the other apprentices and the bunch of them had looked very unprofessional in front of a group of visiting dignitaries.

"Somehow I still can't picture you having a temper," Archer mumbled as they crossed another footbridge. His clothes had settled down to warm dampness now, and he was only cold when the wind blew. "I think you're just saying that to make me feel better."

"I would never embellish on a story, even if it was to make you feel better," Ongel promised. "Even the one with the blue unicorn."

"Okay, there's no way that one is real."

"I take it that I've lifted your spirits a little," Ongel said, and Archer crossed his arms uncomfortably. "I propose a new strategy: I can read over Wick's list of instructions with you, and we can divide the work between us. Since I'm fairly well known through the territories, I can arrange some meetings with a few people. That way we can get a start on some of the other territories, especially with the fair folk, seeing as how we have a deadline coming up with that one. How does that sound?"

Unused to having people help him, Archer managed, "That works."

Together they made their way back toward the Hessen house.

"The family that offered to host me is down the road from here," Ongel said. "I'll send you up for the list, and then we can sort out our plans at my host's house. I'd go up myself, but I don't know if your family would want an unexpected guest. Not to mention I see quite a few stairs from here. I'm getting old, you know."

Archer gave him a funny look and ran up the stairs to get the list. Judging from all the noise, he guessed that everyone else was also home, so he kept a close eye out as he climbed up to his room. The door to the library was open, and as he passed he got a glimpse of Fowl in a tall backed chair, his attention fixed on another book.

Archer made it up to his room without being seen. Huffing a quick sigh of relief, he dug through the heap of ruined letters to find Wick's list. He would probably need the rest of the blank stationery as well. He tucked the stack in the crook of his arm and headed for the door. Then he remembered his father's mail. By now Ochre would have noticed that it wasn't outside his door. He ran back and snatched the opened mail off his desk. Maybe if he left them in the front hall everyone would assume they had overlooked them. The open envelopes would probably defeat that plan, but he could hope.

He raced back down the stairs, trying to avoid the main hallways where he could. As he passed the library, Fowl shouted his name, but Archer ran faster. He skidded down the stairs and past the kitchen.

"There you are!" his mother said, stepping out of the kitchen as he went racing past. "Will you be home for dinner?" she asked as he headed for the door.

"Maybe. I don't know." Archer dropped the opened mail on the table next to the door and darted back out. So much for going in and out unnoticed. He trotted back down the stairs to meet Ongel, one hand skidding down the railing for balance the whole way. Better to avoid a repeat of the earlier slip and fall.

"Okay," he said, skidding to a stop at the bottom. "Got the list, ready to go."

"I thought I heard someone call you," Ongel said, gazing up at the house.

"Yeah, I know," Archer said, flapping a dismissive hand toward the house. "Don't worry about it."

"You took care of it?"

"Sure." Ignored it, more like, but what was the difference?

Ongel took the list and read it as they crossed the cool grass to Ongel's host's house. After a moment, he smiled. "I can see our influence on his plan. The centaurs," he clarified. "This is exactly the kind of approach we would take."

"Yeah, I can imagine you starting with this rather than what I did," Archer said.

Ongel's face broke into a grin. "Imagine me trying to break in through a window."

"I can't imagine you thinking of it, honestly," Archer said, and Ongel guffawed.

They reached the house and started up the ramp. The sun was starting to set sooner these days, and it was already at the point where it shone in a flat line into Archer's eyes. He shielded his face with every turn around the tree trunk, his eyes watering.

"Like I thought," Ongel said as they reached the top, "the best way to divide this up is if you sent out those first two letters and then worked on a few more to some of the other leaders, and in the meantime, I'll arrange the meetings with the fair folk. I believe one or two of the human representatives are due to tour their territory soon as part of a new agreement among their people. If our messengers catch them at a village that's closer to their borders, it would cut down on travel time. Meaning we would get a faster response."

The hostess at the house met them as they entered the door. She wore a dress of reds and blues as bright as her smile and as vibrant as her auburn hair. Either she didn't know who Archer was, or she didn't care. She welcomed Ongel and greeted Archer in the same delightful, warm tone, and offered to bring an extra chair into the study Ongel was using.

"You should probably read the letters before I send them," Archer admitted reluctantly, sitting in the padded dining chair the woman had brought in for him. "To make sure they aren't bad. I'm not Wick; I'm not an expert letter writer."

With great difficulty, he let Ongel have the letters, and he tried not to squirm as Ongel read them.

Ongel handed them back with a nod. "They'll do fine."

"You mean they're bad."

"I said they'll do," Ongel said gently but firmly. "Everyone you're writing letters to right now already knows who you are, and they know that you aren't an elegant dignitary. They aren't expecting a fully polished letter from you, and if the letters were perfect, I think it would seem suspicious. Better to leave them as they are."

Somehow that didn't make Archer feel any better. He put the letters in envelopes and addressed them to the Crowned Head and Queen Frey and tried not to think about them anymore.

After that, Ongel launched off talking about the meetings they could arrange with some of the important people in seraph territory. He grilled Archer on who he knew of and what kind of connections they had with his father. If they liked Ochre Hessen, they would want to keep in good with his son, or at least that was how Archer understood it. But as Archer pointed out to Ongel, anyone who didn't like Archer's father might still side with Archer. They might want to forge their own fame off the coattails of Archer's success. Maybe.

Ongel worked hard at his tall desk writing notes and

suggesting meetings, and Archer worked hard at the glass-topped end table beside it, slaving over the letters and making sure that all the sentences sounded right before he even bothered putting them on the page. He thought about asking for advice several times, but it seemed too weak to ask for help, so he struggled on his own.

Sometime later, Ongel looked at the sun and said, "A messenger should be coming through the city soon. We should finish what we can to send with him." He gathered up his little pieces of paper from all over his desk, and Archer stuffed one last letter into an envelope and sealed it.

"After all the work we put into these, this had better work," Archer said as he handed his letters to Ongel, stretching out his cramped writing hand.

"It might and it might not," Ongel said. "Once we send the letters, they pass beyond our control. It's up to the others now."

"Yeah, well, I don't trust the others," Archer said. He squinted out the window at the sun fading beyond the horizon. "They're all chasing after fame and ambition and stupid things like that. Once they're all about ambition, people never do the thing that's right anymore, they just do the thing that makes them look good."

Ongel grunted in agreement and put all the letters into a little canvas sack. "The messenger should be here any minute now, so I'll go down to the street and keep an eye out for him."

Archer nodded and watched Ongel leave the room. Once Ongel was gone, he sighed and leaned back in the chair. He didn't want to think about any leaders or tiny little people who had a democracy anymore. He had used up all the brain power he possessed.

The hostess appeared in the doorway and placed her hand on the door frame. "Will you be staying for dinner this evening?"

Archer sat up straighter. "I—No. Thanks though. I'll be going." He picked himself up out of the chair, offered the hostess an awkward smile, and slipped out of the house. Crickets chirped in the grass and the crooks of tree roots, and a few evening birds were making their soft calls as well. The night seemed slightly damp, but maybe that was the remaining stream water sticking to Archer's clothes.

He glanced up at his house, at all the lights streaming out of the glass windows, and thought about never going back in. It wasn't too late. He could run away and go live in his grandfather's old house and never have to come back here if he didn't want to. Or he could find a flattish empty tree branch somewhere and sleep there.

He didn't have to go inside.

But for some reason, maybe because he knew Ongel would be relying on him to help with more work tomorrow, he went inside. He sat quietly at dinner and didn't say anything to anyone, except to thank his mother for the meal as he stood up to leave. He didn't storm into the library to confront Fowl for pushing him into the stream. He climbed up the stairs, closed the door to his room, and fell asleep as quickly as he could with the window open to catch the breeze.

CHAPTER NINE:

This is Why I'm Never Home

TWO DAYS LATER he was woken by the sound of a fist pounding on his door.

"Go away," Archer called and buried his head further under the pillows. If the sun would stop shining through the blankets, he could go back to sleep, and everything would be all right.

But no, the pounding continued, followed by the sound of a door opening. The crinkle Archer could feel in his brow deepened.

"Good morning," his father's voice said. "Now get up. We have an event today as a family." Something dropped onto the bed next to Archer's head.

Archer peeked out of a crack between the blanket and the bed and saw it was a stack of clothes, all vibrant shades of red and caramel-brown and black. Nice, respectable, well-behaved clothes, the kind that people who went to events as a family wore.

"No thank you," he said, making no move to get up. "I don't enjoy events much anymore, thank you, Father."

"You'll come. In fact, I don't think you have another choice."

"I can find another choice."

"If what I hear about the plans you're making with that centaur fellow is true, I don't think you'll want to find another choice," his father said, and in the slice of the room visible between the blankets, Archer saw him gliding toward the door. "Many of the city's fair folk will be there. Not to mention it will show our family, yourself included, in a favorable light."

Then he was gone, and Archer found himself climbing out of bed, hating himself. He stood next to the bed, eyeing the clothes that his father had left for him. They were nice clothes, and probably expensive, too.

It occurred to him as he pulled the shirt over his head that he hadn't had clothes like this ever before, and the pants weren't cut long enough to be something borrowed from Fowl's closet. Someone had bought them specifically for him.

That thought could have made him feel warm and fuzzy inside, but then he realized that his father had bought these assuming that he could weasel Archer into coming today. The threat of warm and fuzzy vanished immediately.

Archer got all his buttons in the right order and straightened his hair in the reflection of his window. There were shoes with the outfit, too, sturdy leather things that looked like they cost a lot of money for all that stitching and lacing. He didn't like the looks of them. Those were suspicious shoes if ever he saw any.

But if he showed up at this event, he supposed he

would have to wear the shoes. He would be given a fit if he didn't. He jammed his feet into the leather prisons, giving up all feeling of the ground and subjecting himself to a hundred tripping hazards, and started down the stairs.

A glorious smell floated from the kitchen. He wandered in and found his mother there, as usual. "Almost ready," she said, turning from the stove with a bit of kindling in her hand and a smile on her face. "It's taking me a moment this morning. I forgot and overslept."

Archer reached for a bowl of apples on the counter. "What are we having?"

The *we* made her face brighten a bit more. "Biscuits, if they'll ever finish browning. I made some preserves that we can have with them." She took in his new clothes. "Don't you look nice? I can't remember the last time you looked. . ." She seemed to forget the word and waved a hand. "It looks very nice."

"At least one of us thinks so," Archer said.

As Archer took a bite of his apple, his father gusted into the kitchen. He looked Archer up and down with a critical eye. "The clothes look all right, and I suppose we can all overlook the bruises. Even the fresh ones." His voice took a judgmental tone.

Archer swallowed the bite of apple. It tasted woody suddenly. "If it makes you feel any better, the recent bruises are tripping on the stairs. After your other son knocked me in the stream and got me soaked."

"Don't say that like you were innocent," Fowl said on his way by the kitchen door. "Not to mention I had nothing to do with your tripping on the stairs. You did that yourself."

"I could make you do some tripping of your own," Archer muttered, but Fowl either didn't hear or chose to ignore him.

Taking a quick step into the kitchen, Fowl got an apple himself and left again, off to the depths of the house to read or ignore the rest of them until it was time to eat. Only a few minutes later, Archer's mother declared the biscuits ready and asked for Archer's help transporting all the food to the dining room. He felt very awkward when she almost took off to fly to the dining room, then decided against it with a brief ruffle of her wings.

Archer decided that helping gave him a free ticket to pick whatever biscuits he wanted as his mother called for Ochre and Fowl. He found the three largest and best and then prodded the shining jars of preserves with his spoon as the others entered.

"They're blackberry, apple, and mixed," Fowl said as he took his seat.

Archer, who hadn't guessed any of that, said, "I already guessed that, thanks." He picked up the one that looked like blackberry. Unless of course, it was the mixed fruit one. How could he tell?

The food made its rounds, and everyone started eating.

Before even two minutes of silence had passed, Archer's father said, "The event we're attending today is to provide the city's fair folk with building materials. Many of them need to repair their dwellings that were damaged in the recent storm."

Archer set his cup down. "Which storm?"

"The one you used to pull your grand heist on the centaurs," Ochre said coldly, and Archer decided that was quite enough talking for one meal. "It was myself and a few of my friends who paid for the materials, so it will be us and a few other families who present the materials to the fair folk. There may be a crowd, or there may not. The turnout is unpredictable at this point." He looked up from spreading preserves over a biscuit. "We should all stand straight and smile, and afterward make pleasant conversation with the fair folk who attend. They may need assistance carrying the materials away, and if questions about transporting the materials arise, be sure to redirect them to the seraphs wearing the blue sashes."

Archer was supposed to redirect any actual work to the lackeys. He was expected to stand there and look good with everyone else standing there looking good. This was what people did for politics? It felt fishy.

But this was what Wick would want him to do, so Archer shut his mouth and kept eating biscuits. Maybe if he ate enough, he would glue his mouth shut and he wouldn't be able to open it again until after the event.

HALF AN HOUR LATER, Archer stood on a wooden platform with the rest of his family. Half a dozen other seraphs stood behind them as his father talked about maintaining relations and providing in times of need and at least eight other topics that Archer forgot immediately. Most of the people in the crowd—because there was a crowd—looked so interested it was almost funny. Archer decided he wanted to find it funny and not appalling that some people thought his father was sincere.

The stage made Archer uncomfortable. He wasn't the center of attention—no one else could be the center of attention when his father was around—but being raised above the crowd by a few feet made him feel like he was on display, like he was something in a glass case for people to observe as they liked. And then there were the shoes. Having gone comfortably without shoes for years, the way most of the other seraphs also did, the clamp of them around his feet made him vaguely want to scream. He tried not to think about them.

How had he ever made it through any of these events and parties when he was younger? How had he been able to bear sitting there as just a face that meant money and influence and not a person with wants and aching muscles and other places he'd rather be? Try as he might, he couldn't remember what that had been like.

People were clapping. His father had finally stopped talking and gestured across the street. The seraph men in the blue sashes flew out of the trees, carrying an air cart between them. As they set down the leather carrying straps, everyone saw the abundance of supplies inside. His father and the other families involved must have paid quite a bit for all of it. Sheets of roofing tiles, piles of wood, stones and bricks. . . Archer suddenly found himself wondering how anyone had ever lifted that cart in the first place.

The clapping increased, and Ochre Hessen smiled graciously. He said something to the little crowd of fair folk standing in front of the stage, and some of them said something back with grateful expressions. With that, Archer's father looked around at the crowd of adoring people and tilted his head slightly in a sort of bow, then stepped off the stage.

As Archer trailed off the stage with all the others, following his father's lead, he found himself a little bit jealous of that nodding bow. It was a signal that he saw everyone and acknowledged them, not quite as equals, but as people that he appreciated for their appearance today. It showed that he was a leader of some kind, and Archer found himself a bit jealous of how such a small motion could communicate so much.

For a minute he understood why people wanted power, and it made him a little bit uncomfortable.

As he stood as close to the edge of the crowd as his father's narrowed eyes would allow, waiting for this part to be over, a young fair folk woman with strawberry gold hair nervously approached him. Even with a little cap on, she only came up to Archer's knee. "Excuse me?"

Archer looked down. "Hello?"

"You're Ochre Hessen's son, aren't you?" she asked timidly.

"Yeah, I mean, yes, I am, why?" Archer said, fumbling for words that sounded like a respectable man's son.

"I wanted to ask him myself, but he seems a little busy," the woman said, turning a little bit pink in the cheeks.

Archer glanced at where his father had been standing and saw that he was, predictably, surrounded by dozens of people.

"I know the supplies are meant for repairs, but my mother's house was almost entirely wiped out by the storm," the woman explained. "I wanted to know if it was all right to take enough materials to rebuild it. My father was the one who normally did the building for our family, but he recently passed away. I don't even know where to get the supplies on my own."

"Did he die in the storm?" Archer asked, knowing immediately that he shouldn't have asked that question.

Fortunately, the fair folk woman was forgiving. "No," she answered. "He died four months ago. A tree fell on him."

Oh. Archer didn't know how to get out of the hole he

had dug, so he pretended that he hadn't asked. "Take whatever you want. It doesn't matter. They can always get more materials if the pile runs out."

"Oh good." Her entire face visibly relaxed. "I was worried we wouldn't be able to rebuild the house before the winter came. It's been so cold lately. Some of our neighbors have been good enough to let us stay with them, but we don't want to impose through the winter."

"That does sound nice of them," Archer said, scrambling for something to say.

"I'm sorry to ask for something else so soon," she said, "but I don't know how I'm going to get the building materials to the right place. I understand if I'm supposed to transport them myself. Maybe I can borrow a wagon—"

Archer glanced at one of the men in the blue sashes for half a second. He decided not to ask for help from any of them. "Don't worry, I can help you carry it all. Tell me what you need."

Archer followed the fair folk woman to the air cart. They discussed the building strategy. Between the two of them, they decided that the stone would be too heavy to carry by hand, so the house would have to be made mostly of wood. She was sure some of her neighbors could build her some new furniture, so all they needed to think about was rebuilding the structure of the house itself. Thus, Archer gathered up as much wood as he could carry and the fair folk woman, whose name was Annalise, collected roofing tiles. No one seemed to be paying them mind, so they took everything they needed and left the clearing. The pressure on Archer's temples released the moment they left the crowd behind.

"It's down this road a way," Annalise said, hefting her pile of roofing tiles a little higher. "We lived at the base of the Blacktree family's home, and the family is all right with the house being rebuilt in the same place."

"Okay." Archer got a better grip on the wood as it threatened to slip. "Do you have anyone to help rebuild the house once we get there?"

"I'm hoping the neighbors will help, but I'm not sure yet. The only ones I can count on for sure are my mother and my brother," Annalise answered, "but my brother is only visiting until the end of the week."

"If you can't get anyone else," Archer said, feeling awkward, "I can help you."

"Oh, you don't have to," Annalise assured him with a brief flash of a smile in his direction. "You probably have more important things to do."

"Not if I have anything to do with it." One of Archer's new shoes hit a rock, throwing him off balance and making the wood shift dangerously in his arms.

"Careful!" Annalise cried. One of her little hands stretched out as though she could stop the lumber from slipping.

Archer clutched the wood tighter in his arms, desperate to keep them from falling. Crouching, he used the tops of his legs to shove the wood higher into his arms and shift it sideways so that it was more or less balanced again. "Don't worry, I have it."

"Thank goodness." Annalise sighed as they continued down the road. "I was worried all the wood would fall and break. Oh, but you probably put splinters right through your shirt!"

Archer, suddenly very aware of all the spines poking him in the stomach, said, "It doesn't matter. I don't even know where this thing came from, anyway." Nonetheless, he tried to watch his step a little more carefully. He didn't want to add any permanent marks to his abdomen.

"Forgive me if I'm being rude," Annalise said after a moment, when they were far enough from the crowd that they couldn't hear the sound of all the chatter anymore. "But aren't you Ochre Hessen's younger son, the one who..."

Archer waited to hear which part of his reputation had made it to her ears.

"The one who everyone's talking about? Who stole from the centaurs and the nixies and everyone else? Your friend can change form," she added, desperately trying to make her meaning clear.

Archer hitched the wood higher again. One of the splinters stabbed at his chest. "Um, yeah. That's me. Why?"

"I thought I heard about you, and I was curious," Annalise said. "Having heard so much and knowing that both the sons would be there at the speech today, I expected to see a certain something when I saw you, and I didn't see it. I found it odd that you didn't look like someone who would steal things and threaten the country and then go to prison." She hesitated. "It was so odd that you looked like anyone else. So I thought I must have been wrong. But you say that's you. What am I not understanding?"

How could Archer explain that to her? *I did what I wanted because no one was stopping me from doing it* wouldn't cut it. Neither would *There was this bag, see, and it helped me cause trouble, but it stopped working so I wanted to fix it.* And he definitely couldn't say *I'm still not sure why I bothered in the first place or why I'm here now, so don't ask me.*

"Is there a part of the story that's missing?" Annalise

pressed. "Were you trying to do good all along and no one knew?"

Archer wished he could say he had been trying to do good all along. It would have made it a lot easier. But really, was that what he had been doing? He had started out seeing the journey as a necessary evil, a tool to get his bag to work again. He had only been looking out for himself. But then once Wick had been involved, he wasn't sure what had made him stick around. He wanted to say it had been more selfish ambition, but had it been?

"I don't know," Archer admitted at last. "Everyone thought that I was out to destroy everything, and it wasn't like that, it never was, but I don't know how to explain it. I made some mistakes the first time and now I'm trying to fix them because that's what I have to do, but. . . I honestly don't know what I'm doing or why I'm doing it."

I just hope it's the right thing.

The thought startled him. Was that what it boiled down to? Did he really want to do the right thing for all these people that didn't know or care who he was? He never had before. He thought of himself as someone who always did what was best for him, the way he thought everyone else did. Was he doing that now?

Or was Wick finally starting to rub off on him?

He couldn't explain it.

"But you're helping me rebuild my house," Annalise said. "And you're helping me carry all these things even though you could have asked anyone else to do it. You didn't have to do it yourself. And yet here you are. I think that means you have noble intentions, and that's enough for me."

They reached the base of a huge sycamore, and Annalise set down her roofing tiles. Archer dropped the pile of wood next to it.

"Here's the house," Annalise said, leading Archer around the tree trunk a few feet to show him the disaster of a house.

The storm had taken its toll. Most of the house was missing, probably blown away in the storm. What was left of it, a few walls and a bit of the roof still clinging to the tree trunk, had been crushed by a large tree branch.

"This is all that's left of it?" Archer asked. "And you're going to try to rebuild this?"

"Most of it will have to be torn down so we can start over," Annalise said sadly. "But I'm used to starting over. My family has moved around as much as any other fair folk family."

Archer got a good grip on the branch and heaved. Little by little, with the smaller branches resisting and bending against the ground, he shoved the branch away from what remained of the house. With all the branches and leaves out of the way, the wreckage was even more obvious. Archer took a careful step into the mess and fished through what was left. Next to his feet, Annalise searched as well.

"I think most of this chair is all right," Archer said, fishing it out from under part of a wall. "You'd have to fix the one leg, but you can still use it."

"I found a coffee pot!" Annalise announced. "And a saucer!"

"Move over, children, let me help," an older woman's voice said, and another fair folk woman with grey-streaked hair waded into the wreck. "One of the blankets was still in the corner when the roof fell in, we can still save it."

When they had finished sorting the remains of the house, they were left with the mostly salvageable chair, three cups that didn't match one another, the coffee pot and saucer, two blankets with only a few splinters in them, and a heap of fabric that Annalise's mother had kept tucked in the cracks of the tree bark for repairing clothes. It wasn't much, but it was more than nothing, or so Annalise and her mother agreed.

As they began moving the rest of the wreckage out of the way of the building spot, neighbors started trickling in from around the rest of the street. The family who had been hosting Annalise and her mother at their house brought milk and fresh cookies for everyone. Many brought small pieces of furniture or linens for the new house, and all that was kept under a blanket at the edge of the building site.

Together the lot of them pried the remaining boards away from the tree and cleared it all away to start fresh.

Then the men took out their tools and got to work on the fresh lumber. As the women measured out the wood and made marks, the men got out their saws and axes and hacked and sawed wherever necessary to get the wood down to size.

Once the wood was cut, Archer was the one who picked up the pieces and got them into place against the tree while others nailed them down. He didn't feel like he was being very helpful, and there were a few times he considered leaving so that he wouldn't be in their way, but all the fair folk declared him a helpful resource, as it would have taken several men to move the pieces of wood that he could move all alone. Despite being three times their size, he felt about as helpful as a gnat in the eye, but at least he could move the wood for them with only a little effort.

He wasn't very delicate in his placement of the wood, but the fair folk didn't seem to care. Thinking about how their houses normally looked, he realized that the fair folk nailed pieces down however they landed and didn't care how the result looked, as long as it kept the rain out. They built most of the house's skeleton by mid-afternoon and would have added the beams as well, but as Annalise's mother Beatrice pointed out they would need the roof off if Archer was going to help them move heavy things inside the house. Everyone agreed.

Work on the furniture began, and this was where Archer was no help at all. Furniture work was delicate and particular, and the men insisted on doing it themselves. As the women pulled out their needles and fabric to start working on new curtains and napkins, Archer decided he was done for the day.

As it was, Ongel would probably be looking for him. If they needed to work on any more letters today, they would have to get a move on. It was nearly evening already.

Archer found Annalise in the chaos and told her that he needed to go.

"Of course. We won't keep you. And thank you for everything you've done. I wasn't expecting this much," she said and gestured for him to bend down. When he complied, she hugged his shoulder. "Thank you."

"Could you hang the tarp over the house before you go?" Beatrice called. "I don't think it will rain, but if it does I don't want the house wet."

Archer took the large blanket the fair folk pointed out to him and draped it over the skeleton of the house. The womenfolk tucked a few of their linens inside the house to protect them in case the rain did come. As Archer turned to go, Annalise waved goodbye.

He waved back.

CHAPTER TEN:

A Few Sparks

ON THE WAY BACK to the center of town, the shoes squeezed tighter than ever, and Archer stopped on the spot to take them off. Underneath, he already had a few blisters. That was what he got for wandering all over the city with them on. He threw the shoes off into the trees and kept walking. As Annalise thought, he'd torn a few small holes in the new wine-red shirt, and it was covered in marks from wood and sweat and dirt.

Not that it mattered. He wouldn't wear these clothes again.

He stopped at the house where Ongel had been staying, but the hostess said he had gone out and wouldn't be back for a while. She offered to let him stay while he waited, but that didn't feel right, so Archer told her no and left the house again.

Beatrice had been wrong. Dark clouds gathered over the city. Desperate to avoid getting wet, Archer raced back home and barely made it through the door before the clouds burst.

"There you are," his father said as soon as he stepped through the door. He took in the devastation of Archer's clothes with a quick up and down glance. "Ruined already, I see."

"Yeah, they weren't very sturdy," Archer said. "How'd the rest of the event go?"

"Surprisingly well," Ochre said, sounding uncharacteristically good-natured. "Although I was disappointed to see you disappear so quickly. I thought you wanted to make a good impression on the fair folk."

"I did," Archer said, and a bitter taste filled his mouth. He'd forgotten all about that in trying to help Annalise. There had been dozens of fair folk at the event; he should have stayed.

He'd let Wick down again. But somehow if he'd been put back there, he couldn't see how he could have done any differently with a clear conscience.

"But I forgot," he went on. "I can do better another time. It's fine."

"If you say so. You're always welcome at any event," his father said, and taking a few quick steps, he lifted off and soared back up toward his study.

During his last few days alone, Archer worked hard. He met with Ongel in the mornings and together they planned everything they had any control over. When Ongel had other things to do, Archer holed himself up in his room and tried to muddle things out for himself.

He wrote a great number of letters to anyone who would listen, and when he got a letter back from Queen Frey asking for more details, he conjured up the most capable and detailed response he could manage.

When he couldn't take any more letter writing and planning, he left in the afternoons to help with the construction of Annalise's house. The main structure of the house was done, and for the most part, the furniture was built. But while the men worked hard at welding a new stove to replace one that a seraph child ran off with, there was painting to do, so Archer took a paintbrush for himself and swiped paint wherever Annalise or her mother pointed.

He only appeared at home for meals, and sometimes he didn't even have to do that. Sometimes the hostess at Ongel's house offered them some food or tea while they worked, and twice the fair folk provided food to thank him for his help. He didn't know where they were getting all the food to feed him with and hoped it wasn't their supply for the winter, but they made it difficult to say no, so he ate whatever they brought him.

The day they finally finished the house, Annalise was the one to haul the door over and hang it on the hinges. Everyone cheered and clapped and her mother hugged first Annalise, then Archer's leg, then almost everyone else within range. Someone brought over a keg of ale the size of a watermelon, and drinks were passed around. When he had finished his small cup of ale, Archer thanked the fair folk for their hospitality and got up to go home. Annalise caught him as he was leaving.

"Thank you so much for everything," she said, and once more beckoned for him to bend down for a hug. "I couldn't have done it on my own, and it would have taken all of us ages without you. I'll not forget this."

"I probably won't either," Archer said. "It's been one of the strangest experiences of my life."

"You've never tried to build a tiny house before?" Annalise said. They laughed together. "If there's ever anything we can do for you, please tell me and I'll do everything I can. I never expected this much."

Archer tried his best to smile at her. "I'll just take your word for it that I did good."

"You did. The best of luck to you, Archer."

"Won't need it. And you probably won't either, but good luck, Annalise."

As he made the trek back to his own house, Archer debated what he would do with the rest of his afternoon. It wasn't quite time for dinner, and if he could he'd avoid being in the house until then. Now that Fowl knew about the space under the bridge, he couldn't go there either. Maybe he would make it his mission to find a new hiding place until he had to go back home.

There was an odd stench in the air. He couldn't quite place it. He raised his face and sniffed a little deeper. What was that smell?

"Is your construction project with the fair folk done already?" Fowl asked, appearing out of the trees. His smooth gait fell into step with Archer's stomping stride.

"Why are you walking?" Archer said without looking at him. "You have working wings. Use them." It smelled something like meat burning.

"Having wings doesn't mean that I can't walk. I have legs, too," Fowl said. He glanced behind them. "I would have thought the construction would take longer, even with your clumsy hands helping."

"As it happens, I sped the process up," Archer snapped.

"Is that so." Fowl sounded disinterested. "You know, you didn't have to carry anything for her. There were people there to do that sort of thing. You didn't have to ruin the new clothes Mother bought for you."

Archer felt a twinge of guilt. He had assumed his father bought the clothes, smugly thinking Archer had no other choice than to come to the event. He hadn't known it was his mother who had bought them. "Well, I don't know when I would have ever worn them again, anyway. Besides, I didn't want to send Annalise to someone else."

"Would it have made you too much like the rest of us?" Fowl said, stuffing his hands in his pockets. His gait grew looser. He was trying too hard to appear casual. "I know that's the way you make any decision: how will it distance me from all the people I don't like? That's why you dress how you do, that's why you act the way you do, that's why you cut your hair. If I didn't know better I'd say that's why you broke your wing."

"Don't you dare talk about that." Archer bristled.

"And I'd be willing to wager that's why you're hiding out with your centaur friend and clinging to him like you don't have a father upstairs who could help you. Our father isn't the important person he is by doing nothing. He's a man of strategy. He could help you."

"I don't want his help, and I don't like his strategy," Archer said. "His strategy was always exploiting other people, and exploiting me."

"Exploiting you?" Fowl laughed. "All he ever did was ask you to show up, the same as he's doing now. Trying to get you to participate."

Archer's head snapped sideways to look at Fowl, genuinely surprised this time. Had he never known? "You must have been younger and more gullible than I thought. You never noticed? At every event, every time I showed up like he asked, I was put front and center as the special child, the one Ochre Hessen selflessly protected, the poor child who couldn't fly. I made him look good, didn't you ever realize that?"

Fowl blinked down at the ground as he took this in.

"You got a lot of attention. . ." he said slowly. Then he recovered. "You're angry. It's making you think everyone's against you. Not everything is about you."

"Pretty sure nothing was ever about me," Archer said. "I'll have you know that I got dragged to more events than ever after the wing broke. 'Look at him, look at his wing'."

"You'd like that these days, I think," Fowl said. "Being the center of attention. Not invisible, like me."

"I'd rather be invisible," Archer snapped. "Maybe if I was invisible he could let me exist, instead of trying to bend me into whatever shape works best for him."

"Don't be ridiculous," Fowl said, but it was obvious he knew he was losing. "You're always so dramatic."

Something large flew over the trees, casting a huge shadow over everything for a moment.

"Not that you want to see it my way," Archer said. "You were never any different. You wanted me to stay on the ground and never even try. You liked that I couldn't do anything."

That was when Fowl turned on him. "Wrong," he growled. "Even if you want to look at our father's work like you do, even if he is wrong, even if I hate every moment spent in the house that he didn't earn but stole, you can *never* say that I liked that you were weak. I wanted you to stay safe and wait like the doctors said. I thought you would get better with time, but you never wanted to listen. You wanted to jump off everything you saw and I stopped you time and time again to let you get better. Hate me if you want, but I just wanted you to be safe and happy."

Archer's head spun trying to process what Fowl had just said, but he couldn't let go of the argument now. He opened his mouth to argue.

Then Fowl's eyes flickered upward, and Archer's followed. They both leaped aside as a huge tree branch crashed to the ground between them, flaming.

Sparks floated past Archer's head as his eyes raked across the treetops. The tops of the trees down the street and beyond flamed. Seraphs scattered in every direction, either on foot or through the air. Motion in the treetops caught Archer's eye. A huge ball of fire shot through the trees, angled like a falling star.

Did it have wings?

Archer squinted after it, but the flaming thing had already disappeared.

I should go after it.

A hand grabbed the shoulder of Archer's shirt and pulled. "Come on!" Fowl shouted, inches from Archer's face. "We have to get out of here!"

"Fine."

Heat blazed against Archer's forehead as they raced down the street. He stuck close behind Fowl as they raced toward a house a few doors down. Up in the doorway, someone was beckoning wildly.

Fowl ran with Archer's shirt still gripped in his fist, face like determination set in stone, his eyes wild. Archer tried to keep up. Sparks rained down from the treetops. One landed on his wing, stinging, and he tried to put it out with a quick smack, still running. Even the grass started to burn. They jumped over blazing sticks and leaves, aiming for the tree where the person waited. They both ducked as a mound of flaming leaves fell from above.

"Let's go!" Fowl took off, flying for the top of the tree.

Still on the ground, Archer threw up his hands. "Well, good for you!" he shouted hoarsely, and made for the stairs. A few seconds later, he heard footsteps on the stairs behind him.

"Stop waiting for me!" Archer shouted. "I can climb stairs by myself!"

"I'd rather not worry about the stairs burning out from under you while I'm all snug and cozy in the house, thanks," Fowl responded, gasping. "Now move faster."

They pounded up the stairs. Fowl nearly fell as he rounded a dip in the trunk too quickly, but Archer caught him by the sleeve, and they kept climbing. Finally, they burst up onto the porch, chests heaving, and Archer dragged both of them toward the open door.

The boy waiting there waved even more wildly. He dragged them both inside and slammed the door. Archer recognized him as one of Fowl's crazy friends, the ones he disappeared with sometimes and came back covered in sweat and grime. Archer was never quite sure where the lot of them went.

The three of them clustered around the window.

"What will we do if it spreads?" Fowl muttered. "The whole city could go up in flames."

"No, look!" The other boy pointed further down the street. The flames were thicker, but a group of seraphs dressed in green were systematically throwing water on the fires. Already the flames nearest to them were vanishing.

Still panting, his mounds of dark hair falling in his face, Fowl straightened. "What *was* that?"

"I don't know," the other boy said. His own copper hair was falling out of the tie that held it back, and Archer realized that the boy was covered in soot, just like he and Fowl were. He had raced in from the outside as well. "It came out of nowhere!"

"See, this is what I'm talking about!" Archer ranted,

gesturing toward the outside. "I go to jail, not once but twice, no one wanted to believe me, I had to fight to get one *single* ally, and now, right there, right outside the door, is exactly the thing no one would believe me about!"

Fowl turned to him. "Look, before I lose the nerve to go through with this, I'm sorry."

Archer stopped ranting and stared at his brother with his mouth open. "What?"

"Things aren't good, and they haven't been for a long time. And I know I've never been much help. That's made you angry with us. I want to apologize now before it's too late," Fowl continued.

With a start, Archer realized Fowl wasn't talking about the fire.

"If it helps, I'll apologize for him, too." Fowl noticed the soot all over his shirt and brushed it off. "Our father will never apologize for himself, so I'll apologize for him. Now are we good?"

"No," Archer found himself saying before he could stop it. His face burned like the anger in his chest. "We're not good, because we can't be."

Fowl's eyes were wide.

"It's way too late for sorry," Archer said. "Sorry can't fix this." He took another look out the window, at the fire trickling down the trees.

"Well, then what can fix it?" Fowl sounded like he was keeping a harsh edge out of his voice. A shard of it still hid behind his tone. "If an apology won't help, what will?"

Archer faced his brother. "I don't know. But not sorry. *Sorry* is for when you spill someone's drink or when you bump into them because you weren't paying attention. Sorry is for small things. I was a kid, and I got exploited and used and manipulated. That is in no way a small thing. Sorry isn't good enough."

"Fine," Fowl said softly, and he flew deeper into the shadowy house, probably to find his friend.

Archer squelched down something that felt like sadness before it could fully form. He didn't regret what he said to Fowl. He meant every word.

He took another look outside. Whatever had brought the fire seemed to have gone. More and more people appeared with buckets to douse the flames. As Archer looked around outside the window, he realized that it wasn't as bad as he had thought. It looked like the fire hadn't spread past the street. If one were lucky enough to have functioning wings, one could probably fly up above the city and see a stripe of smoke cutting down the middle.

A shadow flashed across the window.

Archer's eyes leaped up to the sky, following the path of whatever had blocked out the sun. Something the color of rust disappeared into the canopy of trees in a puff of leaves and smoke.

What was that?

Archer threw the door open and dashed out onto the deck.

"Archer!" Fowl's voice shouted from behind him.

Archer didn't pay him any mind. He watched the tree rustle where the thing had disappeared. What was that thing? He eyed the next house over. It was close enough. He could make it. Bracing himself, he dashed across the length of the deck.

The wood burned under his feet. Sparks still fell from the leaves above. He kept his eyes trained on the other porch, on the other side of a ten-foot gap. He pounded across the roof.

As he reached the edge, he pushed off.

"*Archer!*" Fowl roared.

But Archer was already airborne, windmilling and on a collision course with the opposite porch. He threw out his wings, catching the air for more lift. The unevenness of the wings made him wobble, but it gave him the extra air he needed. He hit the other porch running, and only stumbled a bit before he caught his balance again.

He turned around and caught Fowl's eye, and noticed with smugness Fowl's shocked expression. "Happy?" Then he took off again, trying to track whatever had disappeared into the tree. But as he reached the other side of the porch, he realized that the branches were no longer moving. He waited, at the ready in case anything would appear out of the leaves, but nothing showed its face.

Whatever had been there had already gotten away.

The door of the house behind Archer opened, and a pair of children peered out, giving strange looks to the stranger walking across their porch.

"What is it?" Fowl called from the other roof.

"Nothing." With his quarry already gone, Archer headed for the stairs. If he was lucky, Ongel's host house wouldn't be on fire. As he reached the top of the staircase, something at the end of the street caught his attention. Where everyone else was flying around putting out fires, one figure was walking down the street unbothered. Archer would recognize that mechanically even gait anywhere.

Wick.

Archer bellowed a greeting and raced round and round down the stairs to meet his friend. Up on the other porch, he heard Fowl make a sound of exasperation.

Archer dodged a group of fair folk forming a bucket brigade and raced down the street toward Wick. Wick barely looked up as he walked, even when a seraph flying with a fallen branch nearly collided with him. He kept his eyes on the ground, both hands gripping the strap of the traveling bag he had borrowed from Archer's parents.

"Wick!" Archer cried, panting, as he raced up to his friend. He'd never thought he'd be so happy to see that unsettling brown face, tree bark lines and all. "How did it go? Do we have the first stone?"

At last, Wick raised his head and looked Archer in the eye, and Archer saw the shadows around his eyes. He was paler than Archer had ever seen him.

"No," Wick said. "I've been named an enemy of my people. My own friends didn't want to see me. I'm not allowed back there, ever."

CHAPTER ELEVEN:

Lukewarm Welcome

ARCHER SEARCHED FOR something to say. He tried to sound optimistic. "Well, at least now we know. Another new challenge, right? Never stopped us before."

"Right," Wick said, but his heart wasn't in it.

After a moment of awkward silence, they started walking again, in the direction of the Hessen house.

*

WICK HAD BEEN NERVOUS the whole trip to leshy territory. Every step brought a new wave of anxiety. What if he wasn't welcome now? What if they wouldn't believe him and wouldn't let him have the Oak Leaf again? What if he really had ruined his entire future?

Traveling alone didn't help. Usually he liked traveling alone. He always had before. But this time, he wasn't confident, and he wasn't able to enjoy the scenery and the quiet. He couldn't believe he missed Archer's nonstop babbling, but the quiet only provided more time for his thoughts to surround him like a cloud, thickening until he couldn't see anything else.

By the time he reached the ring of red trees at the border, he was terrified.

He practiced his speech in his head as he passed gardens and clay dwellings. This wasn't anything like his past homecomings. People peered out of their houses, but they didn't recognize him. No one greeted him. There were no children eager to hear a new story or old leshy willing to congratulate him on more work well done. Just wary eyes.

Only his mother recognized him.

As he approached his family's dwelling, she dashed out of it. "Wick?"

He tried for a smile. "I'm back, Mother."

Having heard the mention of his name, Wick's sister raced out of the house as well. "Wick's home?"

When she saw him, Reesa skidded to a halt, her eyes wide. "Why are you. . . you're. . ."

She hadn't heard. "I changed my face like I said I would," Wick said. "It worked, see?"

"I see." But Reesa didn't run to hug him the way she usually would. She stayed where she was, with her arms at her sides.

Wick's mother embraced him, though her arms felt stiff. Had they always been this stiff?

"Your father is off working today," Wick's mother said as she released him. "So it's just the two of us here today."

"That's all right," Wick said. "I'm actually here to see the royal family, but of course, I had to see you first. I want to see Twill, too."

"How are you these days?" his mother asked. "Are

you taking care of yourself?"

Wick heard the real questions hiding in her voice. *Are you safe? Is anyone following you?*

Is it true what I heard about you?

"There's a lot I wish I had time to tell you," Wick said. "But I have to talk to the royal family first. Even if I don't see anyone else, I have to see them."

"Excuse me," said a soft voice from behind them. Wick turned.

Behind them stood a pair of tall, strong leshy, wearing the arm bracers signature to servants and guards for the leshy royal family. One of them nodded his head in greeting.

"If you're Wick, please follow us," the guard said. "The royal family has asked to see you as soon as possible. They're waiting for you in the palace."

A flutter of fear squirmed in Wick's stomach.

"I understand," Wick said. He could find Twill after. He embraced his mother once more and tried to give Reesa a reassuring smile. "This is what I came for. I'll be back to talk more later."

"Of course," his mother said.

Wick turned to the guards. "Lead the way. I'm right behind you."

The guards fell into step with one walking ahead of him and the other behind him. While Wick knew that this was what he came here for, the pit in the bottom of his stomach gaped wider. His fingers grew cold as they gripped the strap of his bag.

The palace was very close to Wick's village, although no one liked to talk about it because it made them sound pretentious. The walk there was only a half hour. As the hulking clay structure came into view, Wick's heart threatened to leap out of his chest.

He had to remind himself that this was bigger than him, bigger than his fear of rejection and terror of discovering he wasn't welcome to his people's stone. He could do this, even alone, with no Archer to back him up and no strength in his quaking heart.

The guards accompanied him inside the palace and down the long halls of swirling carvings to the throne room, which was airy and round and open to the sky. Crumbling autumn leaves clustered around the base of each throne encircling the room. Wick had only been here once before, like all the other leshy children, when he had been assessed and sent off to try out a job that matched his skills and virtues. The royal family didn't actually need to be involved in the process, as the assessments and selection were done not by them but by the children's teachers, but it was an old tradition that parents loved.

Now Wick stood here again, but not for anything as simple.

The heads of the royal family turned to him as he entered with the guards. They sat tall and slender in their chairs, their matching gold eyes watching his approach. Every one of them wore a delicate wicker crown that wove through the sticks and leaves of their heads into an arch shape at the front.

Rule of leshy territory was passed down through the eldest child in the family, with the oldest child's offspring inheriting the thrones when their predecessors were deemed too old to rule anymore, or as soon as the first of the previous royal siblings died. The oldest child of each royal family was expected to have seven children, who were trained up by their parent and their six aunts and uncles until it was time for the children to rule in their places.

When Wick tried to explain all of this to Archer, before he left for leshy territory, Archer had said it sounded needlessly complicated and stupid.

"Why not just say that the eldest child in the family gets to rule and leave the others out of it?"

"Because dividing the power up among several people lessens the likeliness of corruption and manipulation of power," Wick had responded. *"And it doesn't seem strange when you've been raised under it. I never questioned it."*

"I don't think you'd question it if it started raining strawberries and squirrels," Archer retorted. *"It's a weird system and I don't like whoever thought of it."*

"That would be the leshy," Wick said.

"Exactly my point."

"Archer, I'm a leshy."

"I know. That's what I'm saying."

Wick had sighed then. *"It makes sense. Siblings always have a variety of opinions and views between them, so there will be no single agenda that leshy territory supports. And allowing them to be trained up by all the previous siblings encourages the same open views being passed down through the generations. It lets them hear all the varying points of view and draw conclusions for themselves."*

"Or lets the previous rulers mold them however they like," Archer had pointed out. *"You could be living under a total conspiracy and never know it."*

Wick could only hope now that there wasn't some great conspiracy. He needed some people on his side.

"We brought him, like you requested, your majesties," one of the guards said. The other had never spoken, Wick realized. A duo where one did all the talking. Not unlike himself and Archer.

He began his speech. "My name is Wick, I'm a messenger from the village near your palace, and I'm here to ask—"

One of the royal family stood up. She was nearly as tall as Wick and held herself like a ruler of the world. "We will ask that you remain silent during your trial."

Trial. Wick's blood ran cold. He was not brought here because the royal family wanted to see him. He was here on trial.

The princess turned to one of her brothers. "You brought the list of his offenses?"

The prince nodded and got to his feet as his sister sat. Slowly he unrolled a scroll with golden edges. It didn't look like a short list.

"These are the charges laid out to you by your fellow leshy and your leaders," the prince said in a deep voice.

Archer was right. Their voices did sound strange in Wick's head, flat with no resonance. No wonder they seemed strange to the other races.

"You have betrayed the messenger's trust laws laid out by the rulers seventeen generations before ours," the prince continued, "and stolen from the leshy's museum of valuable artifacts, a location that has always been safe in the hands of the public. Those are the most serious charges," he said gravely. "The others are as follows: lying to an officer of the museum, refusing to be taken into custody, multiple jailbreaks, thievery and banditry of other races and breaking of multiple treaties, conspiring with a known criminal, assault on creatures of multiple other species, threat, joining forces with an enemy of the state, and lastly betrayal of the seal of trust bequeathed to you by the centaurs."

With that, the prince sat down and another princess stood. She was visibly younger than the other two had been, with a softly flowering crown. "Would you like to explain yourself in the face of these accusations?"

"I would," Wick said. His hands shook. Everything he had planned to say vanished from his mind, along with all the evidence he had hoped to present to them. "I was. . . I was doing what had to be done. There was strong evidence that a disaster was coming to our country, and I acted as quickly as I could so that it could be prevented."

The princess looked to one of her sisters. The one by her side stood as well. "And did you succeed? Did you prevent the thing like you hoped?"

"No," Wick admitted. "I was stopped."

"Then why has the disaster not happened yet?" the older princess asked.

"Because it's still on its way."

"Who is 'we?'" the older princess asked, as her sister sat again. "Yourself and—?"

"Archer," Wick said quietly. "My friend."

"The other criminal in question," said one of the princes, the tallest of the group, and Wick flinched at the word.

"Yes." Wick gripped the strap of his bag, trying to stop the shaking of his hands. "He was the one that told me that the Scorch was coming back. And it is. The evidence is all around us; you must have noticed. The trees are going grey. The rain is dark. Something went over Tor while we were there, and fire fell from the sky. The evidence is unmistakable."

"And this friend of yours told you all this?" asked the first princess who had spoken. "This was the evidence he provided to you?"

"He told me about it," Wick said. "But later I saw for myself. The Scorch *is* coming. If we do nothing, it will kill us all." Better now than never to ask. "I didn't really come here for this trial. I didn't know that you had this planned. I came to warn you."

None of the royal family stopped him this time, so Wick went on.

"My friend and I know that we were wrong by trying to collect the Heather Stones the way we did in the past, and we're trying to get them together again, with the permission of the respective guardians. So I came to you first, in the hopes that my people—"

"You want the Oak Leaf again," the oldest princess said, her tone suddenly frosty and sharp.

Wick's heart beat faster. "Yes, your majesty."

"After all that you did to break our trust in you, you want us to trust you like your crimes never happened?"

Seven pairs of empty eyes stared back at him, and Wick could almost see his plans starting to catch fire.

"Wick," said the princess, "in the light of all your accusations, we have no choice but to act with discipline."

Wick's heart sank.

"With the agreement of my siblings, I am moving that we formally banish you from leshy territory. You won't be harmed by anyone in our territory, but we will do nothing for you if anyone else tries to harm you." The eldest princess looked around at her siblings. "Are we in agreement?"

One by one, her siblings nodded their agreement. The youngest princess hesitated the longest, then finally nodded her assent.

"Then we're agreed." The eldest princess turned to

Wick again. "From this point on, you are no longer allowed to cross our borders. All our people will know your name, and none will allow you to enter our territory until or if the ban is lifted. The title of leshy is taken from you. You may not invoke the name of leshy as your own, and none of our people will claim you. Immediately after this trial, you will be invited to leave the territory, and you won't be allowed back." Her eyes softened for a moment. "I'm sorry, Wick. But many of the people are worried that their territory is not safe anymore, and for their sake, we need to take action."

"I can't explain myself further?" Wick asked, desperate now.

"Can you provide any further evidence to support your claims?" the princess asked. "Anything at all?"

Even Wick hadn't believed the Scorch was coming ages after Archer told him, and the events that had changed his mind couldn't be duplicated. He had been convinced because he saw no lie on Archer's face as he tried to explain everything. And since no one else would ever see that same look, it would not defend him.

"And what if we were to send to the centaurs in the valley?" she went on. "Would all of them agree with what you've said here? Do you have other allies who can vouch for you?"

"Our friends among the centaurs aren't in the valley at the moment," Wick said quietly. "And you would be the first of our allies."

"I see. Then we ask that you leave our territory now."

Wick heard a soft footstep over his shoulder as the two guards who had accompanied him to the palace fell into place behind him.

"I'm sorry, Wick," the eldest princess said, "but we

can't trust you anymore. Your life here is over."

With that sentence, Wick's world shattered.

One of the guards laid a hand on Wick's shoulder, and the suddenness of it made him jump away. Both guards lunged after him.

Wick started running.

As he reached the doors of the palace, one of the guards caught the back of his shirt. As soon as Wick felt the tug, he spun around and punched the one who had caught him in the throat. As the other came after him, he swung his fist at the leshy's head.

With the two guards temporarily taken out behind him, he ran for the border. His new lungs scrambled to keep up with the sudden change of pace. As he passed through his village, he heard a sound behind him. Startled, Wick caught his foot on a root, and he went sprawling. The footfalls behind him were catching up.

He scrambled behind a tree and crouched there, clutching his bag to him like old times and panting desperately.

Footsteps raced past. Wick waited another moment, heart pounding in his ears, then he got up and prepared to run again. Only then did he notice.

Across the road was Twill, staring at him.

Wick recognized the look in Twill's eyes. He had seen it when they were small and things didn't turn out according to her mad schemes. And again when he told her about the councilor job in centaur territory which would keep him away from home.

She was disappointed. And maybe even a little sad.

Still, Wick was relieved to see her. He needed a friendly face. "Twill," he said.

Her round yellow eyes blinked at him slowly, and

Twill took a step back. "If you're going to run," she said in a dull voice, "run."

Wick didn't want to run. Not from her, not from his people, not from manghar with spears or arrows or anyone else. He was sick of running. But he knew that if the guards found nothing up ahead, they would circle back.

And it was clear that Twill didn't want to see him.

He ran.

*

WICK WALKED past Archer, back to the Hessen house.

Archer debated what to say to him. Sure, Wick was back now, but he hadn't come back in the high spirits Archer had expected. He'd never seen Wick like this. When they had been thrown out of seraph territory before, or even when they had been arrested and thrown in jail in centaur territory, at worst Wick had been disappointed and frustrated. This was different.

This was a new level of darkness that Archer had never seen in Wick. Archer wasn't sure what to do. Whenever his father or Fowl were upset, Archer avoided them. Crossing their paths tended to result in backlash, especially with Fowl. Wick, even when he was upset, had always adapted no matter what. But not now.

He didn't know how Wick would react to anything now.

Still, he headed up the stairs to Wick's room.

"Hello?" When Archer pushed the door open, Wick barely looked up. He sat on the far edge of the bed, elbows on knees, staring at the wall.

"I brought your list back," Archer said, waving the

piece of paper through the doorway. "I did everything you wanted. Well, almost everything. What's our next move?"

"I don't know," Wick said. "I don't know. I don't have a plan."

Archer blinked, then he tried to laugh. His fingers tapped anxiously on the doorframe. "You always have a plan. If there's one thing you always have, it's some kind of mad scheme to get whatever you want."

"Well, my plans never work anyway, remember? That's what you said."

Archer squirmed. He wanted to push Wick further, but he didn't know how that would end. "Well, I was wrong. That's nothing new. Come on, let's figure out what we're doing next. The fair folk assembly, right? Ongel and I figured out a lot of that while you were gone. He's here, by the way. I don't know for how much longer, but he was here most of the time you were gone."

Wick nodded. "Good. Then you two can figure out what the plan is."

Archer's fingers stopped tapping on the door frame. "What? You're not helping?"

"I'm sorry," Wick said, looking up at Archer.

Wick's face was unsettling. It was probably something leftover from being a leshy, but Wick's skin and eyes had visibly tinged with grey. He looked like a tree losing all its color for winter. Wick smiled an empty smile. "I think you'll have to take over for a while. I've been trying to think of something new since I left leshy territory, but I don't have anything. I'm out of ideas."

Archer swallowed. He had hoped that when Wick got back, everything would be back off his shoulders again, and he could go back to being reckless and wild and could do anything he wanted.

It wouldn't be like that now.

Something in their friendship had shifted when he wasn't looking, and it hadn't asked him for permission first. It had just changed.

"Okay," was all he could say.

For a moment, he stood outside the door without moving. Maybe if he stood still long enough, everything would start to make sense again.

A faint sound floated from Wick's room. Archer frowned and peeked through the crack of the door.

Wick still sat on the edge of the bed with his head down. But as Archer looked, Wick put his head in his hands, and his shoulders started to shake.

Wick was crying.

A prickle of fear ran down Archer's arms. Wick had come back totally different than when he left for leshy territory, and there was nothing he could do about it. He didn't have the first idea of what to do.

He left without doing anything.

"Hey," Archer said as he sat down at his little glass table in Ongel's sitting room. The hostess of the house had kindly dedicated this room solely to their joint study. "I'm back."

Ongel looked up from a sheet of paper. "I thought you'd bring Wick with you. I heard he returned to the city, but I haven't seen hide or hair of him yet."

"Yeah. He's. . ." Archer grasped for the words. He couldn't stop thinking about Wick's grey face, his shoulders shaking as he sat alone. Eventually Archer settled for, "he's not coming."

"Oh," Ongel said, sounding more than a little surprised. He set the piece of paper down. "Well, I was hoping to have both of you here when I had to relay the information, but here it is. I'm needed back in the valley, right away."

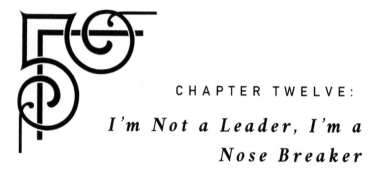

CHAPTER TWELVE:
I'm Not a Leader, I'm a Nose Breaker

ONGEL WAS LEAVING.

It was all Archer could do not to pick up a chair and hurl it across the room. He clutched the edge of the table until his hands hurt.

Wick was back, but he was no use. And now Ongel was leaving.

"I'll be back," Ongel assured him. The assurance wasn't working. "I just have some things I have to do. My people are still depending on me, even if they don't agree with my decision to come here and oversee your plans. While I'm there, I may even get to discuss your plans with some of the other centaurs. I know that several of them were still thinking everything over when I was there last. Once I'm through with all that, I'll be back, I promise. But it may take some time."

"You know that's what they all say," Archer said, his

voice coming out even sharper than he had intended. "That's what they all say when they don't plan on coming back."

"I *will* be back," Ongel repeated. "I would stay here if I could, but I don't have another choice."

"I've heard that one before, too. Fine, do whatever you want," Archer said. Then he turned and left the house.

The fair folk assembly was a few days away, and they planned to meet with someone who could potentially get them into it. He could get them that far on his own.

Archer nearly stormed past the kitchen and up the stairs before he realized who was in the kitchen. Stopping short, he half leaned on the doorway and asked, "What are you doing?"

Wick, slowly stirring something with a wooden spoon, turned without looking up. "I'm making something. I think."

Archer craned his neck to see from the doorway. "You made slop. That looks disgusting."

Wick inspected his lumpy mass of poorly mixed flour and egg and frowned only slightly. "I'm trying to follow a recipe I found on the counter. I may be doing it wrong." He returned to the counter to read the recipe again.

Archer ventured in and leaned over the table between him and Wick. "Ongel's leaving for a week or maybe more."

Wick said nothing.

"He left some instructions, but. . . what are we going to do? I can't—I don't know what to do. I'm not you."

"I don't know either."

Wick's tone was all wrong. Archer looked up.

Wick leaned over the counter, staring into his disaster of a recipe in the bowl. His eyes had gone grey again. "I don't know. . . I wish I knew. But everything I could do before was through the resources I had and the people I knew. Now that I don't have any of that, I don't have anything."

Archer didn't know what to say.

Wick's hands, balled into fists on either side of the mixing bowl, carefully unclenched and spread flat on the counter. "I need time to figure things out for myself. You have all the plans Ongel laid out for you. Work with those, okay?"

With that, he walked out, leaving Archer alone in the kitchen. The sound of his footsteps climbed the stairs, too quickly, and faded away.

Archer didn't know how to say that he didn't want to do it all on his own. He didn't know how to do it without help. But Wick was already gone, and even if he wasn't, Archer couldn't bring himself to make Wick feel even more guilty.

Archer climbed the stairs and started working on plans by himself. He could do it. Of course, he could do it. Not because Wick said he could, not because Ongel thought he could handle it, not because everyone needed him to, but because he had to prove it to them. He had to prove he could do it.

The next day was the scheduled meeting with the fair folk. While dressing he realized with chagrin that maybe the red shirt would be better suited for this than his regular clothes—or at least it would have been if it wasn't riddled with holes and basically ruined. All the same, he put on his own clothes and thudded down the stairs to get Wick.

"Wakey wakey, we have a meeting with that fair folk family, and they won't wait for us." A pile of nice clothes sat on Wick's dresser, borrowed from Fowl and stitched up the back to hide the wing slits. Archer tossed them at Wick's motionless form. Wick jumped a bit as the stack hit his head.

"Come on, we're going to be late pretty soon," Archer said.

Wick sat up, his hair a tousled mess. The dark circles ringing his eyes didn't look good, either. It must have been a rough night of sleep. "Are you sure about this? I doubt I'll be helpful."

"Are you kidding? You're the only one who knows what to say." Archer ran a hand through his hair. "I'm nervous too, but one way or another this has to happen. Get yourself dressed, and I'll meet you downstairs."

Roughly twenty minutes later, once Wick had slowly made his way down the stairs and Archer's father deemed them both presentable enough, they set out for the arranged meeting place.

The fair folk family had asked to meet in a public place, so they (or rather, Ongel) had suggested a nearby park. It would take several minutes to walk there, which gave Archer plenty of time to dread the whole thing, and to assess the state of Wick.

Archer observed Wick discreetly as they walked. Wick looked more cleaned up than he had before, with his hair washed and brushed back from his face. Fowl's clothes were a little too long at the sleeves, and the sewn-up wing slits on the back looked a little funny if you looked directly at them, but overall the strong charcoal grey and the flowing sleeves suited Wick.

Wick's face was another story. He never looked up from the ground, and even after washing his face, the darkness around his eyes hadn't lightened. He looked far away, like he was in some other place entirely.

Part of Archer wanted to talk to Wick about it. Another part of him knew that other people's emotions were a nest of snakes he shouldn't stick his hand in. And they had a meeting to worry about. He said nothing.

The park came into view up ahead, little more than a sunny clearing surrounded by a short iron fence, and Wick's steps slowed. "I don't think I can do this."

Realizing he was leaving Wick behind, Archer stopped and turned around. "What do you mean? Everything is hanging on us doing this. We don't have a choice here."

But Wick's eyes were wide, unfocused, not looking at Archer but through him. He shook his head quickly as he began to back away. "I can't. I can't right now."

"Wick, come on." Archer reached for Wick's shoulder to pull him along, but Wick sprang away. Something in Wick's eyes was new, and not a good new. New like back in the kitchen, when he had admitted he had no ideas and then left without speaking. It was like a whole piece of the Wick Archer knew was missing. Where had he gone? Who had taken him?

"I'm sorry." The fear glistened brighter in Wick's eyes. "I can't do this. I need more time." He turned and walked away.

Archer grabbed onto his arm this time. Fowl's shirt crinkled under his grip. "Hang on, you can't—"

Wick knocked Archer's hand off his arm. "Please. Leave me alone."

He sounded even more unlike himself than before.

Then he walked away.

The back of Archer's knuckles stung. He watched Wick disappear into the shade of the trees with his head down.

Uncertainty shot through Archer's mind like lightning. He couldn't do this on his own. There was no version of this where Wick wasn't involved. He thought about running away alone, or getting someone else to help him, but there was no time. And Wick had been the one to say that it was important not to be late. They had to be on time.

Or at least, Archer did.

He didn't want to go by himself. He would mess it all up. But Wick was already gone and might be for a while. One way or another, someone had to talk to the fair folk family.

Archer's stomach turned.

It would have to be him or no one.

He took a deep breath, clenched his fists, and walked up the slope into the park. As he passed through the gate, he easily spotted the large group of fair folk gathered around a semi-circle of iron benches. Archer's heart bumped a little bit. He didn't like being the one that everything rode on. He'd avoid doing it at all once all this was over.

The eyes of the tiny people latched onto him as he approached. There were more of them than he had expected, almost two dozen of varying ages. More than one generation? Wick would know.

"Welcome." A man with a black beard half as long as he was tall climbed onto the back of one of the benches and extended a hand. "My name is Otho, and this is my family."

Archer took the tiny hand he was offered and shook it. It felt like shaking the hand of a flower, or a lizard. His hand swallowed the hand of the fair folk man a dozen times over. "Archer. Archer Hessen," he corrected himself.

Otho hopped down from the back of the bench and sat on the edge of the seat. His family gathered around, sitting cross-legged on the seats of the benches.

Archer scrambled for the next thing to say. "Thank you for meeting me. I wasn't sure if we could get anyone to agree to this, honestly."

Wick wouldn't have said it like that.

"I had planned not to agree," the fair folk man admitted. "But my daughter heard a glowing endorsement from some friends of hers, and her friends insisted that we should meet the famous Archer Hessen after all. So here we are. Do you know the Iselberg family?"

Archer, who had only just remembered to sit, frowned. "I don't think I know an Iselberg family. Maybe they know Wick?"

"No?" The lines in Otho's brow deepened in confusion. "They mentioned you specifically. You don't know Annalise and Beatrice? They live in this city."

Annalise's smile appeared in Archer's mind. *Thank you for everything. I'll not forget this.*

Relief rushed through his chest. "Oh, Annalise! Yeah, I know her. I helped her rebuild her house after the storm." He paused. "Sorry, I didn't know her last name."

"Don't worry," the fair folk man said, flapping a hand. "I'm relieved. I was worried I had the wrong person. Annalise gave you a full endorsement when my daughter spoke with her, you know. She said you were one of the most honest, decent people she had ever met."

Archer didn't know how to answer that. He'd never heard such lofty words aimed at him in his life.

"What did you want to talk about?" Otho asked. "I'm listening."

Archer realized he didn't know how to lead up to this.

This wasn't as simple as copying letters from his father. He leaned forward and rested his elbows on his knees. "I can't jump around the topic like other people do with this sort of thing, so here it is: Wick and I want to gather the Heather Stones again, and we want to borrow the fair folk stone as part of that. So we're hoping we can get some people to take us to the fair folk meeting in a few days."

Otho looked at him for a long moment, then slowly scratched his beard. "Not what I thought you would say when you asked to meet us here, I'll grant you."

The dark-haired woman at Otho's elbow, who had been knitting a stocking cap that matched the one on her head, finally spoke. "What do you mean? You want to get the stones together, again?"

Archer swallowed. "Well," he began, "you might have heard about how some people tried to steal all of them a little while back."

The wife looked wary. "That was you?"

Otho's gaze also grew uncertain. "Is that so?"

Usually, once someone got suspicious, this would be the part where Archer took what he wanted and made his escape. Several of Otho's children were watching him with narrowed eyes. If only he could run away.

"Yes," Archer said. "That was us. It was my idea and I
. . . It was a bad idea. You probably know how that turned out. We're trying to do it the right way this time."

"And what is the right way?" Otho asked, his voice still guarded. The eyes of the whole fair folk family were fastened on Archer now.

Archer wondered what on earth Annalise had thought she saw in him. He was clearly not meant for this. He searched for something like what Wick would say.

"We want to borrow the stones this time, with the owners' consent, and when we've cast the barrier spell with the stones, we'll return them. We're not asking for anything else, just the stone. We'll take good care of it," Archer promised.

"But why should my people give it to you?" Otho asked. Archer watched him, trying to decide if Otho's tone was hostile or if he was just testing for a reaction. "You didn't prove yourself trustworthy before, and you even brought your friend down with you. As far as we know, you're criminals, and considering how quickly you seem to have been released from centaur territory, you may even be criminals on the run."

One of the younger men, probably one of Otho's sons, leaned forward. "Why should we believe a thing you say? You should be in jail right now."

The corner of Archer's mouth twitched. *I should, should I?*

Another one of the young men caught the movement. "And you know it, don't you?"

"We were. They let us out," Archer said. "You can take that up with them."

"Maybe I will." The first son got up hastily. Archer tensed. Were they going to fight?

His eyes darted around. Only the two sons who had already spoken looked hostile. The rest of them just appeared to be on edge. If it was going to be a fight, he would only have to punt the two sons into the treetops to settle it.

Then he remembered why he had come. He was trying to give himself and Wick their best chance, and Wick wouldn't want him to fight with anyone. Wick would try to de-escalate everything.

He searched for what Wick would say. "Hey—"

Then he heard the running footsteps behind him.

An ambush?

Archer spun to face backward on the bench on his knees, facing the runner.

It was Wick.

Wick, who had come back from leshy territory unpredictable, who must have been watching from the woods and seen what looked like someone about to attack Archer, was charging toward the fair folk with a big stick in his hands.

One of Otho's sons exclaimed something that Archer couldn't make out as Archer made a split-second decision and leaped over the back of the bench. He dove past Wick's swinging stick and slammed his shoulder into Wick's stomach.

They both hit the grass hard. Pain shot through Archer's crippled wing and down his spine. Despite it, he struggled to a sitting position and hissed, "What do you think you're doing?"

Wick's eyes were wild. "They were going to—"

"No, they were being stupid. I know stupid. *I'm* stupid. I was trying to make them calm down, like you would. You're ruining it." As the last few words left his mouth, Archer knew it was a mistake.

"I—" Wick's face went empty. He winced and wrapped his arms around his bruised stomach.

"Forget I said that. Give me a second." Archer felt a little bit remorseful but mostly stressed as he turned back to Otho. "I'm sorry, he didn't understand. He's not usually like this."

Otho cast warning glances toward his two sons. "Mine were out of line as well. I would rather nothing like that happened again, but I understand."

"Look," Archer said, climbing back over the bench and sitting again. "I know you have no reason to trust us, but I'm asking anyway because the Scorch *is* coming back, and that puts everyone in danger. Including your family. We want to get it right this time, and keep everyone safe." He hesitated. "If it makes any difference, my father is Ochre Hessen, and he can vouch for Wick's character."

Otho eyed Archer for a long moment. At last, he shifted and said, "Frankly, I'm more concerned about you as a pair than individually, so vouching for Wick wouldn't be much good. But you're being honest, and I admire an honest man. Not to mention, Annalise seemed to genuinely believe in you, and I trust her judgment. Therefore, I'll do what I can for you."

Excitement surged through Archer's veins. They'd done it! Somehow, they had made it into the fair folk meeting. "Thank you," he managed.

"You're welcome," Otho said. "But don't get too excited. Outsiders aren't allowed into the fair folk meetings, so you'll have to write your full case down for me to read to the others. You need a lot of people to vote in your favor, so you'll have to be convincing."

"We can't show up in person?" Archer asked. He wasn't sure if he was ready for strangers to present his case for him. This could be some kind of scheme.

"Not likely. A letter is your best bet."

"I'll figure something out," Archer said. "Thank you."

"Good luck," Otho said.

Having found at least partial success, Archer hauled Wick up off the ground, and they started the trek back to the Hessen house.

On the way back, Archer said, "They're not that upset

about what you did. I think it'll be all right. We just need to get the letter written like they asked."

All Wick said was, "Yes."

On their way to take some more paper from Ochre's study, Archer said, "We need to come up with a game plan to write this letter. I've never made a convincing argument in my life. You've heard how I talk. We need a plan."

Wick said, "Hm."

In Archer's room, sitting against the wall with some books he had also taken from the study and trying to find helpful information, Archer said, "This is going to take forever. How do you even find what you're looking for in a book without reading through the whole thing?"

Wick, bending over a piece of paper and tapping the tip of his pencil against it, made a soft noise and said nothing.

Now finally frustrated, Archer scowled. "Wick, *help* me."

Wick's head snapped up. "*I'm trying.*" He slammed his palm down, clapping the pencil against the floor. "I'm trying to help, I'm trying not to ruin everything, I'm trying to even find the energy to *do* anything about our world burning when I feel like I'm crumbling into nothing. I'm *trying*."

Archer didn't know what to say as Wick got up and walked out of the room, running his hands across his face over and over. Looking around, Archer realized he was alone in a room full of half-formed plans and information he didn't know how to understand.

CHAPTER THIRTEEN:

The Only Place In the Whole World

EVENTUALLY, Wick returned and finished writing down his list of points for the assembly. Neither of them apologized. They just went on ignoring the elephant in the room like they hadn't shouted at one another. Wick offered to help Archer find what he needed from the books, but Archer had already given in and gone to Fowl for help.

He had found his brother in the library, in the same tall backed chair as always. When Archer grudgingly asked for help in his research, Fowl looked up with cold eyes.

"This is what you get for running away before any of your tutors managed to teach you anything useful."

"This is what they get for not teaching all of it to me when I was younger," Archer responded. "Are you going to help or not?"

"It's called an index," Fowl said, like the unhelpful lump he was. Meeting Archer's infuriated expression with a long-suffering sigh, he took one of the books off the stack beside his chair and opened it to the back. He showed Archer a long list with page numbers. "Find what you want to look at on the list, and it will tell you what page. Now, can I go back to my book, or while I'm at it should I show you how to use a spoon without hurting yourself?"

Somehow Archer couldn't believe that this was the same brother who had tried to apologize for everything a few days ago. He took the advice and went back to his room, where he managed to find a few helpful pieces of information. He scrawled these on Wick's list of useful points for the letter.

Now, with their list fully written down, the two of them worked on the statement itself. Once again, Archer knew he wasn't helping much, and it was obvious Wick was struggling from how he rubbed his forehead and how often he hesitated mid-sentence, but Archer tried to offer suggestions wherever he could.

By the end of the evening, they had something resembling a polite letter, with the correct greetings and pleasantries, eventually winding around to the point they were getting at and containing a strong argument for 'their case' as Otho had put it. Archer told Wick he would take it to Otho's family in the morning. For the time being, they put the letter in an envelope and sealed it, and Archer left it on top of his dresser.

"I'll figure out things from here," Archer offered, although halfheartedly. His head felt too full to do anything else.

"Thank you," Wick said, and getting up slowly, he left the room.

Archer sucked in a deep breath and blew it out,

scrubbing his eyes with his palms. That had been plenty of stress for one day.

"How did it turn out?" Ochre breezed into the room and scooped up the letter from Archer's dressertop. In a second he had it out of the envelope, bright eyes scanning the page. He didn't react as he read the first page, or the second. Finally, he turned over the second page and read the back of it. "Hmm."

Archer sighed. "What is it?"

"It's a good letter," Ochre said. With a nod, he folded up the letter again and tucked it back in the envelope. "Plenty of solid points, and your friend made an excellent argument. I can't imagine you did any of that. But it won't make the fair folk side with you."

Archer's brow furrowed, half in confusion, half in annoyance. "Why not? What's wrong with it?"

"You're planning to send this to their assembly, aren't you?" Ochre asked, tossing a glance in Archer's direction. "Letters like these would be the best for the nixies or the manghar, who are more of a political state and will make their choices based on reasoning and advantage. The fair folk are small people. They're a true democracy, and they vote emotionally. Your letter isn't personal enough. It won't convince enough of them to get the majority vote."

Archer forced himself not to say anything too quickly. Steeling himself, he asked, "Then what would you have done?"

"I wouldn't have stolen things from people, because then I wouldn't have made so much work for myself when I wanted to write letters later."

Of course.

"But, if I found myself in your predicament, I would rewrite this letter to sound less cold and calculating and more like a personal appeal. You need to make them feel something. And no offense meant to your friend, but Wick doesn't feel things very deeply. You, on the other hand, let your feelings control you. I think if you were the one to rewrite the letter and then have your friend edit it for clarity, it would come together nicely." Ochre flapped the envelope. "But don't give the fair folk this letter."

"Fine," Archer said, shaking his head. When his father didn't move, he added, "Not tonight, though. Wick's tired. I'll tell him about it in the morning."

"Very well." Ochre reached into one of the deep pockets of his silk robe. "In the meantime, I believe it's in your best interest to take this." When Archer didn't move, Ochre beckoned impatiently with his other hand. "I don't have all evening to wait for you."

Feeling used and stupid, Archer held out his hand. A chunk of cool green rock dropped into it.

"Your letter, if you can make it personal, should win over the fair folk," his father said as Archer looked up at him in confusion. "I still don't think that you're correct in all your rambling about the Scorch, but if you succeed in banding together the races of Aro, it will be something important. If you succeed, I want to be remembered as a backer to your cause. I'll write you the correct papers in the morning to let you travel where you like unhindered."

As much as Archer knew the correct thing to say was *thank you*, he couldn't bring himself to say it. Not to his father, and not when something in his gut told him this wasn't his father being thoughtful and supportive.

"But remember," Ochre continued, "if you're imprisoned again, I won't have the rest of this family dragged down with you. If you fail, I don't want my name even mentioned in your little venture."

There it was.

"Gotcha." Archer closed his hand around the stone. "If we do good, people can know you helped, but if we don't do good, you don't want anything to do with us." *With me.*

"Exactly. It isn't complicated, is it?"

Archer held in a deep sigh. "No, it isn't." Actually, it was exactly what he should have expected. As his father left the room again, Archer jammed the seraph piece of the Heather Stone into the unfillable bag and scrubbed his palms against his eyes.

Since he couldn't sleep after that, Archer sat up for the rest of the night and tried to scrape together a meaningful message for their letter. How did one write a letter to sound personal? It had been hard enough to get the original to sound right. This was even harder than writing a letter *humbly*.

You need to make them feel something, his father had said.

How was he supposed to know what would make the fair folk feel something? He didn't like to worry about other people's feelings. They always got in the way. But seeing how Wick was in no state to do the talking, it would have to be Archer. Archer rested his chin on his fists and thought harder.

Somehow, he had made Annalise care about him. And she was a fair folk. How had he made her like him?

You didn't look like someone who would threaten the country and go to prison.

But you're helping me rebuild my house. And you're helping me carry all these things. You didn't have to do it yourself. And yet here you are. That's enough for me.

He had convinced her with. . . what exactly? His

existence? Being unexpected?

Archer tilted his head back and thought about what Otho had said.

You're being honest, and I admire an honest man.

So it was honesty they wanted. Honesty and integrity.

It was a shame that those weren't really Archer's best qualities.

Not to mention, Annalise seemed to genuinely believe in you.

Annalise believed in him.

Archer slumped. "Make it sound like a personal appeal," he muttered to himself as he reached for the remaining stationery. "Easier than trying to sound like Wick."

This letter is addressed to the fair folk of Aro. Hello to all of you, individually. My name is Archer Oak Hessen, and I'm the son of Ochre Hessen of Tor. His father, my grandfather, was Oak Hessen of Eri. I'm writing to you about the Heather Stone thefts not too long ago. You probably heard about it. Me and my friend Wick were the ones who committed the thefts. This letter is to explain why we did what we did and to ask for your help.

If he even knew how to ask for help. The only reason they had made it this far was because Ongel had volunteered to help. Before that, Archer had done everything using Wick's smarts. Everyone had spoon-fed Archer instructions since the beginning.

I'm here to tell you that you and your families are in danger. Everything you know is in jeopardy. The Scorch is returning, and this time it's hidden from the centaurs' visions. No visions means no specifics, but the signs I've seen around me are obvious. Have you noticed that your trees are dying from the root? And the rain is coming down black. The smaller plants are dying already, too. I wouldn't be surprised if we started getting earthquakes soon.

Caihu the centaur warned me about this a while ago, and since then I've seen the signs myself. I started stealing the Heather Stones because I knew no one would give me enough of a chance to explain. I got Wick to listen, and he joined me because he saw the same things I did.

He can spot a liar when he sees one. And I wasn't lying.

You've probably heard, but we nearly succeeded the first time. We had all the stones, and we made it to the cavern to put them in place. We didn't use them for anything else. All we wanted to do was put the stones in place and cast the barrier spell so that we could keep the Scorch out.

But we were caught, because we were thieves, after all. But that doesn't change the fact that Aro is in danger. The Scorch is still coming, and it's closer than ever. You must have seen the fire that came down from the sky. It's only a taste of what's coming for us if we don't do something about it.

I'll get to the point of this letter. I'm sending this with Otho, who has promised to help us as much as he can. I'm asking for two things: your trust, and through your trust, your piece of the Heather Stone. If we're going to keep the Scorch from destroying us, we're going to need all the stones we can get. We'll understand if you only want the centaurs to handle it or if you want to add other restrictions so you know nothing happens to your piece of the Heather Stone.

Think about the danger before you make your choice.

The Scorch is coming. Both Otho's family and the Isleberg family can vouch for me, and there are a lot of people who can vouch for Wick.

Archer thought for a minute. He had no idea how to end his letter.

Respectfully,
Archer Hessen

Would it be enough to convince them? Archer read the letter back over and concluded that he couldn't do any better. And his back ached from leaning over the toy chest. Sitting up slowly, he folded the letter into thirds and tucked it into the envelope. After thinking for a moment more, he also tucked the letter he and Wick had written together into the envelope, with a note that said, *If you need more technical information, read this.*

By this time, it was so late that he could barely navigate to his bed and under the covers. Through the open window, he heard someone singing out in the city. It was an old nursery song about monsters made of fire and death.

Eyes of fire, skin of flame, creatures rare that overcame—

Sleep took him before he could hear the rest.

The following morning, with great trepidation, he brought the finished product to his father. Archer stood across the room with his arms crossed tight as Ochre breezed through the letter.

"It's better." Ochre slid the letter back into the envelope with his usual expression of indifference. "Not perfect, perhaps, but I imagine it will do the trick more than the previous version. Although your penmanship is the same scrawl as when you were small."

"I like it that way." Archer crossed to the desk and

took the envelope back before his father could change his mind. "I'll go give this to Otho now."

As it turned out, he didn't have to go far to find Otho. Otho was already at the base of the stairs with the rest of his family. The confrontational son eyed Wick once again, but neither of them made any quick movements, so for the moment Archer could assume they were safe from any fights.

"Thanks for doing this," Archer said. The statement felt a little forced, but it seemed like the right thing to say.

Otho tucked the envelope under his arm. Compared to his size, the letter was as big as a cupboard door. "I wish you luck."

"Thanks. You too, I guess."

With a nod, Otho walked away with the letter. And so the waiting game began for Archer. He took a long walk around the town to kill the time, and then when he was hungry enough he wandered back to the Hessen house, where Wick appeared to have made real biscuits this time instead of grey slop. Wick himself was in a strangely cheerful mood as he stirred a pot on the stove. It seemed bizarre after his despondent attitude the day before. And his skin was still grey.

"How long is the assembly going to take?" Archer demanded as he spread blackberry preserves on his third biscuit. "It's taking forever."

"They don't meet until this afternoon," Wick said. "And we probably won't hear anything about it until the evening. Don't worry about it yet."

Later in the afternoon, they received a message from the nixies, thanking them for their letter but requesting more time to consider.

"It's not a bad sign," Wick commented, glancing over

the reply again. His eyes were still grey and hollow as they glanced up at Archer. "She didn't ignore your letter. The queen is seriously thinking about what you said."

Archer checked back through the stack of letters again. Still nothing from the manghar.

He cut open another biscuit.

Shortly after dinner, where the conversation was still stiff and Archer still couldn't manage to be good enough for his father, Wick appeared in the doorway of Archer's room with news from the fair folk.

"What did they decide?" Archer asked.

"Nothing. The vote was too divided. They're going to think it over and vote again tomorrow afternoon. From the sounds of it, every other vote went well, but ours will need to be taken again."

More waiting. "Great."

A feeling nagged at the back of Archer's mind. Maybe it would help to talk about what was going on with Wick, about what had happened in leshy territory, but he had already gotten yelled at once, which had been no less than he expected. He wasn't someone that people wanted to talk to.

Wick still stood in the doorway, hovering like he was thinking about something. The strangeness of the silence built a lump in Archer's throat.

Not too long ago, Archer and Wick had been so close. They had talked about anything and everything. But already Archer felt a distance growing between him and his friend like it had grown between him and Fowl, and there was nothing he could do to stop it. He wanted to help Wick, but the fear gnawing at his stomach made him stop. He was no good for emotional support. He had proven that.

Archer looked up at Wick. "I guess we'll find out what happens, then."

Wick nodded and left the room.

Archer suddenly found the room too stuffy. The air was too still. Shoving the floor-length window open, he sat on the sill and stared out at the city.

The tension at home was getting to be too much. In the past, he would have gone to his grandfather's house for the day to get away from the rest of them, but now that the house was empty, it wouldn't do any good.

Instead, he tried to think about their next step. Who should they talk to next? Who would ally with them before anyone else? Who would believe them based on their word and their word alone?

He tilted his head as he remembered something from years ago. They might be able to help. It was a bit of a gamble, but maybe they would.

"Huh," he said aloud. "That could work."

Getting up, he found Wick in the library where, for once, Fowl wasn't.

"If you're going to pack anything, do it tonight," Archer said. "We're heading for human territory in the morning."

Wick looked up from the picture he was studying, his brow creasing. "The fair folk are voting again tomorrow. We shouldn't leave now."

"They'll vote whether we're here or not. It won't make a difference."

"But you said it wasn't safe to leave seraph territory," Wick protested.

"Well, we're risking it anyway. I might know somewhere else we can stay for a while."

Wick looked suspicious. "Where?"

"Just a town," Archer said defensively. "It should be safe, so long as things haven't changed since I've been there. We're leaving after breakfast."

Then he climbed back up the stairs and collapsed into bed to sleep off all the mental strain the day had brought him.

As it turned out, sleeping in the middle of the day made him wake in the middle of the night fully conscious. He tossed and turned, trying to get back to sleep, but try as he might, he always ended up staring at the ceiling, bored.

After waiting three-quarters of an hour for sleep to return, he got out of bed and crept down to the kitchen. As he had suspected, no one else seemed to be awake. The only other thing in the kitchen was the cluster of baked goods from where Wick had spent several hours cooking in a slow fog. Archer got down a pot from its hook above the stove. Stirring up the few remaining embers, he threw on a log and a bit of kindling and got to work.

A jug of frutelken had been left on the counter, so he poured himself a glass while the pan of milk on the stove warmed. He took a sip. Just enough cinnamon, just enough peach, just enough everything. Perfection.

He went through the ceramic ice chest to find the fruits he needed. It was almost past season for most of the fruits he needed, but he was lucky. The ice chest still had a little bit more of everything.

Archer filled his arms with fruit and dumped it out on the counter. The milk was warm when he stuck a finger in it, so he got out a knife and started cutting the fruits, one at a time, into first slices, then into cubes. Then he dumped the whole lot into the pot, hoping for the best. As the fruit slowly softened in the pot, he dug through the spice rack.

A soft sound came from the hallway. Archer turned

and looked over his shoulder. His father stood in the doorway, wrapped in a grey silk robe with his hair loose and unruly and his eyes screwed up tight against the light in the kitchen. "What are you doing?"

Archer set the cinnamon down on the counter and lamely gestured to the pot on the stove. "I'm. . . giving it another go."

"We have plenty," his father said.

"I know," Archer said. "I want to learn how to do it, that's all."

"You're overcomplicating it." Archer's father brushed past him and took a small box from the shadows beneath the counter. Plucking out a single piece of paper, he slapped it on the counter. "Use the recipe like everyone else."

Everyone else.

As soon as his father's hand lifted, Archer threw a towel over the paper. The recipe disappeared from sight. "I don't want to use the recipe. I want to figure it out for myself."

Ochre Hessen looked up with tired eyes. "And why is that better?"

'Everyone else' learns family recipes from their family. Directly from their family. If I learn it from a piece of paper. . .

"I'd rather figure it out myself."

Because one day, if I get it right, maybe it will mean something.

Ochre shook his head as he started back for the dark stairwell. "You always have to be different."

Archer blinked. He was too tired to start a real argument, but he had to say something. With only a touch of bitterness, he asked, "Would you rather I was like everyone else?"

His question was quiet, but Ochre heard. He turned, and the half-light of the lamps Archer had lit accented the hard planes of his face. "Don't play the victim with me. You know that's not what this is about. I just don't see why you can never take the obvious action. Things can be simple, you know."

How dare he make it sound so easy.

"I was born with bones that wouldn't let me fly," Archer said, without a pause, "in a place where flying means everything. I don't think being different was up to me. And in this family, simple is a little out of reach, too." He paused. "Whatever. Go back to sleep. I'm not bothering anyone."

His father sighed as he left the kitchen. "Have it your way, then. You're so hardheaded."

"Yup. Just like you made me." Archer flicked a fruit rind off the counter and looked up after his father's departing form. "Better that than hard-hearted, I guess."

Ochre paused in the doorway. Then he left without another word.

As silence smothered the kitchen, Archer realized his pot was almost boiling over. Grabbing the spoon, he did his best to salvage the drink, choosing to focus on that over thinking about how the conversation had gone. At the end of it all, he had one glass of the good frutelken that his mother made, and a pot full of some drink that tasted all right, but nothing like hers.

He had got it wrong again. Like every time before.

He pushed all the spice jars back into the cabinet and fell back into bed, where he slept soundly until morning.

*

BY THE TIME the sun had risen into the treetops, Archer busted into Wick's room, demanding he get up.

Wick winced and buried his head under his pillow. That tired, empty feeling still weighed on his body. Like he didn't want to get up now, or ever again.

"Come on," Archer said, "we're going." Something thudded against Wick's side. Probably his bag, which he had packed the night before, hoping that come morning he would feel more willing to leave.

When Wick still didn't move, Archer tried a different tactic. "Get up or I get the cold water, and I'll dump it on your head."

Wick forced himself to roll over so that the pillow no longer covered his head. He rubbed at his eyes, trying to summon the energy to get up.

Archer waited for a moment before leaving without a word.

After much hesitation, Wick dragged himself out of bed. He stood in the sunlight pouring through the windows, feeling the warmth on his skin. Only his skin, though, no deeper.

He missed how the sun gave him energy. He should have known that would be what he missed the most.

He had slept in his clothes, so all Wick had to do was to make the bed (or at least a rough approximation of making the bed), then put on his shoes and started down the stairs with his bag over his shoulder. He felt impossibly less ready to travel to some unknown village than he had when he woke up.

Archer's mother stopped him on his way down the stairs, holding out some brick red garment. "It's much too cold outside today. You'll need this."

Wick took whatever it was and realized it must be a jacket or something of the like. "Thank you." He continued down the stairs, putting the jacket on as he went. It was fleecy to the touch and provided an extra layer of warmth that he hadn't quite expected from its light weight.

He found Archer in the kitchen, pulling various food items off shelves and stashing them in the unfillable bag. "About time," he said when he saw Wick. "Get what you want for breakfast. We're eating while we walk."

An unhappy horse snort came from the bag as a whole loaf of bread went tumbling inside. Archer stuck his nose inside the bag and apologized to Sasha.

"Did you ever take Sasha out of the bag while you were here?" Wick asked, trying to select a peach from a basket of peaches.

"Of course I did," Archer said. He tilted his head. "Or, I think I did. Did I? I don't remember now."

Wick sighed and shook his head.

The walk to human territory was strangely uneventful. Even with their papers from Archer's father, Wick expected to find enemies behind every bush, tree, and small rise. But as it happened, they met no one and were able to travel in peace all the way to human territory.

As they crossed the border from seraph territory into human territory, Wick asked, "Do I get to know where we're going yet, or am I still in the dark?"

"You probably don't even know where it is, so why do you care?" Archer asked. "It's just a place where I know some people. It's not an important city or anything."

Wick raised his eyebrows. "*You* know some people? When have you ever known anyone?"

"Why do you say that like you're surprised?" Archer

said, taking offense. "I'm a person, I know people. Why does that surprise you?"

"Because I thought you liked being a force of impassive detachment," Wick responded, utterly deadpan. "A will of the wisp, as I recall. Someone without responsibilities such as knowing and caring about ordinary people."

Archer snorted, and for a moment Wick saw a glimpse of their older energy, the way they were before everything went wrong, before he left for leshy territory and returned feeling like he'd never be the same again. For a moment, he got a glimpse of their old banter. "Don't be dumb," Archer said. "I have some people. I have my family, even though I hate them. And every so often, I make some friends, like you."

With his head still down and eyes fixed on the path, Wick blinked in surprise. Archer never talked like that.

It made him feel strangely warm inside.

"I'm still thinking about how you said it wasn't some great city," Wick said, "like I'm too good to go to common places. In my job, I went wherever I had to go; it didn't matter if it was big or important."

"Well, you thought you were someone fancy," Archer said with a laugh. "You got on my nerves because you reminded me of my father."

"I think you were jealous of my fanciness," Wick mused.

"Never." Archer snorted. "I'm not the fancy kind."

"Says the son of a noble."

"Says the guy who was going to represent the *entire leshy race*."

"But not anymore," Wick said, and the horrible aching tired feeling came back. He felt weary in the very shadow of his soul. "Sorry," he said, trying to take back how he had darkened the mood.

Archer didn't say anything, but Wick assumed he didn't know what to say. Wick didn't know what to say himself.

"We'll be there soon, if that makes you feel any better," Archer said. "It's not far. That's why I wanted to go. If things go south, it's only a few days from seraph territory, and we could even run all the way back."

"Good," was all Wick said.

As more time passed, Wick found himself hoping that whatever happened, the fair folk received the letter they wrote for the assembly with good spirits. It had been on his mind for their entire journey. Whenever his mind was idle, it always came back to thinking about the letter.

He couldn't help but think that if he was still a messenger and still important, maybe he would be at the assembly right now, presenting the letter himself. Back then, they probably would have let him come without a second thought. But now everything had shifted. He was untrustworthy. Slippery.

Dangerous.

He didn't like being dangerous. He had never wanted to be a threat.

And yet, something in the back of his mind whispered to him that now, maybe *now* he could finally be the one in charge.

"I think this is it here," Archer said, interrupting Wick's train of thought. They came over the crest of a small hill and there, in the valley on the other side, was a village.

Wick didn't know if he was surprised that the village they had come to visit looked a lot like any other human village: boxy wooden houses with thatched or straw roofs, dirt roads, the last struggling remnants of gardens as the fall crept in. Some running children, some bleating livestock. What looked like a small market on the far side.

This was what they had come to see. A village.

"Archer," Wick said. "I'm finding myself a little underwhelmed."

"Wait for it," Archer responded, walking ahead.

Wick chased after him. "I know you said that it wasn't an important city or anything like that, but. . . how can these people help us? This isn't even where the human piece of the heather stone is. How is this going to help at all?"

"Wait for it," Archer replied. Stuffing his hands in his pockets, he sauntered down the hill toward the village.

Wick, having waited for it more than a second and seen nothing, said, "Archer—"

"*Wait* for it."

They passed through a slatted gate into the village with Wick close on Archer's heels.

Archer looked over his shoulder at Wick and smirked. Swinging around again to face the empty street, he inhaled and shouted, "I'm back!"

As his shout echoed down the barren street, Archer turned to Wick with a smile on his face.

"Listen," he said, "we didn't just come here for help with the latest grand scheme. Honestly, I don't know if they can help us at all. We came here because I wanted to. Because believe it or not—" he threw open his arms and shouted up to the sky— "this is the one and only place in the whole world where everyone thinks I'm awesome!"

CHAPTER FOURTEEN:

It's Not Often That People Like Us

PEOPLE BEGAN TO APPEAR.

One door cracked open, then another. Somewhere in the village, a dog burst out into loud barking. Some men appeared from a barn and took off their hats to wave them in the air, shouting loud greetings. A gaggle of children raced around the corner and plowed into Archer's legs, not stopping nearly fast enough to avoid a collision. Archer lost his balance and vanished under all the children.

In the space of a few moments, half the village had arrived to welcome Archer back.

Wick was approximately two days' travel past confused.

"Go on, shoo!" A round woman old enough to be Archer or Wick's mother waded into the crowd of children and pulled Archer to his feet. "Other people want to see Archer, too."

A smaller boy still clung to Archer's leg. "Did you bring me a present?" His toothless lisp made it *prethent*.

"Uh, I forgot," Archer said, and the youngsters tackled him once more. He went down under a pile of about twenty small children.

The round woman plucked them off one by one and sent them off down the road. "Go on! I mean it!" She pulled Archer up again, with a little girl climbing up his shoulders. Archer laughed as the round woman pried the little girl off his shoulders, and he ruffled her hair before she was set down and sent on her way.

Still laughing, Archer finally saw Wick's face. He held up his hands. "Okay, okay, let me give you the grand explanation of what's happening here."

"Please."

"Not before I get my hug," the woman said, pulling Archer into her arms. To Wick's surprise, Archer didn't immediately pull away.

"Here's the situation," Archer said, working his way back through the crowd of friends to Wick. "I may have saved this entire village from flooding."

"Ah, I see," Wick said numbly. Then the words processed. "What? You did what?"

"Listen, listen," Archer interrupted. "Just let me get through the story, okay?"

"Are you hungry?" one of the other women asked. "My husband shot a deer a few days ago. We plan to salt it so it keeps over the winter, but there's more than enough to share."

Archer ran a hand through his shark's fin of hair. "That would be nice. We've been traveling for a few days, it would be good to have a real meal again."

"Done." The woman gave him a warm, fond smile

and disappeared back into her house to begin meal preparations. Some of the others had already vanished, maybe to spread the news of Archer's return. The children had already forgotten about the excitement and tumbled over one another as they kicked a rock back and forth across the road.

"So here it is," Archer said, coming to stand beside Wick and looking out over the town. "A while back, a long while back I guess, soon after I left the seraphs for good because. . . well, you know. Anyway. I was roaming, trying to find a place to end up, and I ended up here."

Another child ran screeching past.

"I wanted nothing to do with anyone at the time, so I hung out on top of the rise up there and only came down when I wanted some food or something. Danna, that's the lady who saved me from the pile of kids, she saw me and she tried to take me in like a lost puppy or something, but I didn't want to be around anyone. This was after I met Caihu and got the bag, so I could keep a few days' worth of food in it and only come down to the village once in a while." He shrugged.

"After a while, there was a big storm, and I hid on someone's porch to wait it out. It was a ton of rain, buckets and buckets, and when it stopped, the whole street was flooded up to your ankles. So I went back up the hill in case it was less wet." He turned around and pointed to their left, toward where the foothills got higher and denser transitioning into the mountains.

"And see, the hills over there are really steep, and there's a pretty severe incline. I happened to look that way, and I saw all this water and mud coming toward the village. And don't ask me why, but it upset me to think about this place getting flooded. I took my bag, and I raced over there, and I caught all the water in the bag. I guess someone saw, because later when I showed up for some more food, everyone was so happy to see me and they gave me a ton of supplies, and they said I was welcome to come back any time I liked. I do come back, sometimes, when I'm in the area. It's a nice place."

"You're saying," Wick said with a comical smile, "that when I met you, it wasn't the first time you'd put a river in the bag?"

Archer tilted his head. "Well, it wasn't a river. More like a huge mudslide. But yeah, I guess. That's how I learned not to dump everything back out of the bag. I tried to get rid of the mud a few weeks later, and I lost everything I had in the bag. I couldn't find any of it once all the mud emptied out."

"I see." Wick looked out at the village, now seeing it through a new light. "You lost all your possessions for these people."

"You could put it that way." Archer squirmed a bit. "But that makes it sound so serious."

Wick frowned. "No offense, but do they know who you are aside from that?"

"With the stealing and the hitting and the escaping from jail? Yeah," Archer said, the picture of nonchalance. "Danna dragged it out of me after the second time I showed up with a black eye. They don't want me telling the kids about some of it, but no one ever overreacted about it." He shrugged. "They like me all the same, you know?"

"Huh," Wick said. "Well, they seem like good people."

"I'm pretty sure they are."

"Archer!" one of the younger boys called. "Are you

coming to play ball with us?"

"Of course!" Archer yelled back. "I'm coming!" He turned to Wick. "Care to play some ball?" Without waiting for an answer, he bounded off after the younger boys, who were racing deeper into the village with their ball.

Wick started after them. "I don't have the first idea of how to play ball."

After an hour or two of the boys trying and failing to teach Wick ball, they were shooed out of the way so that the village could set up tables down the center of the street, end to end. Wick watched from a porch as they set vases of autumn leaves and plates of food all over the tables. Since becoming human, he had never seen so much food in one place. It was clear from the amount of salted pork and dried fruit that much of this had been stored for the winter.

A dog barked at Wick's feet, and he bent down to rub the dog's head.

"We scraped together what we could," Danna said, reappearing out of the house behind him. "But winter is still coming, so we can only feast on so much."

"We weren't expecting anything like this," Wick admitted. "It's more than enough. Thank you."

He remembered again that he didn't know why they were here. He wondered if Archer had only come to get away from all the tension in seraph territory with his family.

"What was your name, dear?" Danna asked. "I don't think we were introduced."

"Wick," Wick said, looking up. The dog took that as his cue to leave and raced down the street, barking.

"My name is Danna," Danna said, her large, strong hand engulfing his to shake it. She took a closer look at Wick's face, and fascination filled her features. "You're something special, aren't you? I've never seen anything like you before."

Wick, who had expected this, said, "I'm a leshy."

Was.

"The tree people," Danna said in a curious voice. "The legends have you looking different."

"I recently changed my form. Although it seems the transformation wasn't a complete one. I'm stuck with these," he said, gesturing to his eyes. He knew they weren't as bright as of late, but they were still clearly gold, and even at the worst of times they were a lighter shade than normal eyes.

"How unusual," Danna said with the right amount of surprise and ease. "I'm pleased to make your acquaintance."

"And I'm pleased to make yours," Wick responded.

Danna smiled and gestured to the table. "Shall we?"

They were the first to sit, at the far end of the table toward the edge of the village. People bustling around the tables gradually took their seats, and the children reached over the backs of the benches to snatch some food for themselves. Archer found a seat a little way down from Wick and Danna.

From the center of the benches, a man stood and whistled for quiet. Everyone turned his way. "Friends, today is a feast day. This meal is to celebrate Archer's visit here, and the friend he brought with him." He looked over at Wick and Archer. "We're glad to have you, and we'll drink to your health. To Archer, and to Wick!"

The town cheered. Glasses and wooden tumblers tapped together, and food began making its way around the tables.

Wick's heart stirred as he watched the townspeople.

He was a stranger here. These people didn't have any reason to look after him. But here they were, celebrating for him and Archer like they had won a war.

"I did mean to ask, Archer," said a light-haired woman, the one who had originally offered them dinner, as she stood preparing a plate for a child, "what brings you to the village this time?"

Wick listened to see how he would answer.

Archer leaned out over the table to see. "We mostly came because we needed some peace and quiet. The world isn't usually peaceful and quiet these days, Ruth."

A deflecting answer.

"What are you up to these days?" Ruth asked. She handed the plate off to her little one, and the little girl raced off to join her friends on a doorstep.

"Adventuring, seeing the sights. You know me."

"Aye, we know you," Danna said, pointing a leg of turkey in Archer's direction. "There were whispers about some huge theft not too long ago. Don't tell me that was you."

"It wasn't!" Archer exclaimed, momentarily pretending to be offended. "It was me *and* Wick."

Ruth sighed and shook her head as she began to prepare her own plate. "You can do better, Archer."

"I'm working on it," Archer said, frowning. "Change doesn't happen overnight."

Or sometimes ever, Wick thought. He couldn't picture Archer changing for anyone.

Danna spotted one of the children making off with a whole plate of salted pork and leaped up with a bellow. The child shrieked with excitement and fear and took off down the street with Danna on her heels.

"If it makes you feel any better," Archer said, "I'm

trying to make up for it. Wick and I are trying to turn ourselves into civilized people and politely ask for the stones again or something like that. Wick has all the plans."

Wick felt a rush of unease at the mention of planning.

"You don't happen to know where the human piece of the heather stone landed this time, do you?" Archer asked. "We're guessing we'll only need a few stones this time, but since we're here I thought we might try to collect the human piece."

Ruth pondered, then shook her head. "I don't think I've heard anything about it lately. We don't get many travelers down here, so there's little outside gossip that gets passed around." She suddenly stopped herself, embarrassed. "Not that I'm a top source for gossip."

The women around her laughed. One of them shouted to a man further down the row. "Daniel! Did you hear anything about our piece of the heather stone when you were traveling?"

"I heard it changed hands recently," the man named Daniel responded, thumbing the brim of his hat higher. Already he had a few crumbs in his mustache. "Whoever had it before had some kind of breakdown. They don't trust him with a spoon anymore."

"Sounds about right," Archer said.

"He didn't seem like the stable type when we met him," Wick added. "He seemed paranoid."

"Probably for good reason, since we knocked him out in the woods and stole his stone," Archer mused. He tapped his spoon against his plate at an irritated pace. "Sounds like we'll have to track it down again. If Prentiss doesn't have it anymore, it could end up with anyone."

He caught Wick's worried look and abruptly changed

the subject. "Okay, where's Charlie? I have a good story for him about how I got out of jail in manghar territory. There isn't any stealing in it, I promise."

A small, dirty face appeared behind him, and Archer made an enthusiastic sound. "Charlie! Just who I wanted to see. I have a story for you." He turned around on the bench to talk to Charlie excitedly.

Danna returned, huffing but triumphantly bearing the plate of meat. "That girl of yours can sure run fast, Eli. Took forever to catch her." A man halfway down the tables laughed. "What are we talking about now?"

Charlie's scrubby little face appeared around Archer's shoulder. "Archer drowned a manghar!"

"Well, maybe," Archer said. "We didn't stick around to see if they were alive or dead."

"I don't think *maybe drowned a manghar* is filling anyone with confidence," Wick said. That earned a laugh down the table.

Later on in the evening, once food had been eaten and tables dragged away, when the sun was disappearing and lights began appearing in a few of the windows, Wick and Archer sat on someone's front stoop talking to the remaining villagers. One by one, the others said goodnight and disappeared back to their homes.

When the last of them left, Archer stretched and yawned. "I wasn't expecting to be this tired. Maybe I had too much turkey."

Wick made a quiet noise. "So the human stone isn't here."

"I didn't think it would be," Archer said, taking Wick by surprise. Wick glanced over at him. "They probably won't be able to help us at all. To be honest, I wanted a bit of a vacation. That's why we're here."

"But Archer," Wick said, "I don't know if we have time for a vacation. We need to be planning and preparing so we can keep Aro safe."

Archer hesitated. Wick seldom saw him wait to say anything. At last, Archer took a breath and said, "You mean *I* need to be planning."

Guilt twinged in Wick's chest. "I'm trying. Believe me, I'm trying to put myself back together to be more helpful. But I need more time."

"I know," Archer said, almost before Wick finished speaking. A light flickered on in the house across from them. "But here's the thing, Wick: I'm exhausted. I've never felt more tired in my life. I'm not meant for planning and sweet-talking and all the things I'm doing right now. Those are *your* things. You know about them. I can't even figure out how to sound polite without it coming out stupid."

A dog barked off in the village somewhere.

"I know that ever since you had to go to leshy territory by yourself, you've been trying to. . . figure everything out. And that's fine. I understand what you're going through. Or I think I do." Archer shifted uncomfortably. "But the way our friendship works is that one of us has to be the responsible one. And I've tried. I can't be the responsible one. It's just not in me. When things come, I want to face them with my fists up. I can't smooth out the tension the way you do because that's what you do. I wait until the moment is right, and then I hit hard and fast. I can try to get along with people, but that doesn't change who I am."

Wick got up off the stoop. Archer sighed and got up too. They walked halfway down the street before Wick got up the courage to speak again.

"I'm. . ." Wick stopped and tried again. "For a long time, I've been the only leshy anyone saw. I was the only one who represented my people and kept us from being forgotten by all the other races. There's always been a lot put on my shoulders, by everyone." Wick paused. "I'm terrified of failing them. I've always been worried that one day I would mess it all up and end everything for my people. We'd sink back into anonymity and we wouldn't mean anything anymore. I've always known I was carrying more than I could handle, but I carried it because no one else could."

"I kind of got that idea when I met you. You were scared of everything," Archer said.

"Yeah," Wick managed. "And I'm convinced now that we did the right thing, even if we didn't do it the right way. But I've been worried for a long time that the choices I made would destroy everything I built, and when I went back to ask my people for their help, and they rejected me. . ." Wick stopped and spread his hands helplessly. Even now his heart beat wildly remembering it. "What can I do? I don't regret what I've done, I still don't, but I—I don't know how my people will go on now."

"They can't find someone else to fill your shoes?"

"Maybe they can," Wick said. He kicked something in the dirt road, scuffing some dirt up into the air. "But it worries me because I don't know anyone has any desire to fill my shoes. They never even leave the territory. Aside from me, do you even know a single leshy by name?"

"If I'm being honest, I've never even talked to any other leshy," Archer admitted.

"Exactly." The tired feeling was back, weighing heavily on Wick's chest. "I don't know what will happen to them. What's more, I don't know what will happen to me. I didn't even realize that the messenger job was all I had. I don't know anything else. I don't have any other expertise. I don't have any hobbies. I need to start over now, but I'm not even sure where to start. I feel like I've lost who I am."

"Here's the thing, Wick," Archer said, and they stopped walking. Archer turned to face Wick. "Not to make this all about me, but I've been where you are, starting again from scratch. You're trying to reinvent yourself because the old you can't do this part. It isn't easy, and no one else can help you."

"But," Archer went on, "I'm going to help you out however I can. So long as you do your best to help me, I'll do everything I can to help you. You're one of the only friends I've ever had. No matter how you reinvent yourself, I'm going to be here to see who you end up becoming. I can do that much."

Wick struggled for something to say. Finally, he settled for, "Thank you."

WICK RUBBED HIS FACE and sat up. His back hurt a bit, but it wasn't an unfamiliar feeling. Danna had no extra beds in her house, but then none of the villagers probably did, so they had slept on the floor in her attic, wrapped in extra blankets. Danna insisted they would stay with her or no one, so how could they refuse?

His heart didn't weigh so heavily this morning. Archer had been right to come to this village. There was a feeling here like no other, an air of relaxation and peace that was different from anywhere else Wick had been. His mind felt freer than it had in a long time.

Holed up against the opposite wall of the attic, Archer snored softly. Wick tried to remember if he had ever woken up before Archer. If he had, he couldn't recall it.

Uncertain about what to do with this new experience and overwhelmed by the quiet, he gathered up the blankets and crept down the stairs to put them away.

Danna was already awake, sitting at the table with a small cup in her hand. "Up already?" she asked.

"Yes," Wick said. "I thought I'd bring the blankets down to you."

"You don't think you'll be here tonight?" Danna took another sip of her drink.

"I'm not sure. I just didn't want to leave the attic a mess."

"So considerate." Danna sipped again, and Wick got the feeling she was sizing him up. "So polite. Although that's not how Archer described you when he was talking to me last night."

"When was that?" Wick asked. "I didn't realize he was ever on his own." Then he frowned. "How did he describe me?"

"To put it frankly, he said you were annoying."

Of course.

"But he also said you were smart and tenacious, and he wouldn't have come anywhere near succeeding if it wasn't for you."

Realizing he was still holding the blankets, Wick set them down on the table. "Well, at least I'm not all bad."

"Not at all. He thinks you're quite an incredible person. I've never in my days heard him talk about someone with so much respect."

Archer. . . respected him? Wick's brow furrowed. He couldn't picture Archer saying anything nice of his own free will, let alone all that. He looked up at Danna. "He said that?"

"He did. He had quite a lot to say, about you and

about everything you've done together. He was in quite the talkative mood last night." Danna smiled. "It seems like you make an impressive team together."

"We do." Or rather, they did. Wick's fingers fidgeted with the hem of the blanket. "Although our teamwork is being tested now. Taking the harder path with the Heather Stones this time is proving a challenge for both of us."

"I see." Danna nodded. "Where are you going after this, if you don't think this is your final stop?"

"Since we're already in human territory, I imagine we'll try to track down the human piece of the heather stone," Wick explained. "No one in the village knows where it is, so it will probably take some traveling around and digging through clues until we find it again. All we know is that it's not with Prentiss anymore."

"I know that much," Danna agreed. She took yet another sip of whatever was in her cup. "Because it's with me."

Wick sat in silence for a moment, waiting for the punch line. "Excuse me?"

"It's with me," Danna replied in a calm tone. Setting her cup down, she rose from her seat and walked to a cupboard in the corner of the kitchen. "I realized last night what you must have been looking for, but by that time both of you were already asleep. If I'd heard at supper last night that you were looking for it, I would have told you then, but I was chasing some little scamp up and down the village for my good crockery back." She stepped back from the cupboard. In her hands, she had a ceramic crock painted with pictures of lemons and leaves. "My father's," she explained as she opened it. Inside the crock, wrapped in a piece of linen, was a shining piece of jade green stone.

"You had it here the whole time," Wick said in a

stunned voice.

"Alva Prentiss is my second cousin. Only met him twice, never liked him. He always seemed a little bit crazy in the head. But it seems that when he lost his mind officially, I was the relative that lived the closest to his house. So now the stone is in my possession." She held out the stone in her palm. "You can take it."

With shaking fingers, Wick took the piece of the heather stone. "I'll be right back," Wick said, still in shock, and he raced up the stairs.

"Archer!" he shouted, pounding up the steps. There was no sound from the top. "Archer!" He threw the door of the attic open.

Archer bolted upright, hair wild. "What? What?"

Wick held out his hand, the stone still clutched in his fingers.

Archer's mouth fell open. "You've got to be joking. It's not even breakfast yet."

CHAPTER FIFTEEN:

Fire in the Sky

"AND WHAT'S MORE," Danna said as they ate breakfast, "I have friends in satyr territory I can connect you with. There's a strong chance they can win over the other satyrs, too. And the neighbors know one of Queen Frey's advisers in the nixie kingdom."

"Good," Archer said, and Wick saw his own need for success in Archer's eyes. "Good, we'll take anything we can get."

After breakfast, the arrangements began. Several of the villagers got their fastest horses and rode out in all directions to find the elected representatives who made up the government in human territory. Still more started the long journey to satyr territory. There were offers to go to nixie territory as well, but as they still hadn't heard much back from Queen Frey, no one knew what her stance was on the matter yet, and to bother her at such a delicate point in her decision would probably do more harm than good.

The goal was to make as many and as good of cases to members of authority as possible. The villagers would vouch for Wick and Archer and their cause of reuniting the heather stones to keep the dark force out. Wick and Archer scraped together the same evidence as they had presented in their letter for the fair folk assembly, as well as some crumbling plants they found in the surrounding forest. As they wished each traveler luck on their journey, Wick hoped that they could get it all done and get the stones together before the Scorch hit again. Because they had no way of knowing how much time they had left, and if they couldn't do it. . .

Well, if they couldn't do it, they wouldn't have to worry about a thing ever again. As Danna put it once they had told her their full story, "Now, either you do what you set out to do, or it won't be your problem anymore. It's all a matter of perspective."

Somehow it failed to make Wick feel any better.

Wick brought up returning to seraph territory, and Archer blew it off.

"Not time yet," he said, flapping a hand. "There's still stuff we can do here. We don't have to go back yet."

Wick had a feeling Archer didn't want to go back because of his family, and because of the impending sale of his grandfather's house. For all they knew it was already sold. Maybe Archer was avoiding facing that reality.

And to tell the truth, Wick liked it better in the village himself. Here they were safe, and no one was trying to attack them, and no fire fell from the sky. He didn't have to face the daily challenge of overcoming his failures and the consequences of his actions. He didn't have to look any important people in the face and know he had broken their trust. He could escape from all of that.

He saw why Archer didn't want to leave.

But still, on the morning of their third day in the

village, they realized there was nothing else they could do here, and they packed their bags to leave.

Danna hugged first Archer, then Wick, and wished them luck. She tucked a little extra dried meat into their bags with a wink, saying she knew how Archer hated eating only leaves and mushrooms on his travels. They thanked her and the other villagers a thousand times, but were always answered with 'of course', 'not a problem', 'we'll miss you', and so much more. One little girl who had taken a shine to Wick's strange eyes clung to his leg as he tried to leave.

Then they were once again on the road, and once again in a lot of trouble if they weren't careful. They slept with one eye open and kept an eye over their shoulders every step of the way. Since almost anyone could be an enemy, they didn't want to see anyone. Twice they heard the sound of voices and had to hide, and once they nearly ran into a group of other travelers, but they managed to dive into a hollow behind a log so they weren't seen.

*

AS THEY CROSSED over the border into seraph territory, Archer suddenly got an odd feeling, a prickle at the back of his neck. Traveling alone and making enemies for this long, he knew to listen to it. "Wick, give me the stones."

"What?" Wick asked, stopping.

Archer swung the unfillable bag off his shoulder and fumbled with the buckle. "Give me the Heather Stones. We're testing them right now."

"Why now?" Wick asked, confused, but he dug through his bag nonetheless. He produced the human stone from his traveling bag and pulled the other one out of the pouch around his neck.

A bright flash lit the sky, and Archer's head snapped up. His heart pounded. Something big and bright was hurtling down from the heavens, headed straight toward them. "Ohhhhhh no." He fumbled in the bottom of the unfillable bag, and finally his fingertips found the stone his father had given him. Dropping the seraph stone to the grass, he grabbed the other two in each hand and knocked them against the first one, shoving his demand at them with every ounce of mental strength he possessed.

Protect us. Protect us!

The stones sparked.

They began to shine, faintly, a pale glow from the inside out.

And nothing happened.

Archer looked up. The fire still hurtled down from the sky from a meteor, now leveling out to head directly toward them. And there was something else in the flames. It was more than a ball of fire. Somewhere in the smoke, something was moving.

"Hide," Archer said suddenly.

Wick's eyes were still fastened on the sky. "What's wrong?"

"It's not working. The stones aren't working." The leaves above their heads began to curl and blacken. "Hide!"

Archer gave Wick a shove, and the two of them scrambled under the cover of some bushes. They threw some leaves over the unfillable bag and crawled inside. By no means a comfortable choice of hiding place, but it provided more cover than the surrounding underbrush. Archer wormed his way closer to the opening of the bag so he could look out. He had a sliver of a view, enough to see the spaces between the branches and some of the trees in the distance. It wasn't much. But it would have to be enough.

The fire burned through the trees and landed in the heaps of autumn leaves in a cloud of billowing sparks.

"Why have we stopped?" a hissing rattle of a voice said. A pair of feet stepped into view. They were faintly golden and arched like a bird's. Between the scales, something glowed from within, like the way lava glowed between cracks in stone.

"There was movement," a second voice said, higher and less metallic than the first. *"I thought there was something to eat."* There was a crackling sound as it searched through the underbrush.

"What if it had been a witness?" the first voice growled, and the two sets of feet moved toward one another threateningly. *"I want no repeat of landing in that 'empty' forest, the forest that was, in truth, a city."*

"I know my own mistakes," the second, less gruff voice responded. *"I don't need reminding."*

Aside from the webbed feet, Archer couldn't see anything. He needed to know what was out there. At the risk of being spotted if the things did another sweep of the forest floor, Archer reached out to shove the flap of the bag a little higher.

Wick caught his arm. In a voice barely above a breath, he whispered, "What are you doing?"

"No one knows what they look like!" Archer whispered back, his face inches from Wick's. "This could be our only chance to see." And if they knew what the things looked like, maybe they could find a weakness.

"But—" Wick protested, but the creatures spoke

again, and Archer clapped a hand over Wick's mouth so he could hear.

"*What news?*" the first, older-sounding voice asked, and Archer's stomach hollowed out to make room for fear. There were more of them? "*Any sight of our quarry?*"

Wick and Archer both stiffened. They were being hunted.

"*No luck,*" said the other voice. "*They're so small, and so easily hidden inside any structure. Other expeditions suggested that they have divided and scattered.*"

Archer's brow furrowed. Maybe they weren't looking for Wick and him. Or if they were, who were they calling small?

"*Legend says that they will gather the stones together when they know we are coming,*" the second voice said. "*Perhaps we could strike once they've already gathered the stones together.*"

One of the sets of webbed feet shifted backward as the other set lurched forward, and the voice of the older-sounding creature hissed, "*Do you not understand that if they get the stones together, they will have the ability to keep us away again? That's why we must stay hidden. While they remain ignorant, we have the upper hand.*"

The feet of the younger-sounding creature shifted uncomfortably. "*The earlier expeditions told us they were divided and considered one another untrustworthy. Wouldn't it be easier to make them gather the stones for us?*"

"*Easier, perhaps, but they can activate them too quickly. We could jeopardize our whole plan.*"

"*But what if we can't find them before the army arrives?*"

"We must. We have no other choice." A stick crackled under the feet of the older creature. They had to be big creatures, judging from the size of the feet, Archer realized. He almost didn't catch what the older creature said next. *"Ryga, try to understand. We've been given these orders because this plan was declared the safest and best. We have to find the stones before the army arrives, and we must remain hidden while we search, so that when the time is right, we can take them by surprise and capture their stones."*

Archer's eyes bugged out, and his breath caught in his throat.

"They can't be allowed to put up their spells. If they put up their spells, it will be too late."

They weren't just trying to get into Aro, weren't out to destroy everything for destruction's sake.

No, they were after the stones.

Whatever these creatures were, they were trying to take the Heather Stones.

CHAPTER SIXTEEN:

Sudden Change

WICK TURNED TO ARCHER with a face of open shock. "Did you hear what—"

The creatures turned. *"I thought I heard something,"* the younger, less metallic voice said.

Way to go, Wick.

Wick and Archer flattened themselves inside the unfillable bag. Archer wished he could pull the flap shut, but that would draw the eyes of the creatures, whatever they were.

His heart stopped as a glowing eye skimmed past the opening of the bag, barely overlooking the open flap and the terrified eyes that watched from within.

Something crawled across the leaves, making a metallic hissing sound wherever the dry edges brushed against its skin.

"Leave it alone, Ryga," the older voice said, sounding bored. *"We want to avoid being spotted."*

The creature named Ryga made a disappointed noise, and a harsh blowing of wind made Archer realize that whatever they were, they were leaving.

This was his last chance to catch a glimpse of them.

He threw himself forward, desperate for a glance. In his haste and eagerness, he overshot the distance. He landed halfway out of the bag, into the leaves. It was too late now to slide back in. He rolled over and his eyes chased after the things that had taken off into the sky.

What met his eyes were two huge, scaly, fiery beasts, with wings like bats and bodies like winter-starved lizards. The gleam of internal fire glowed inside skin that stretched across prominent ribs. Crests of smoldering flames streamed back from their heads as they strained towards the sky. Their wings, membranous and vast, beat rhythmically as they pulsed ever upwards.

From that glimpse, Archer knew what they were.

Dragonkin.

The things that were after their lives and their means of protection were dragonkin.

As the dragonkin passed the treetops, heading for the clouds, Archer thought he saw one golden, glowing eye pointed down toward him.

But no sooner had he seen it than the dragonkin were gone.

"What were those?" Wick breathed, and Archer realized Wick had managed to stick his head out and catch a glimpse of the creatures as well.

"Dragonkin," Archer said.

Wick looked at him curiously, and Archer realized it was the first time he had known something Wick hadn't. Archer searched his brain, trying to come up with where he had drawn that name from.

"They're. . . they're in a song," he managed. "An old nursery song that the seraphs sing. I've known it forever."

Eyes of fire, skin of flame, creatures rare that overcame,

Dragonkin, lizard-like, drakon, come from airy flight.

The song also went on to describe how a dragonkin would devour all your best food and burn your left shoe if you didn't lock your doors at night, but that was probably one of those nonsense things that songs left in because children thought they were funny.

"A song?" Wick asked.

Archer explained the whole thing to him, with the hand motions and face-making that went with the song in case it provided any more context. Wick looked unimpressed with his memory of the song.

Archer realized how stupid he looked and dropped his hands. "I don't know, that's how they're described in the song. Down to the glowing eyes and everything. Those were dragonkin, I'm positive."

Wick stared at the ground for a long moment, thinking. He stared for so long that Archer finally had to say something to him in case he had somehow frozen in place. "Wick—"

Wick looked up. "We have to move faster. We need to get back to Tor, now." Then he started walking again, so suddenly that in the time it took Archer to snatch his bag out of the leaves and swing it onto his shoulder again, he had to run to catch up with Wick.

Archer jogged up next to Wick. "What are you thinking?"

Wick's face was closed up tight, serious as death. "I'm thinking we need to change our plan, again. From what we overheard we can gather two things: they're after the Heather Stones, and they're trying to take us by surprise. They plan to take the stones the moment we have them all in one place. If they do that, they'll have the power of the Heather Stones, and we won't be able to cast any spells to keep them away."

Wick went on. "And for our plan, now we know that just using a few stones won't work. Firstly we need to move quickly and get the stones before their army arrives, and then we need to get them to the valley and activate the spell without them noticing."

"Okay," Archer said. "How are we going to do any of that?"

"I don't know." A tinge of the grey came back into Wick's face, but his stalwart expression only wavered for a moment. "I've got to figure something out."

"Hey, no. *We* have to figure something out, because you can't do anything without me, remember?" Archer had meant it as a joke, trying to lighten the burden they were now both carrying, but with all that was weighing on his mind, it sounded much too serious.

Everything had gotten so much worse.

Tor looked even more awful when they returned. Or maybe Archer had never realized before how much the fire had destroyed. Only charred tatters remained of the autumn leaves in the treetops. Burn marks raked down the sides of houses or across porches. The scorch marks down the street caused a noticeable change of texture in the ground when they walked across.

All this from just two dragonkin.

No sooner had they entered the street where Archer's family lived when a centaur with a flash of red hair came galloping down the street. "Wick!" Eland shouted.

As he reached them, he saw the expressions on their faces and skidded to a stop. "What is it?"

"It's a long story," Wick said.

"Here's the short version." Archer extended a hand, fingers spread flat. "We saw what's coming for Aro, and it's worse than we thought. They're coming for us, but they're not after us. They're after the Heather Stones."

Eland's eyes darted from Archer's face to Wick's and back again. "You're serious."

Really? Archer's face went slack. "No, I lied."

The sudden change of attitude made Eland hesitate, but only for a moment. "Then what do you want to do?" He stopped himself. "Wait, don't tell me now. Ongel is due to arrive this afternoon. We'll talk about everything when he arrives. For now, both of you should get some rest. You look like you've had a long journey."

In the end, they didn't get much time before the excitement started again. They returned to the Hessen house, where Willow pointed them to some fresh-baked tarts on the counter and Ochre proceeded to act as though they had never left.

No sooner had they eaten and sat down to rest for a while before Willow poked her head in and announced that some fair folk were here to see them. It was Otho and a few of his sons. Archer eyed the one who had tried to start a fight the last time they met, but everyone seemed to be in better moods today.

"The vote went in your favor," Otho announced, and Archer's heart soared. "It took a lot more deliberation than we were expecting, but after enough discussion, the majority was in your favor. The personal insight of your letter seemed to do the job."

Archer's father made a self-satisfied noise as he passed through the hall.

"I should also say that Annalise said a few words in your favor, and so did some fellow named Fergus," Otho added.

Archer frowned. "Fergus?" The ambush in the woods hadn't exactly given him the impression that Fergus was on their side.

"It seems he noticed you helping a girl rebuild her house for days on end," Otho said. "He said your dedication was admirable. Ah, but let's not forget. . ." Otho held out a canvas sack. It looked so heavy in his hands. Archer bent and took the bag. Loosening the opening, he tipped the cool green stone out into his palm. It felt good to see the stone again.

"We agreed to give it to you," Otho said, "under the condition that you always have a fair folk representative with it. If the representative thinks you're up to no good, they'll take it away again."

Archer nodded.

"We understand," Wick said.

One of Otho's sons who hadn't tried to start a fight with Archer stepped forward and took the stone back. As he slid the stone back into the bag, Wick said, "If we're going to have representatives, they'll need a place to stay."

Archer shrugged. "Don't look at me. The house is big, but if we're going to end up with a lot of reps, there won't be enough guest rooms for everyone."

Unless, of course, Ongel's host was willing to look after some more guests. His head tilted. "Give me a minute."

He abandoned Wick and raced down the street to talk to the red-haired woman. She seemed delighted to have more guests, especially if it would be helpful to Ongel. "Ongel and I are old friends," she said. "If there's any way I can help him, I'm happy to do it."

Archer left Otho's son with her, and no sooner was

that settled than Eland appeared, having seen Archer from the window of his own host house.

"I didn't expect you to be out and about so soon," Eland admitted.

"It's not by choice," Archer said wryly. "Things happened."

"Where's Wick?" Eland asked. "Since the two of you are already back out and about, I have news that will be important to both of you."

As if summoned, Wick appeared behind Archer. "What news?"

"I didn't want to overwhelm you with more news as soon as you arrived home, so I saved it." Eland took a small, excited breath. "Ongel is arriving this afternoon with your allies from the valley."

Wick's eyes widened. "Really?"

Archer was still trying to understand. "There are more of you coming to help us?"

Eland nodded eagerly, grinning. "Yes. Like I said, you have some supporters in the valley, and some of them were even willing to come and help you directly."

Wick put a hand to his head. But he was smiling. "This will be such a great help."

"And," Eland added, "I've been trying to talk to as many of our messenger friends as I can. So far eight of them are convinced."

Wick nodded quickly, and Archer could see the wheels in Wick's head turning. "Then we could create our own, smaller force of messengers, and get the letters to the leaders much faster."

"A little faster, at least," Eland said. "And this way, our messages are less likely to be confiscated. Fewer changing of hands means a safer delivery."

Archer realized how useless he was in this conversation. He didn't know what would be helpful to them or how to strategize with any of it. For the moment Wick seemed to be recovering, but Archer had no way of knowing if it would last.

"We have news as well," Wick said. "Good and bad. But the bad will have to wait until Ongel gets here."

Eland's happy expression wavered for only a moment. "Well, then what's the good news?"

"While we were in human territory, we met some friends who know the elected officials in human territory, and one of them also knew Queen Frey of the nixies. They're traveling right now to meet with the leaders and vouch for our cause. If all goes well, it may convince them to join our side."

"That's great!" Eland paused. "In that case, how many stones do we have now?"

"Three."

"Then we can try putting up the barrier spell with only a few stones, can't we?" Eland asked.

"That's part of the bad news," Archer said, relieved that he could finally contribute. "Like Wick said, it'll probably have to wait until we can tell everyone at once."

"I see," Eland said. "Well, I'll wait. But you seem to be making strides."

"Some strides," Wick agreed. "Let's hope they're big enough."

That was when a messenger arrived, a thin seraph boy with golden hair and a hawkish nose. To Archer's surprise, the envelope was addressed to him. "It must be an answer to one of the letters I sent while you were gone," he told Wick. "Took them long enough."

"This is Dell," Eland said to Wick as Archer cracked

the envelope's seal. "He's one of the more recent messengers to join our little messenger force."

"It's good to have you with us," Wick told Dell.

Archer was only half listening. He slid the paper out of the envelope and scanned it quickly. It looked like most political letters: name of recipient, polite greeting, a bit here and there about what was happening in their part of Aro. Finally, in the third paragraph, the letter got to the point.

"The nixies want to meet us at the edge of their territory in three days!" He glanced back at Wick. "Do you think we can get there in three days?"

"It can probably be done," Wick said. "But should we both go? Once the centaurs are here, we'll have a lot of things to manage. Maybe one of us should stay here to oversee everything."

Archer knew what he was trying to suggest, and he didn't like how he looked on either end of that. He didn't want to travel to nixie territory and negotiate the heather stone away from people who might still not like him, and he didn't want to stay in Tor with his parents and now several huge centaurs, being fancy and in charge.

"If you want to go to the meeting with the nixies, I can stay here and look after things in Tor," Eland said. "Or Ongel could when he arrives."

Wick hesitated. "Yes, that could be done."

"So long as we don't get any more offers for meetings before then," Archer muttered to himself. The last thing they needed was another direction to stretch.

"Wick!" a booming voice shouted.

The three of them spun around. Coming down the street was a tall, smiling centaur with skin the color of chocolate and a head full of long braids. Behind him were four other centaurs.

"Ongel!" Eland called, waving.

"Eland! I'm glad to see you made it," Ongel said as he approached. The four centaurs behind him made their greetings as well. "Friends, this is Wick, and his friend is Archer. Wick, you know Hirim and Cohn, Fariss believes you've met before, and Oman has heard a lot about you through me and Eland."

Wick might have met these centaurs before, but Archer hadn't. Because he knew it was what Wick would do, he tried to memorize names and faces on the spot. Oman was a strong, blond centaur wearing sky blue and carrying a bag full of books and papers. Cohn was a brunette female, dressed in berry red, and had skin that would have been the same copper tone as Wick's if Wick's skin had looked normal. Fariss had a stern face but kind eyes, and his brown hair was shaved close to his head.

Hirim was obviously related to Eland. They had the same square jaw and the same wispy red hair. They even held themselves with the same tall posture, though Hirim was still much taller than Eland and Eland's face lacked Hirim's many lines and creases.

"Father," Eland said, embracing Hirim and confirming Archer's suspicions. "I was so worried you wouldn't be with us."

"You did half the convincing," Hirim said with what sounded like a laugh. "If it weren't for you, I wouldn't be here."

Archer clamped down on the jealousy before it started. He had more important things to think about than Eland's relationship with his father.

"Wick," Ongel said, embracing his mentee. Then he turned to Archer.

Archer didn't know if he liked being hugged, but he got a hug regardless.

"How has it gone without me?" Ongel asked earnestly. "Easily, I hope."

"It looks like we're starting a collection of representatives," Archer said. "The ones we have so far are staying in your friend's house. Apparently it's our base of operations lately."

"Good, good," Ongel said. "Many hands make light work. The more the better."

"But there's bad news, too," Archer added. "We were waiting for that part until you got here."

Ongel nodded. "Let's get to our base of operations, as you're calling it, and we'll set up a meeting."

Don't even get me started on meetings, Archer thought, but he agreed and followed everyone back to the house of the red-haired seraph woman.

Once they had all situated themselves across chairs and lounges and whatnot in the sitting room, leaving Wick and Archer standing against the fireplace when they ran out of chairs, they all compared updates.

"So far we have these four centaurs with us," Ongel said, "and three more thinking it over."

"We have several people going out to the elects in human territory to vouch for us," Wick said. "And one going to Queen Frey of the nixies."

"Some of the messengers are on our side," Eland said, "although I doubt they would tell anyone since our plans to collect the Heather Stones are a divisive topic at the moment."

"Tell me about it," Wick murmured.

"Even now, I haven't seen a single warning in any visions," Hirim said, resting the side of his pointer finger against his lips. "Why is that? Is it something the Scorch is using to shield itself?"

"I don't know," Wick said. "It's been like this from the beginning, and there's still no way of knowing."

"Let's forget it for now and focus on something we understand," Archer said, "Sure, it would be helpful to see things coming, but most of us survive without visions. No offense," he added.

"What was the bad news you had?" Eland asked. "You wanted to tell everyone all at once."

For some reason, Wick looked at Archer, prompting him to explain.

"It's. . ." Archer stopped and started over. "You saw what happened to the street out there. Something fiery fell out of the sky and burned up a lot of things. Well, on our way back from human territory, we saw the same thing coming down from the sky. I didn't want to burn to death, so tried to put up a barrier spell with just the stones we had. It didn't work. It didn't do anything. The theory failed."

A general sigh of disappointment came from around the room.

"But it wasn't a total loss, if that helps," Archer said. "While we were hiding from the things, we could hear them talking, and I got a glimpse of them. They're dragonkin. I don't know if anybody here knows what the dragonkin are, but I know them from a nursery song. They're creatures of fire and destruction and apparently they're the ones that are bent on destroying Aro."

Cohn, who had been looking at the floor as she listened, looked up at last. "Do you think these things are connected with the Scorch?"

Her voice was deeper than Archer had expected.

"It's more than that, I think," Wick said. "I think they *are* the Scorch. From what we overheard, it seems to me that what we call the Scorch are actually what Archer knows as dragonkin."

"There are a few legends in the valley like that," Eland said. "About creatures with claws and fiery breath. They're stories for children though, or at least that's what I always thought."

Everyone was silent a moment.

"They were talking," Hirim said. "What did they talk about?"

"That's the other part of the bad news," Archer said. He shifted against the mantelpiece behind him. "They didn't spell it out, but they were looking for something. It sounded like they had gone ahead to scout for the others before they arrive. According to what they said, they're not just after the country." He paused. "They're trying to take the Heather Stones."

Everyone blinked. Some of the centaurs' legs tapped restlessly.

"Did they say what they plan to do with them?" Hirim asked.

"No," Archer said. "Maybe they want the power, or maybe they want them as some kind of trophy. Maybe they like them because they're shiny. I don't know."

"But considering that some of the creatures are already here, that might mean that the Scorch is closer than we ever guessed," Wick added, speaking up for the first time in several minutes. "We'll have to move fast from here. It'll take all of us and then some to get everyone on our side. And then there are still the Heather Stones to gather before time runs out."

"I see," Ongel said, rubbing a hand over his chin.

"And as much as it might be a risk to recruit others to help, we may have to," Wick said. "If we're going to beat the clock."

Ongel tilted his head. "Why would it be a risk?"

"Because by now anyone could be a traitor. Anyone could try to trick us because they think that Archer and I are thieves and criminals," Wick said. The way he said *thieves and criminals* sounded like he was echoing someone else.

"I think we can trust our countrymen," Ongel said. "Everything will be fine."

Archer thought of all the times their countrymen had tried to kill them, maim them, insult them, or throw them in jail. That somehow didn't strike him as trustworthy. Still, he said nothing.

"It comes down to one question," Wick said. "What are we going to do?"

"Our forces will be spread thin," Eland said. "We have a lot of things to do, but not a lot of people to do them with. Like I said, you and Wick could go to the nixies together. Ongel or I can take over here. Everything else we need to do can be done either by letters or face-to-face negotiations."

"Some of the people might be more willing to lend us their stones if they could also send a representative with it," Fariss mused, his hands folded under his chin.

"It might ease their minds to have one of their own people protect their stones," Wick admitted. "And we do already have one representative. It's too late now to tell the other races that they can't have one."

The way Archer saw it, they could tell anyone anything they liked.

"I'll see what I can do to arrange a meeting with the

manghar," Oman said. "Considering the. . . history here, it might be best if the Crowned Head remembered the both of you in fond nostalgia rather than face-to-face. And since he has a personal vendetta for Archer, I wouldn't let them meet until we're certain that he doesn't still want Archer's head."

All things considered, the Crowned Head probably would have taken eight of Archer's head if it was possible. But Archer didn't want to stare death in the face again anytime soon, so he agreed alongside Wick.

"Then we'll go to the nixies and talk to Queen Frey personally," Wick said. "And Oman will go to the manghar while Ongel and Eland handle things here."

It was settled. They planned routes and agreed that everyone would aim to be back in Tor in ten days. That gave those of them with farther destinations less time to negotiate, but with limited time and more limited communication once they left Tor, ten days it would have to be.

As they wrapped up their plans, a knock came at the door of the room, and the host put her head in. Her eyes sought out Wick and Archer. "There's a messenger here for you."

Wick shot a look at Archer. Archer pushed off the mantle and skirted the edge of the room to the door. Outside, a young satyr waited with a creamy envelope.

"Archer?" the satyr asked.

"Yeah, that's me." Archer held out his hand for the message. The satyrs seemed to believe in only the highest quality paper. Even his father didn't use paper as thick and heavy as this. He slit the envelope open with a knife that the host handed to him and scanned the paper. It was from some satyr he didn't know named Barban, speaking on the behalf of the satyr people. Archer's eyes skimmed down the paper.

Name of recipient, polite greeting, half a sentence of small talk (couldn't even bother to act like they wanted to talk, could they), then the satyrs finally got to the point.

Archer's eyes snapped up to the satyr's face. "They want *us*, in person. Seriously?"

The satyr nodded. "In three days' time. They were very specific."

"Yeah, I know they were, because—" Archer flapped the letter instead of completing his sentence. "What I mean is, why? What difference does it make whether we keep talking through letters or whether we go in person?"

"Archer," Wick said quietly but disapprovingly as he stepped through the doorway behind Archer. He took the letter and skimmed it. "We'll be there," Wick said to the messenger. "Thank you."

"Wick," Archer said, exasperated. "You just said we'd be there, at the same time as we're supposed to be meeting with Queen Frey. We can't do both."

"We didn't tell Queen Frey we would go to her ourselves," Wick said. "We can send Ongel or someone instead. We just have to change our plans a little."

He started back toward the room, but Archer blocked his path. "Why are we going to them, specifically? Why can't we tell them we can't make it and we'll meet them two days later than they asked? Why do we have to meet them face-to-face at all when it apparently doesn't matter if Queen Frey sees us face-to-face?"

Wick sighed. "It's a matter of context. It's important to understand what each territory wants from you before going into anything. The nixies are a race that respects power and tenacity. By sending someone in our place, we assert our equality with them and acting like a nation of our own, which I suspect Queen Frey will appreciate."

Then he took a breath. "The satyrs were used as slaves by other races for decades, so they're a society that's built on equality and respect. If we were to tell them that we won't come to meet them as they asked, it will be an insult to them, and we may destroy our only chance to negotiate for their stone. If we don't show them the respect they want from us, we'll ruin our chances. So we'll meet them personally, and someone else can go to the nixies. It's the best course of action."

Archer nodded once. "And this is why you're the better planner than me."

Wick slid the paper back into the envelope.

"Because you're pretentious and think you know everything."

"I try," Wick said dryly.

"That's why you get along with all the leaders, too. You get on their level of pretentiousness, and then once you're thinking the same way they do, it's like you're reading their minds. . ."

Wick made a faint agreeing noise and walked back into the sitting room, seeming to hope that if he ignored Archer long enough he would quiet down.

"You're a pure legend of pretentiousness," Archer continued, trailing after him. "A pillar in the house where pretentiousness is kept. In the hall of fame with all the big wigs, sorry, the big egos, if you will. A timeless legacy of self-importance and—"

Wick shoved the envelope in Archer's face, forcing him to stop talking. "We've had a change of plans," he announced to the room. "The satyrs want to meet with Archer and me face-to-face, three days from now.

Someone else will have to meet Queen Frey for us. The rest of the plan can stay the same, but we have to work out who will go to the nixies now."

"Ongel could go," Eland said. "He's a good negotiator."

"I'd rather have him here," Wick said uncomfortably. "To run things while I'm gone."

"I would send Fariss," Cohn said, adjusting her four legs on the lounge. Archer's eyes flickered over to the imposing dark-haired centaur on her right. "He has the strength and confidence the nixies would be looking for."

Wick gave Archer a look of 'I told you so'. "Then Fariss it is. Fariss, do you think you can get to the nixie kingdom, do the proper negotiations, and get back to Tor in the ten days we're hoping for?"

"I'd have to run," Fariss said. "But it can be done. I'll send word if I think the negotiations will take longer."

Wick nodded. "Just what I was thinking. We'll do the same." He looked around at the room overflowing with allies. "Now let's just pray we can do this in time."

CHAPTER SEVENTEEN:
Hello Again, Mother, Are You Disappointed?

ARCHER WOKE UP after another night of deathly deep sleep and remembered they had to leave again.

"Great, more traveling," he muttered.

Head still bleary, he traveled down the stairs to wake Wick. Wick, predictably, was in a sleep like death, and it took a solid kick to the bed frame to even get him to stir. Wick had seemed to be improving lately, but by the slow, slow way he rubbed his face, staring at the sheets, the improvement had only been temporary.

Rather than wait for breakfast, they took some food from the kitchen to eat while they walked. Once Archer had tucked some extra supplies from the kitchen into the unfillable bag, they started for the door.

It struck Archer that maybe they should bring the letter from the satyrs, in case they needed to reference it. He mentioned it to Wick. "I'll go get it," Archer said and turned around to run back up the stairs. "I'll meet you outside."

He raced back up and found the letter exactly where he had thought it would be, on the dresser across from his bed. Stuffing it into the unfillable bag, he ran back down the stairs and grabbed the handle of the door.

"You aren't going to say goodbye?"

Any cobwebs of sleep still clinging to Archer's brain flew away as he spun around, nearly slipping on the thick rug in the entryway. "Mother." It came out more as a gasp than anything. "You scared me! I could have fallen down the stairs."

His mother looked unmoved by his theatrics. "I wanted to see you off." She tilted her head. "I miss you when you're gone."

Archer struggled, but like he always did when faced with things like this, he couldn't conjure a thing to say.

"You don't miss us," she said. It wasn't a question. Just a simple observation. "We do love you, you know. I love you very much. And your father does, too."

Archer snorted before he could stop it.

"He does," his mother said firmly. "And so does your brother. But they don't know how to show it any better than you do." Her tone turned pleading. "Can't we forgive one another and be a family again?"

A family? When had they ever been a family? Archer couldn't even remember a time when they had acted like family. They had always been broken. "I don't think we know how to, Mother."

"And that means we can't try?" Willow stepped forward and took Archer's hand. "Listen, my son. I don't want all of us to look back on a time when we could have forgiven one another and didn't. Will you look at me?"

Archer lifted his eyes to his mother's face and was

surprised. Her eyes, creased with time and with care, didn't have the same lukewarm gaze from his childhood, topped with a smile like a painting, only real from a distance. The eyes looking at him now were full of tenderness. Not overflowing, but full.

"I'm truly sorry for everything that has happened to you in life, and I want you to know that if I was ever the cause of your unhappiness, I apologize. I see I've failed you in more ways than one, but I never wanted to make you unhappy; I only want to see you thrive. I could never be anything less than proud of what you've become."

Proud? Archer looked at her miserably. "What's there to be proud of, Mother? I'm nothing like what you wanted me to be. I'm just this."

"No," his mother insisted, wrapping both her hands around his own. The familiarity of the gesture felt strange. "You are individual and unique. You have become a wonderful, strong young man, and when you see something that's wrong, you act. Maybe your choices aren't ones your father or I would have made for you, but I love you as much now as I ever did. I'm proud of what you've made for yourself. I watch you improve every day. What is there not to be proud of?"

From beyond the door, Archer could hear Wick shouting his name. "I have to go, Mother. We have to be in satyr territory in a few days."

Willow released Archer's hands and smiled weakly. "Then I wish you luck."

"Thank you." Archer hesitated, then quickly pecked his mother on the cheek and raced out the door.

"Took you a while," Wick remarked as Archer reached the bottom of the stairs.

"Sorry." Archer jammed the letter further into the bag

with severity. "I'm just slow, I guess."

And so the expedition to satyr territory began. They ran into several of their friends on their way out of the city, and each time they wished one another luck before they parted.

Archer tried not to notice, but the grass under their feet crunched as they walked, like dry charcoal stalks, and the sky was darker than ever.

He did his best to ignore it.

Two days later, as they neared the border of satyr territory, tired of hours of silence and even more tired of chewing over the conversation with his mother, Archer said, "Let's talk about something. It's too quiet and I'm sick of it."

Wick barely looked up from the path. "Like what?"

"I don't know. Whatever you're thinking about. It's got to be better than what I'm thinking about."

"I doubt it."

"I don't."

"I'm thinking about what you said back in the village," Wick said. "How I have to be the responsible one. I don't feel like I'm improving at all."

The abruptness of the statement took Archer by surprise. Wick was always slow to open up. Usually his thoughts needed to be dragged out of him, but this had come out of the blue.

"You're doing fine. You just need time," Archer said, floundering for the right words. "I wouldn't worry about it if I were you."

"But we don't have time, do we? All we have is a crisis on our hands, and I'm barely helping. It seems like no matter what I do, everything keeps going wrong. *I* keep going wrong, and there's nothing I can do to stop it."

Wick's grey skin paled further as he spoke. "I know everyone needs my help, but I can't even make myself think straight."

Archer, at a loss for words, listened with his heart beating frantically.

"I'm such a disappointment and everyone knows it. But whenever anyone comments on my mistakes or how I've changed, I want to lash out. I want to break them to make them shut up. Archer, I'm out of control." Wick slowly stopped walking. "Is this how you feel all the time?"

He looked over at Archer, and Archer was startled to see moisture glimmering in Wick's eyes. Sure, Wick had been upset before, plenty of times, because that was his way. He got worked up over even small things, and once Archer had found it annoying. But Wick had never cried in front of Archer.

His father had been wrong to say that Wick didn't feel things deeply. Wick felt deeper and cared more than even Archer did. That was why he worked so hard and did his best for everyone—he cared so much about doing the right thing. And now he was paying for it.

"No, you're wrong," Archer said.

Wick sighed, frustrated. "Never mind then."

"Let me finish," Archer went on frantically. "Stop interrupting me and let me finish. I know what you're saying, but that isn't why I'm like this. I act like this because I don't think anyone has the right to criticize me. They don't know me, and they aren't any better than me. And I lash out because I'm childish and angry. Any of my family could tell you that." Not that he cared about their opinion, either. "You though, you actually *are* better than me, a lot better. And you've worked so hard to be that way, so you're angry and you're scared now that everybody's trying to take what you earned away from you. I'm angry that they're doing that, too. I want to destroy all of them. They deserve it."

Wick rolled his eyes, then swiped at them when another tear fell.

"You're not losing control, Wick. You already lost it. And you're used to having control over everything, so now you're relearning what to do without it. I'll admit, I'm not having a good time covering for you. It's not where I'm comfortable. But like I told you before, I'll watch out for you as long as it takes until you recover. I've got your back because you're my friend." *My best friend.*

"But what if I can't put myself back together again?" Wick asked softly, after a long pause.

Now having run out of the right words to say, Archer managed, "You can do just about anything else, so I think you'll do fine."

"And if it takes forever? You can't handle my job forever."

"Nope, but if that's what it comes to, I'll figure it out. I'll get help from Ongel or Fowl or something. Maybe even some of your friends from the valley. I want to see how you turn out. I'm willing to wait."

Wick ran a hand down his face once more, blinking hard. Taking a deep and shaky breath, he said, "Thank you."

"It's fine."

"No, I mean it. I'm not sure that anyone has ever cared if I couldn't handle something before."

Archer hesitated, not wanting to sound vulnerable. But this was about Wick, not him. He spoke quickly. "And I've never once had anyone in my life who cared about just me and not what I could get for them. But you do, somehow, so thanks to you, too."

With all that said, they gathered their wits again and entered satyr territory.

Satyrs met them almost as soon as they crossed the border, pointing them to the hall of valuables further into the territory. The other satyrs would meet them there to decide whether the satyrs would collaborate or demand justice.

"You're going to be the difficult part of this negotiation," Wick said as they walked. "If you could think before you talk, it would help."

They broke out of the trees, and the hall of valuables appeared before them. Archer realized now that he had only ever been to the hall of valuables under the cover of night. It looked very different in the light.

In the dark, it had always looked like a long shape in the darkness, cut in places by slices of light from the windows. The windows had been the only thing that gave it any definition. But in the light, Archer almost liked the design. A series of shapely wooden pillars and beams supported the walls and roof, obviously old but still clean and crisp. The walls were painted a fastidious white and scrubbed glistening clean. Carvings of moons and stars decorated the peak of every windowframe, and the glass of the windows had been left open today to let the crisp autumn air into the hall.

A reddish satyr Archer didn't recognize met them at the entrance to the hall. On either side of the doors, satyrs in chest plates watched, their hands gripping stout fighting staffs. The staffs were a new addition, if Archer recalled correctly. There had been plenty of guards before, for all the good they did, but they had never been armed.

It was good to see he was adding something to the world, even if it was only armed guards.

"Welcome," the satyr said to Wick in that slightly tense tone that said they weren't really welcome. "You will understand if we request you make no sudden movements. Our people don't trust you or your companion, and many are concerned that we will be robbed again while you're here."

Archer didn't understand why, since the satyrs had been the ones to invite them here, but he said nothing.

"We understand," Wick said, but a faint grey tinge appeared in his face.

Archer realized the satyr was staring at him. "No sudden moves, no stealing. Got it."

"May I take your bags?" the satyr asked, in a tone that made it sound more like an order.

Wick slid his traveling bag off his shoulder and handed it to the satyr, who took it and slung it over his own shoulder. Archer handed over his bag as well.

"Please be careful with it," Archer said. "My horse is in there."

The satyr looked appropriately confused, but he led them through large wooden doors into the hall of valuables and handed them off to a different satyr with white fur.

"Ambrack," Wick said. "It's good to see you again."

The white satyr nodded his goat head with a face of indifference. "My people are gathered through here."

He led them through the antechamber and into the hall itself. The inside of the hall, too, gave a different impression in full daylight. Each row of identical stands glistened with fresh lacquer, and they glowed in the light pouring through the windows.

Throughout the hall, scattered among the stands and

gathered in droves at the far end, were the satyrs. It seemed that most of the satyr territory had come to say something. They crammed themselves between the stands and across the walls and sat in the windows, watching. It reminded Archer too distinctly of how the manghar had eyed them on their visit to the Crowned Head, although where that had been a crowd of shadowy colors, the satyrs looked almost like a collection of autumn leaves in their different shades of browns, reds, and greys.

Between them and the crowd of satyrs, the Satyr's Crown glistened on its podium with the heather stone now restored to its setting in the middle. Archer tilted his head, and the sheen of a new spell glistened around the stand. A part of him wondered what kind of security they had installed this time and how easy it would be to break.

But Wick was talking.

"Thank you for agreeing to meet with us. We appreciate your invitation to come here."

"And we thank you for your compliance in leaving your trick bags at the doors," Ambrack responded.

Like it had been waiting for the right moment, a dark cloud rolled over the hall, and rain started to pour on the roof.

One of the other satyrs, one with black fur and a large white patch across his chest and snout, opened a piece of paper. Archer recognized it as one of his letters. "In your letter, you stated. . ." The satyr scanned the letter, looking for a specific line of text, "you wish to heal all rifts from past events and to come to an alliance."

Archer squinted. He didn't remember saying it quite like that, and he knew he hadn't used the word *alliance*, but since he didn't have a copy of the letter himself, he couldn't argue with it.

"We did," Wick said, even though he certainly didn't know what Archer had written either.

"How do you aim to do that?" the satyr asked. "We would want to play a real role among your allies. How are the other races involved in your plan, and how will our part contribute?"

It was just like Wick said. The satyrs were anxious to be equal to the other races.

Wick didn't miss a beat. "Currently, we're involved with the humans, the seraphs, the fair folk, and the centaurs, and the nixies are negotiating with our friends as we speak. Several of the other races have sent a representative with their stone as a safety measure. You're welcome to send a representative to accompany the stone back to seraph territory if you choose."

"But first we have to agree to join you," said the voice of an older satyr toward the back. "I'm not convinced. What steps will you take to make up for what you've done?"

"Whatever you would have us agree to, once the threat is gone and the Scorch is driven away." Wick's voice was steady. He was doing well. "We want to make up for our crimes however we can, and once the Scorch is taken care of, we'll do whatever it takes."

"Would you go back to jail?"

CHAPTER EIGHTEEN:

I'll Answer Your Questions, But I Won't Like it

BESIDE ARCHER, Wick stopped breathing. Archer's shoulders tensed for what came next.

"The things you've done deserve more time in jail than a few days. After all of this, even if you turn out to be right," the satyr said, "would you go back?"

"Yes," Wick said. He spoke so softly that the rain on the roof almost drowned out his words. "We would."

"Now hang on a second." Archer spoke before he thought about what he was doing. Everyone's eyes were on him in an instant. Wick turned to him with an expression of masked horror.

It was too late to stop talking now. "I don't think you can put us in jail on behalf of Aro, not realistically. Everyone wants us in jail. There's probably a waitlist by now. But that's not my point," he added, realizing he was going wildly off-topic. "If you want to hold someone responsible, that's me. But you can't say anything to Wick because he didn't do anything to you."

Out of the corner of his eye, he saw the muscles in Wick's shoulders coil even tighter. He didn't doubt that the tree desperately wanted him to shut up. But it was too late for that, and Archer had to finish.

"The only person who did anything to you was me. I stole from you a bunch of times. But Wick hadn't even met me yet when I took your crown. He had nothing to do with my plans back then, so he's not accountable to you for anything. All of that's on me."

The satyrs didn't look pleased, but they didn't look very condemning either. They didn't look like anything. Archer adjusted his wings uncomfortably.

"And I get it if you don't want to help because I'm involved. I know I haven't proved that I'm worth trusting. But don't think of Wick any differently because of me. That's all I'm asking for."

The black satyr with the patch of white cleared his throat. "I wasn't expecting so much. . . insight."

"And I must say," Ambrack added, "it's good to know you would understand if we wanted nothing to do with you." A few of the satyrs nodded.

Archer's deep-seated hatred of being criticized wanted to fight back, but considering the circumstances, he kept his mouth shut.

"Their crimes were still against all of Aro," a voice said from the back of the crowd.

A few people nearer the front nodded.

"Not to mention how our trust was betrayed," a white satyr in particular pointed out.

Archer's mouth quirked. They wanted to throw blame around anyway. What had he gone and opened his mouth for?

"And we have another problem," another satyr said from off to their right. A pale grey satyr speckled with white produced a piece of paper and settled some spectacles on his snout to read it. "We received several messages like this from the centaurs a few days ago."

Beside Archer, Wick's face tinged grey again. The rain poured down with renewed vigor. Archer had the feeling in the pit of his stomach that whatever had made the centaurs send that many letters couldn't be good.

The grey speckled satyr read aloud. "While it has come to our attention that the thieves are using the death of the plants and trees to claim that the Scorch is once again a threat, that is not the case. We in the valley have taken samples of the trees and plants and done extensive research to find the cause of the problem." He glanced further down the page. "We have now discovered that the source of the dying plants is a blight. Granted, this blight spreads quickly, but we know of a cure and soon we will send instructions to all the territories so the disease can be treated."

Someone in the valley was trying to convince everyone that the dying plants meant nothing. Archer glanced at Wick. He had that careful blank look again.

"Out of curiosity," Wick said quietly, "who signed that letter? Who does it say sent it?"

The grey speckled satyr glanced at the bottom of the page. "Tinor of the centaurs."

Wick nodded. "I see."

Archer's blood boiled. Tinor again. The next time he saw Tinor, Archer decided, he would get what he deserved.

"What have you got to say about this letter?" the grey

satyr asked. "Can you explain it?"

"They misunderstood," Wick managed, still in a flat voice. "The plants are dying and the trees are going grey because the Scorch is getting closer. Even if the centaurs send treatment, it won't work or it won't last. The plants are burning up. Nothing will stop them from dying if the Scorch is coming."

"There isn't a blight," Archer repeated, more to the point because Wick seemed to be dodging it. "They're trying to explain it away because they don't agree with us, but there isn't a blight."

"Interesting." The grey satyr looked around at the crowd of his people, and when no one else spoke, he said, "If there are no other questions, we can convene."

"I have another question," said a younger satyr from the back. Archer watched Wick as he looked in that direction with an air of hope but also fear.

"I wanted to know, Wick, if you really understand you've let everyone down."

Something changed in Wick's posture, something so small that Archer couldn't pick it out.

Archer watched carefully to see what Wick would do.

"Yes," Wick said to the silent room. His voice bounced off the walls, sounding suddenly small and cracked, like a bowl that had been dropped. "I understand that very well. But I've always done what I thought was right. And I can't apologize for trying to keep everyone safe."

Archer noticed that the younger satyr wasn't meeting Wick's eyes, like he couldn't do it. Did they know each other?

The black and white satyr cleared his throat. "If that was the last of the questions, we'll convene."

This time, no one spoke up. Wick nodded, a little too hard, and he beckoned for Archer to take several steps back with him, into the middle of the hall, while the satyrs massed into a more concentrated crowd to talk. Even from the distance, they got brief snatches of conversation whenever anyone spoke louder than a whisper. Archer tried to catch what they were saying.

". . . not again. . ."

"Long trusted. . ."

"—have changed. . ."

The rain pounded on the roof as the satyrs talked. Puddles formed around the windows from the spray that made it in.

"They're taking a long time," Archer said. He tried to lean on one of the stands but stopped when it wobbled under his weight.

"They'll take as much time as they need." Wick rubbed at an itching eye. "The last thing we want to do is rush them."

Someone's voice rose a bit in the crowd of satyrs, and both Wick and Archer turned to look. But as quickly as it had risen, the voice fell silent again.

"Don't more satyrs live in their territory than this?" Archer gestured to the crowd. "There's no way this is all of them."

"This isn't all of them," Wick replied. "Some of them live too far north to come, and some of them won't care at all about what's happening. The ones you see are the ones who wanted to come."

"Huh. The satyrs are so high-strung, I would have thought all of them would have something to say." The wheels in Archer's head started whirring. "But if there are fewer people, isn't that good for us? It might change their vote."

"No." Wick shook his head. "The satyrs who didn't come are the ones who don't have strong feelings about us or would vote neutral. With a smaller crowd, we end up with a higher concentration of informed and passionate votes. That's all."

The tension in his voice made Archer frown. Wick was staring at the ground with his arms crossed, his brow furrowed. What had him so tense? Was it what that young satyr had said? It had to be.

Archer frowned. Maybe that kid needed a good beating.

As if hearing his thoughts, Wick turned Archer's way and said, "Don't do anything stupid."

Archer sighed. He missed being able to do something stupid.

"Archer," Wick said suddenly, in a quiet voice, "what if this doesn't work?"

Archer glanced over. Wick was slowly rubbing his forehead with one hand, staring at the floor.

"It was complicated enough to get a few stones, but now we need all of them. I don't regret what we did before, but it made sure that a lot of people stopped trusting us. If even one of the territories refuses to lend us their stone, we have no backup plan. What will we do then?" Wick crossed his arms tighter against his chest. When he spoke again, his voice was quiet and rushed. "I've already been rejected by my people, Archer. I don't have the job that I committed my entire life to. I'm losing everything for this. If I can't keep my country from burning, I'll die with nothing but failure to my name. I don't want that."

"No," Archer said, more abruptly than he meant to,

making Wick jump.

"You'll be more than a failure even if everything goes wrong," Archer went on. "I'm not good with words like you are, but no matter what, you'll be fine. We'll get all the stones, and even if anyone says no, that's what we have you for." Wick flinched. Archer backtracked quickly. "And Ongel. And Eland. All of your friends want to help you, and that's what they're going to do. Don't worry so much. We'll get this right."

Wick's brow furrowed a bit. "You're not worried?"

"Worried? No. Maybe. A little. This is the only thing I've ever done for somebody other than myself, and it's the only big thing I've ever committed to, so if it goes wrong, yeah, I'll feel like nothing I did was ever worth it. I'll die with a success rate of zero. So yeah, I'm worried about that a little bit. But the advantage is, if we don't get this right, we die, so I won't have to live with it for long." Probably not what Wick wanted to hear, and probably not helpful, but it was too late to rethink.

Wick smiled wryly. "That's true. At least I won't have to live with it if we fail." He looked up at the dark ceiling. "Still, I'd rather we didn't have to—"

One of the satyrs waved them back over, interrupting Wick's thought.

"We've convened," the grey satyr said as Wick and Archer approached, "and though some still voice some discomfort, more than half of us agree that you may borrow our piece of the Heather Stone once we have safely removed it from the Satyr's Crown."

Archer's heart leaped inside of him. Who could have known that talking the satyrs over to their side would be this easy?

"But there are two conditions of this agreement," the

satyr went on.

Archer's excitement dulled.

"Firstly, since we're still uncomfortable letting you walk away with our most valuable possession, we will be sending two representatives with you on your journey. If they think for any reason that you can't be trusted, they will take the piece away from you and return to our territory. But if you can convince them that you're truly doing the right thing, you will be allowed to keep the stone until it's no longer needed."

"Thank you," Wick said, with obvious relief.

That was all well and good, but two more people would slow down their travel. Not to mention they would just get in the way back in Tor. Archer frowned, but Wick sent him a warning glance.

"It's a reasonable request," Wick said. "We would be happy to have your representatives accompany us. What is the other condition?"

"The other condition regards when you're through with the stone," the grey satyr said. "If you can successfully cast the spell like you say you will, we will take the piece back, and then we want to speak with the centaurs about putting both of you back in jail."

Archer's blood boiled. After all that? Even if they saved everyone from the Scorch, the satyrs would still put them back in jail? That would never happen. Not on Archer's watch.

He stared the grey satyr in the eyes and lied. "All right. We'll go back to jail when it's all over."

They had time. He could work out a way to get out of it by then.

The satyrs all looked somewhat surprised, which gave Archer a little prickle of pride. They hadn't expected him to agree so easily. To Archer's right, Wick's eyebrows rose.

"How soon can we leave?" Archer asked, cool and calm. "We're kind of in a rush."

The black and white satyr seemed taken off guard, but he answered, "We can choose the representatives now, and once they retrieve whatever they need from their homes, you can leave immediately."

Immediately sounded good enough. "Then go ahead and pick whoever you want," Archer said. "We'll be outside." With that, he breezed toward the exit with Wick in tow.

"We need to discuss how you handle delicate situations," Wick said under his breath.

"I think I handle them fine, thank you very much," Archer said proudly, stuffing his hands in his pockets. "After all, I've gotten us this far. When do you think they'll give me my bag back?"

"You can get it back on your way out," Wick said, looking over his shoulder. "I'll be out in a moment." He split off and walked back toward the crowd, headed for the younger satyr who had taken him off guard.

The satyr looked a little worried as Wick approached, but as they talked, he looked less scared and more conflicted. Archer stuck around for a moment to see if Wick was going to give the kid the beating he deserved, but it seemed that Wick was trying to explain something to him.

That was Wick for you. Trying to get everyone to like him. That was how he had got in this mess in the first place. He needed to be less worried about what other people thought of him.

Archer strolled back out of the chamber, casting a

longing look at many of the shiny baubles they had on display, and took his bag back from the satyr at the door with a little smile. "I'll take that, thank you."

He wasn't outside long before Wick joined him.

As they waited under the edge of the roof, staying near the wall to stay dry, Wick said, "I never would have expected you of all people to agree to that. You're really all right with going back to jail when this is over?"

Archer shot Wick a hard look. "Of course I'm not. No way am I going back to jail after this. It just made them agree to help us, so I said yes."

Wick didn't look happy with that answer.

While they waited for their satyr representatives to arrive, they received a simple message from Farris: they had a sixth stone.

"Good," Archer said to Wick. "Now, once we get your people on board, all we have left is the manghar. You know, the people who want me dead."

"You should have thought of that before you committed crimes in their territory that were worthy of the death sentence," Wick said.

Archer huffed. "What did they expect with such unreasonable laws?"

"Unreasonable?" Wick asked in a 'really?' voice. "You went back into their territory after you had been banned, you made personal enemies of several of their people, you disrespected their rules and their leader as you were about to steal one of their most revered possessions, and then you were sentenced to death and didn't stay for the death penalty. Oh, and you also tried to kill one of their people with your bare hands, in case you had forgotten."

"It wasn't with my bare hands," Archer said patiently. "It was a knife. His knife. And I didn't forget, I just don't count it as a crime because they were trying to kill you. It was more or less self-defense."

"That's not what self-defense is. You weren't defending yourself."

"Self-defense is what I say it is."

Wick's brow furrowed for a moment. "How did you get yourself banned from their territory in the first place?"

"A story for another time," Archer replied breezily. "But it was one of my best thefts. I didn't know it was physically possible to swallow an entire—"

"Shh," Wick said quickly. "Here come our representatives."

Just as he'd been getting to the good part. Archer sighed.

Their representatives were two satyrs, a young female and an older male.

"It's good to have you with us," Wick said to them. "We appreciate you volunteering for this."

Luckily, Wick didn't waste much time standing around talking, which was also good because Archer didn't listen to a thing anyone said. As they walked, Wick got to talking with the male representative, and they walked along ahead, leaving Archer with the other satyr. The other satyr in question was a female, a little older than he or Wick, with silky cream-colored fur and a delicate face. Something about her seemed strangely stern, but maybe that was why she had been chosen.

"What made them choose you to come with us?" Archer asked, attempting to be friendly like Wick wanted. It also seemed like something his father would do, so unfortunately it had to be good for their cause.

"Because I don't know you or Wick personally," she said, without missing a beat. "Therefore if either of you turns out to be lying or tricking us, I don't have any reservations that will keep me from beating either of you senseless."

Archer deeply wished he had said nothing.

"If it matters to you," she went on, "my name is Kanri."

"Archer," Archer said. "But you probably knew that."

"Everyone in our territory knows your name. If we put out arrest warrants, your face would be on every tree."

He should have let well enough alone. Archer told himself he wouldn't try to fill the silence again as long as he lived.

Somehow they made it back to Tor without Kanri feeling it necessary to beat anyone senseless, and in that time Archer was introduced to the other representative. He was a snow white satyr named Frost, who found the whole situation an interesting article of study and was a cousin of the satyr named Ambrack. Wick also managed to make Kanri open up, and they discovered that she was fond of knitting and nights looking up at the stars. Wick said that she should meet Eland, and she said she would like that, she would like to meet any of their allies.

Archer concluded that Wick had to be working some kind of sorcery.

As they reached the outskirts of Tor, the other group caught up with them and introduced their own representatives, a group of three nixie siblings who were curious about Wick and Archer and had been charged by their queen to guard their stone with their lives. They asked if the manghar had joined the cause yet, and Wick swooped in to say that they were currently in negotiations with the manghar and hoped they would arrive in the next few days. Archer wasn't so hopeful and he doubted Wick was, but maybe that was the point, to make everything sound better than reality.

When he got the chance, Fariss quietly shared with them that the negotiations had gone well, and that the only time he had been genuinely afraid for his life had been when he had first arrived in the territory. The queen had thought he was some manner of spy and had him dragged into the palace by the neck. But the queen had listened to his story with a more open mind than most, and she had readily sent the stone, but threatened to have Wick and Archer hunted down by her best general if she was betrayed again.

Archer guessed that the general in question was the one who had tried to slice his throat out before. Because his luck just ran like that.

"He didn't try to slice your throat out, he threatened you with a knife," Wick said when Archer mentioned this to him. "Don't be so dramatic."

That sounded rich coming from someone who turned a lovely shade of ash whenever he was tired or depressed, but Archer kept that to himself.

Archer was thoroughly overwhelmed and tired of people by the time they reached the street where their Rep House was. Wick had said not to call it the Rep House, but Archer conveniently forgot he said that. Archer stuck around for a bit, but as the red-haired woman led all the guests away to their rooms, he seized the opportunity to leave.

Finally, a little silence.

Archer strolled down the road with his hands in his pockets until he arrived at a little stream where he could let Sasha out for a bit. She seemed a little ruffled from all her time in the bag, and she whinnied at him with more than a little venom before guzzling water from the stream.

"I get it, I get it," Archer said. "Maybe I didn't let you out the last time I had a chance, like I thought. I forget things sometimes, okay?"

Sasha snorted at him once more and bent down to drink again.

"Good point." Archer bent over the water and took a long drink himself. Walking so far without any kind of water pouch was thirsty work after a while. Straightening, he swiped his mouth on his sleeve. "What do you think, girl, should we wander for a while before we go back home?"

Sasha said nothing.

"I agree, we shouldn't go back until everyone's in bed." Archer leaned back against a rock beside the stream. "You always have such good ideas, Sasha."

Sasha finally lifted her head, apparently having drunk her fill. She approached Archer and nibbled at the sleeve of his shirt.

"Hey, I need this," Archer said, batting her away. "It's the only one of my shirts that still fits. You don't get to chew holes in it until I'm done with it."

Sasha let go of his sleeve and switched her attention to the brown grass on the stream's bank.

"Don't worry, I'll leave it to you in my will." Archer leaned his head back against the rock too, and his mind wandered off into the darkening night. How he would survive around all these people, people that he had to keep happy, no less, until they had all the stones was beyond—

Down the street, something smoky flashed across the gap between two houses.

Archer bolted upright. His eyes remained locked on the gap between the houses. If it had been a branch swaying or someone's curtains blowing in the breeze, he would see it again. But he saw nothing.

He leaped up and charged at the gap between the houses. If Sasha even noticed him going, she paid him no heed. Archer raced through the gap and swung his head from side to side, scanning the street.

What was that?

Where did it go?

Movement caught his eye down the street. Something long and dark darted behind another house. Archer raced that way. It rounded a corner and he hooked a post with his elbow, swinging around the corner and shooting into the shadows in the forest. Whatever that thing was, he had to catch up with—

Something appeared out of the dark and rammed into his chest.

Archer slammed down onto the leafy ground. The breath nearly flew out of him. A mass of swirling black and cracks of red filled the space above him. He couldn't make out a shape. Something was digging into him through his shirt. What was this thing? Was it a dragonkin?

Then a snout appeared out of the swirling darkness. It *was* the dragonkin. Somehow it was darker, made more of soot and ash than smoke and fire. In the eyes and the spaces between the uneven scales, the fire still glowed from within, but it wasn't as bright as it had been in the forest.

Could they camouflage themselves? Or was it hurt?

The glowing eyes of the dragonkin pressed closer to his, and the lizard snout wrinkled in a snarl. Archer could smell its breath, all smoky, yet sour.

"What do you think you are doing, foolish thing?"

"Right now, or in general?" Archer asked, wincing

against the heat on his face. "Because the answer to both of those is that I'm trying to stop *you.*"

"*You can never beat us,*" it said. Archer thought he recognized the voice of the younger creature they had seen in the forest. "*We are too many, and already too close for you to prepare in time. We'll overwhelm your little country and pillage your castles.*"

Archer coughed smoke out of his lungs. "Good luck. We don't have many castles. Palaces, sure, but not castles."

The dragonkin's whip of a tail lashed. "*Castles or no castles, your stones can't save you. My kind will scorch all your green grass and turn all your pretty trees into torches. Everything you know will become ash.*"

"The plants are already sort of turning into ash, if you missed that," Archer said. "That's how we knew you were coming."

The dragonkin's head twisted to look around at the forest. It peered at the charred grass.

"*That will be interesting to share with my superiors,*" it managed.

"You didn't know about that?" Archer asked. "We've known about that for centuries. When your people are coming, the plants are the first things to let us know. It's not that hard to spot, actually."

A cruel gleam entered the creature's eye. "*Then why aren't you already prepared?*"

"Some of us are stupid, okay?" Archer waved his hands, and the wings of the dragonkin came rushing down to pin his arms to the ground. Archer hissed. The claws were so hot. He could picture the muscles in his forearms cooking.

"*No matter what you say or what you do, you and everything you know will come to an end.*" Flames flicked from the dragonkin's mouth, licking dangerously close to Archer's face.

Archer frowned as something occurred to him. "What are you doing here, actually?"

"*That is no business of yours to know!*" the dragonkin hissed.

"Well, not here *specifically*," Archer corrected himself. "I meant in Aro. How are you already here when none of your other people have even made it to our borders yet? If you can travel that fast, why aren't all of you here yet?"

"*That is no concern of yours!*" the dragonkin insisted.

"What, are you worried about me?" Archer said. "What damage do you think I can do to your army? I can't even fly, I'm not going to take down your whole army all on my own."

The dragonkin considered this.

"And can you let me up?" Archer said, flinching. "Pretty sure you're cooking my wrists."

The dragonkin hesitated.

"Look at you. Big scary dragon and you're scared of little old me," Archer said sadly, then winced as a twinge of pain shot through his arms. "You won't tell me anything, you won't let go of my arms since you're slow roasting them. . . I've gotta assume you're scared of me."

The claws wrapped around his arms released all at once, and the dragonkin's face drew even closer. "*My kind,*" the dragonkin said, "*fear nothing. There is nothing on this earth worth the time your kind sacrifice for fear. I fear nothing, and least of all I don't fear you.*"

"That's what I thought," Archer said, forcing the dragonkin to withdraw a few feet as he sat up. He got himself into a comfortable position with his hands clasped atop his knee. His burned arms screamed. "But seriously, you didn't answer the question. How are you here?"

"*I don't have to tell you anything,*" the dragonkin said. Its bright orange eyes were trained on Archer from only a few feet away, where it sat upright with the support of its wings. "*I'll gain nothing from telling you.*"

"No, but you sure won't lose anything," Archer said. "And I'll still think you're afraid of me if you think I can use that kind of information against you. Just saying."

The dragonkin adjusted its wings. Then its head shot forward, its eyes only inches from Archer's. "*Very well. I will tell you this: I was sent here by the army because I'm a faster and more vigorous flier than most. They sent me ahead to understand your land and find your weaknesses—*" Its eyes gleamed— "*so that we can destroy you and take everything you hold dear. We want to leave you defenseless.*"

They wanted the stones, Aro's means of protection. This confirmed what Archer already suspected.

The situation shifted in Archer's mind, and two questions seemed clear to him:

One, did the dragonkin know about Archer's suspicions? Would it try to blackmail him into giving up the stones if it did? Maybe if he was careful, he could get it to admit why the Scorch wanted the stones.

Two, what else could he get out of the dragonkin?

CHAPTER NINETEEN:

You Can Burn Off My Eyebrows But I Still Won't Be Impressed

"YOU'RE A SCOUT." Archer ripped up some of the dry grass without breaking eye contact with the creature in front of him. "Sounds fancy. Prestigious. I have a friend who's sort of like you. He's a messenger. And if you're anything like him, I'll guess that you know all sorts of secrets."

"*I'll tell you nothing more,*" the dragonkin said.

"I know. You said that. But I wanted to know what you figured out about us. You know, since you're scoping us out and everything."

The dragonkin said nothing, its eyes hard.

"Here's my guess, okay? You're probably looking at all the territories trying to figure out where you can hit us so it'll hurt. More results for less work. And I could tell you," Archer said. "But just like you won't tell me anything, I won't tell you anything. And you can't make me."

The dragonkin's head tilted. "*I could make you. But there would be no point. You would lie to me.*"

"Yup. Like there's no tomorrow."

"*Furthermore, I already know what your biggest weakness is.*"

Archer's spine crawled a little. What had this thing figured out? Was it even something important? He kept his face neutral. "Do you?"

"*Your people are divided. There are clear borders where you've divided yourselves into sects, and therefore you can agree on nothing, even now that you know we're coming. You're unprepared to meet us because you have no army to meet us with.*" The dragonkin's eyes glinted. "*Am I right?*"

"Sure, but you missed something," Archer responded. He ripped up another chunk of grass. "You didn't realize we've always been this way. We've been split into territories since forever, and you know what? It never stopped us from keeping you out before." An idea occurred to him. The dragonkin seemed to like talking. Maybe if the question was simple, it would give Archer more information than he asked for. "But anyway, here's my question: what do you want? You keep coming back over and over, obviously you're after something. What are you trying to get?"

"*We want your downfall,*" the dragonkin growled, and this time Archer jumped. Its voice sounded angrier this time, almost bitter. It stared at Archer with a burning gaze. "*We want your destruction and our triumph. Nothing more, and nothing less.*"

"How come? What do you get out of it?"

A stick crackled further off in the woods. Both their

heads snapped toward the sound. All of a sudden the dragonkin leaped forward and pinned Archer down again. Its breath was hot and fiery on his face as the eyes bored into his own. *"Know this, little broken thing,"* it whispered as Archer struggled beneath it. *"No matter what you do, all your efforts will be in vain. This time, our strategy is like none your people have ever known. Nothing will be able to stop us."*

The cracks in the blackness of its skin glowed brighter, and Archer knew if he didn't escape soon, he wouldn't walk away from this.

The dragonkin snarled in his face. *"Prepare to meet that which made you, because this country of yours will burn."*

Archer's scrabbling fingers found a stick on the ground. "Cool," he told the dragon, then smacked the stick into its ear.

The dragon leaped away with a screech. Archer tore into the trees.

"Hurry up, hurry up, hurry up," he singsonged to himself anxiously as he dodged through the underbrush. "If it catches you, you're dead."

After a minute of helter-skelter running, he stopped and listened. Nothing. No loud crashing, no hissing, no trees breaking. He scanned the sky. No smoke. It appeared that the dragonkin had decided against hunting him down.

"Good job," he told himself. Ruffling his fingers through his hair to knock the ash out, he walked back into town.

His arms *hurt*.

Sasha hadn't budged from the stream bank. Archer patted her on the nose, telling her she was a good girl after all, then led her back to the Hessen house, where he left her to feast upon whatever she found growing around the house. If she ate the garden, so be it.

Wick was waiting on the stairs for him, with a book open on his lap. "Where did you disappear to?" he asked, sounding a little accusatory.

"I took Sasha for a walk. She hasn't been out of the bag in a while," Archer said.

"Well, luckily none of the representatives noticed you were gone," Wick said.

"I'm sure they're all dying for my company." Archer leaned against the railing. "I ran into one of those dragonkin in the forest."

Wick's spine straightened. "*What*?"

"Dragonkin," Archer repeated, extending his arms to show off the burns. "In the forest. I think it was the younger one. It didn't seem sure of itself. Kept fidgeting."

"Did it see you?" Wick asked.

"It sat on me and made a strong point of telling me that everything I know is going to burn to a cinder," Archer said, "so yes, I think it's safe to say it saw me."

Wick made a spluttering sound and then fell into flabbergasted silence.

"But the good news is, I think there's only the two of them so far," Archer said. "The rest of the army is still on its way. The two we saw were scouts, and I'm still sure they're out to get the Heather Stones. I'm not sure why, but that's what they're after."

Wick's mouth tightened. "They won't get them from us."

Archer's eyebrows rose. "I think that's the most aggressive I've ever heard you. Or, that's what I would say if you hadn't tried to attack people twice recently."

"Right." Wick rubbed his temples. "Well, it's good to

hear that the dragonkin aren't all here yet. If they were already here, it would be too late. I asked permission to experiment while you were gone to see if we really need the last two stones, and we still couldn't put up the barrier spell."

"Let's just hope," Archer said slowly, "that it's not working because we still need the last two stones, and not for any other reason."

Wick's gaze snapped up to Archer's face. "What kind of other reason?"

"Seeing how we don't know how to work the spell, we could be doing anything wrong and wouldn't know it," Archer said. He felt a little relieved to finally say what had been on his mind for days. "Nobody ever wrote down how to use the spell."

Wick was silent for a moment. "Yes, let's hope it's not any other reason."

"The centaurs wouldn't have given us a bogus stone, would they?" Archer asked, feeling a little ashamed for even asking. "We got that stone first, after all, and it was the easiest one to get hold of."

"They wouldn't," Wick said with certainty. "Maybe. . . maybe some of the others would, but Ongel and Eland wouldn't do that. They're on our side, I know that much."

"Then I believe you," Archer said. He pushed off the railing and started up the stairs. "But I still feel like there's something here that we're missing, and I don't know what it is yet."

When he entered the house, they found Ongel speaking to Archer's mother.

"Archer," Willow said. "Your friend has been waiting for you for some time now."

"I truly don't mind," Ongel assured both Willow and

Archer at the same time.

"Sorry." Archer pushed the door shut. "I was a little busy with the dragonkin I met in the woods."

Ongel's expression instantly leveled into a grave one. "What do you mean?"

"I mean I met a dragonkin in the forest and we had a nice little conversation." Archer realized too late that he was being rude. He cleared his throat. "I'm okay, though. And it's gone now."

"Your arms!" Willow exclaimed.

"Yeah." Archer inspected his burns, which were starting to look like shiny raw meat. "It wouldn't let go."

"Wait here." Willow hurried away.

"What did you learn from it?" Ongel asked.

Archer shrugged. "Not a lot. I know that the two we saw were only scouts, not the start of the real army, and the army is coming, but I don't know when they'll get here. It wouldn't tell me anything about what they want or why, but it made sure I knew that they're going to burn everything to the ground."

"Nothing else?" Ongel probed.

"I don't think so," Archer said, his gaze returning to Ongel's face. "I could tell it knew more than it was saying, but it didn't have a good reason to tell me anything. Wick said you tried the stones again and it didn't do anything. When he and I were traveling around, I did a couple of little spells with the stones and it went fine. Now that we have six stones, they should be doing *something*. We should at least be able to cast smaller spells. Why can't we?"

Ongel sighed. "I don't know. Neither do any of the others. You're right; based on the limited historical records we have, something should be happening. But I inspected the stones and they're all genuine. None of them appeared to be damaged, either."

Archer ran a hand through his hair, cringing as the burns on his arm wrinkled. "Here I was hoping you'd have more answers." Then he paused as he remembered something from a long time ago. He looked at Ongel. "Did you know Caihu?"

"I knew *of* him," Ongel said, "but I didn't know him personally. I was involved in a lot of outside affairs while he still lived in the valley, and when everything went wrong for him, I wasn't really involved. But it was a sad day when he decided to leave."

"Yeah," Archer said.

His mother reappeared with the bandages and started gently spreading some sticky stuff from a jar on his burns. Archer squirmed as the wounds blazed with pain.

He watched his mother with a touch of confusion. She never would have done this when he was growing up; she always sent him to some doctor and never touched his injuries. Her hands felt awkward as she tried to take care of his burns.

"Caihu was the one that gave you your bag, wasn't he?" Ongel asked. "I think I remember Wick telling me about that."

"Yeah, he gave me the bag." Archer flinched. "And ages ago, I found a notebook inside the bag, full of scribbles and notes and everything. He must have forgotten it was in there. I wanted to use the bag so I took it out. Since he was the only one who saw the Scorch coming back, maybe he wrote something useful in that journal."

"Perhaps," Ongel mused. "I assume you still have it."

Willow finished wrapping Archer's arms and disappeared again with the bandages.

"Maybe I do." Archer shrugged his shoulders and pulled on one of the bandages where it was wound too tight. "I left it in my grandfather's house. You know, the one where all the furniture is already sold and long gone. But if you want, we can walk to Eri and see if it's still there."

"In all honesty," Ongel admitted, "if you can find it, it might be the last remaining piece of his work. I think most of his papers were thrown away when someone else took over his office."

"Figures," Archer muttered. "I'll get my bag."

IT TOOK ALL NIGHT, but they walked to Eri and knocked on the door of Oak Hessen's home. The caretaker appeared at the door in such a state of shambles Archer assumed he had been in bed.

"Sorry," Archer said. "I think I might have left something here."

"We'll borrow a candle and let you go back to sleep," Ongel said apologetically, as a damp breeze gusted across the porch. "It shouldn't take long."

Once the caretaker had handed them a candle and disappeared into the house again, Archer and Ongel climbed the stairs to the sitting room on the topmost floor. Archer looked around and tried not to remember how it had looked when his grandfather still lived there.

"Welcome back, my boy—gracious, what happened? Sit. I'll be back in a moment."

Archer blinked, and the memory was gone. It was for the better if he didn't think about that right now. He jumped atop the stone hearth and fished around on top of the mantelpiece. Sure enough, his fingers found the worn pages of the book he had hidden so long ago.

"Got it," he grunted, jumping down from the fireplace. The book was ancient now, covered in dust and split across the spine. But it was still here. Somehow it had been left behind.

Archer started to open the front cover, then stopped and handed the book to Ongel. "You'll probably find what we need more easily than I will."

"Two pairs of eyes will be more efficient than one," Ongel said, and the pair of them sat on the floor and studied the pages as Ongel flipped through. Just as Archer remembered, Caihu's handwriting was sloppy and uneven, and lines of it sprawled in every direction across the pages. No page seemed to have any rhyme or reason, or even a topic. Grocery lists rambled alongside words like *past? Hand? Mountain (USELESS)*. Three pages went on in excruciating detail on a flood in satyr territory fifteen years ago, which he had predicted down to rivulets on certain hills and who would spot them first.

Archer's eyes hurt trying to read the messy hand. He scrubbed the heel of one hand against his eyes. "This is a mess. We're never going to find anything."

"We will," Ongel said. "Caihu was the only one who saw the Scorch coming. Maybe we won't find exactly what we're looking for, but we will find something."

Archer focused on the page again. Three-quarters of an hour later, as Archer was about to throw in the towel for good, Ongel said, "Look here."

Taken off guard, Archer looked where Ongel pointed. In the upper corner of the page was a note so small it took him several heartbeats to decipher the first word.

Return of the Scorch: Archer and Ongel, I knew you would be here. Instructions inside the flap of the bag.

He *had* known. Not only had he known that they

would be here, and what they were looking for, but he had also known where to leave the instructions. He had known Archer would never give up such a useful tool, so he could guarantee Archer would never lose his instructions.

All that from only knowing Archer for a few minutes.

Caihu hadn't been crazy.

"I hope he meant in the actual flap of the bag, not in the bag itself," Archer muttered as he felt around the edges of the bag flap for an opening. "This bag has been washed out a bunch of times, so if he put anything in the bag, it's long gone."

"We can certainly hope." Ongel watched Archer feel around. "But he did specify the flap."

Having found no clear opening or catch, Archer tried a different approach. He grabbed hold of the first loose thread he found and started picking out stitches. Slowly but surely, the flap of the bag peeled into two pieces.

"There!" Ongel reached out and drew a small roll of paper from between the pieces of leather. Carefully, he unrolled it, holding it tight at each end to keep it flat.

Archer squinted at the paper by the light of their candles.

If anything, the little slip of paper was a worse mess than the journal. Caihu's heavy scrawl covered both sides of the paper from top to bottom, made denser by the number of cross-outs, underlines, and extra words packed between the rows of text.

After frowning at it a minute, Archer shook his head and took a step back. "I can only make out a couple of words. It's too late at night for this."

"I think I can read it to you." Ongel brought the paper closer to his eyes. Archer held up his candlestick to provide better light.

Ongel and Archer: You want to know why the stones aren't working. Here is everything I can glean from my visions, though it never stops shifting. The more it appears in my visions the more my mind seems to slip. You will need all the stones to succeed; every vision of your success involved all the stones. Stealing the stones won't work. Watch over the manghar; they need your help even more than you need theirs. Tell Wick to watch his head when he casts the spell; danger will come from above. When you need to take down the dragonkin, stab them in the ear or under the chin. Guard Ongel with your life. Get out of Tor as quickly as you can. I don't know why the stones won't work, and all the scrolls I read about them are now missing, but I know you will succeed in the end if you push through. For Archer alone: I gave you the bag because you have the power to keep Aro from burning. You also have the power to let it all turn to ash. Make the right choice. You will have to learn more about the stones yourself. This may be the last vision I write about; the future is heavy behind my eyes. Good luck.

Ongel glanced at Archer. "This is less helpful than I hoped."

Archer rubbed his forehead. "Maybe he *was* just a crazy old centaur. It kind of looks like he was crumbling away even while he was writing the note."

"In a way, yes. But he accurately predicted that you and I would be here looking for this," Ongel said. "He knew something."

"But he barely told us anything."

"Yes," Ongel agreed grimly. "We have volumes of instructions on how to describe visions so that everyone can understand them just as they appeared, in every detail. This is oddly vague. Caihu was unconventional, but even his notes in the journal were less abstract than this. He seems to imply that the future kept changing, with the only constant being the return of the Scorch."

"And I don't like that he said all the information on the stones disappeared." Archer looked at Ongel. "Why do you think that would happen?"

Ongel shook his head. "I have no clue. Though he seemed to know that using fewer stones was folly from the beginning."

"Would have been nice if he had said something sooner. You know, 'Here's an unfillable bag and oh also my legacy, and don't forget that when the fate of the world rests on your shoulders, I left instructions in the bag!'" Then Archer's shoulders slumped. "It wouldn't have made any difference if he had said that, would it? I wouldn't have listened. I'm stupid, so the only way I could have ended up here was the long way around."

"Stupid, that I doubt," Ongel said. "But I agree that even if this had been Wick, giving the instructions before there was any visible danger would hardly have been more helpful than letting you arrive here in the end anyway."

Ongel glanced up at the window. "It's nearly sunrise. We need to return to Tor and help the others before they realize we're missing."

Sometimes Archer wondered if all of this was worth it. As they walked the miles back to Tor, he tried to think over the note.

"Maybe there were other notes we never saw," Ongel had said when they started out. "Perhaps they would make it clearer."

Archer doubted it. If anything, finding the journal made him wonder more than ever if Caihu had just been crazy. And yet, with the grass still crunching under his feet like charcoal, he knew that somehow Caihu had predicted the dragonkin would be back, and that they would be back now.

As they arrived back in Tor, Eland raced down the street to meet them. "I've been looking for you everywhere! No one knew where you went!"

Archer knew enough to assume that Eland was only talking to Ongel.

"I'm sorry for the lateness of our return," Ongel said. "We meant to be back sooner."

Archer squinted at the sun. It had to be almost noon now. Suddenly he felt exhausted. The overnight journey was taking its toll.

After this, sleep. A lot of sleep.

"The manghar have agreed to join us!" Eland cried. "We received the message first thing this morning."

Archer's mouth dropped open.

"Their only condition is that Archer doesn't touch their piece of the heather stone as long as it's with us," Eland continued. He stopped and gave Archer an apologetic look. "Sorry."

Archer shrugged. He expected as much.

"They'll arrive tomorrow," Eland said. "Once they've arrived, the only piece of the heather stone remaining will be the leshy piece."

"THEY WON'T give it to us," Wick said, leaning back against the headboard of his borrowed guest bed in the Hessen house. "I already tried. And I doubt they'd give you a warmer welcome than they did me."

Archer adjusted his seat against the side of Wick's bed. "Then how will we get the leshy piece?"

"We won't. They won't give it to us."

"Can we. . ." Archer shrugged. ". . .write them another letter?"

"I've been trying." Wick looked down at his hands. "I've sent two separate messages to them since I returned from their territory because Ongel said I should. They haven't sent any response."

"Has Ongel tried?"

"Yes. They haven't responded to him, either. There's nothing we can do."

"And Caihu made it painfully obvious that we need all the stones to survive," Archer said with a sigh. He tipped his head back and stared at the ceiling. "Do you know how you'd like to die, Wick?"

Wick's brow creased. "What was that?"

"Ever thought about how you'd like to go, when you go?"

Wick took a deep breath. "I try not to think about that if I can. Thinking about dying doesn't exactly help me sleep well at night."

"Well, it doesn't help me either, but I think about it anyway," Archer said. "And considering how I almost got killed in manghar territory, it's been on my mind a lot since then. I don't want to go out like that."

"Like what?"

"With someone else deciding the timing. Someone else saying it's my time to go and making sure it happens. I don't want that." Archer frowned at the wooden beams of the ceiling. "I want to make it matter. I'm going out on my timing, and it's going to be spectacular. It's going to be the biggest thing that's ever happened to this rotten country. Sorry. Not rotten," he added quickly when he caught Wick's venomous glance.

"But really," he went on. "I want to have the biggest

and most exciting death that anyone here has ever seen. With my luck, I'm not likely to be an old man, and that's fine by me. I'd rather be able to run while I can."

Wick made a soft noise. "Sounds like you."

"I'm going to live a life so big and bright it'll burn across the sky. I'll be a legend. I'll die like a falling star. The moment I go is going to be so big and brilliant that it'll make them all look up and wonder who I was. If the only way I can make anyone notice me is by dying, that's fine. It'll finally show all of them exactly what I'm capable of." He reached up over the side of the bed to slap Wick on the knee. "What about you?"

"Like I said, I don't think about it much," Wick said. He thought a moment. "I suppose I haven't thought about having options now that I'm human."

"Human-ish," Archer said.

"Humanish." Wick took a breath. "Leshy all die the same way, unless we break our necks or something. We don't get diseases or die in a lot of the ways you can. We get old and tired and then one day they lay us down to rest. But now that I'm more or less human, I guess anything could happen." He made a face. "I'm not sure I like the sound of that."

"Get over it," Archer said. "Go on. Pick something, anything. Eaten by a sea monster. Falling from the top of the tallest tree. Killed in battle against a dastardly political figure who thinks he's even bigger than my father is. If you could choose how you go, how would you go?"

"Honestly," Wick said, "I think I'd rather grow old and die in my sleep. That way I can get the most out of the life I've been given. I'd rather die old than young."

"Then I guess we'll have to get that last stone so you can make it that far."

The two of them fell into silence, their thoughts now heavier than before.

After a long moment, Archer said, "I guess there's only one option left."

Wick looked up with a question on his face, then the look in his eyes changed. "We can't. We know better." He searched for another reason. "There has to be another way."

The note Caihu had left for them drifted through Archer's mind. *Stealing the stones won't work.*

He ignored it. "You've talked to the leshy, and they didn't listen. We've written them letters, and they won't listen to us. We've tried every angle, and nothing's worked. Sure, we could keep waiting and keep contacting them until they change their minds, but do you think they will? Do they accept anything new that fast? Because from what you've told me, they won't. And if we're missing even one stone, we can't cast the spell, which means everyone will die, including the leshy, and you, and me, and anyone we care about." Archer's heart pounded. "I hate it too. It seems so stupid to do this after all our hard work. But I can't see any other way. Can you?"

Wick struggled for something to say, distress in his eyes.

"Wick." Archer felt sick trying to convince Wick to steal things all over again, especially when that was what had ruined Wick's life in the first place. "We're running out of time. We have how long, a week or so, until the earthquakes start? If we wait much longer, there won't be any Aro left to save. Maybe if we get their stone, and then we save everyone, the leshy will see we were right and forgive you."

Still, Wick hesitated. "Give it a little more time. I

have a terrible feeling that you may be right, but we have to save taking it by force as a last resort. All right?"

Archer nodded. Getting Wick to agree brought some relief, but somehow that relief didn't feel quite right. "Fine, we won't do it unless you think we have to. And I understand if you don't want to. I just can't see any other way."

Slowly, with tired limbs, Archer climbed the stairs and tumbled into bed to catch up on some sleep before the next big thing happened. Before he drifted off he heard the sound of Wick's even footsteps pass by, heading downstairs.

He hadn't been asleep for two minutes before the whole tree shook.

Archer was nearly thrown out of his bed as the whole tree shuddered from bottom to top, bending and swaying like there was some great storm outside. Too startled to even make any kind of noise, Archer clung desperately to the bedframe with both hands. Downstairs, he heard a sound like a bookcase falling over. Something crashed on the floor above him. After only a moment, the shaking stopped, and he tumbled out of bed. Racing to the doorway, he shouted into the house.

"What the devil was that?"

The falling books noise came again, and Fowl's voice bellowed, "How would I know?"

Fear raced through Archer's chest. Had Wick still been on the outside steps? He could have been thrown down all those flights of stairs. He dashed down the stairs, nearly falling in his haste, and threw the door of the house open.

On the other side, with his hand where the handle of the door should have been, was Wick. His eyes were as large as Archer imagined his own were. A smudge of dirt ran up the side of one of his cheeks where it seemed he had fallen, but not far.

"We're going," Wick said.

"Yup." Archer grabbed his bag off a hook on the wall, and they ran down the stairs to start their journey to leshy territory.

CHAPTER TWENTY:

More Poor Life Choices

LESHY TERRITORY wasn't far. It would only take them a few days to travel there, get the stone, and return to Tor. They gathered their things, and so it would seem less strange, Archer suggested they should tell Ongel and Eland that they were leaving.

"We're going to talk to the leshy in person," Wick said, and Archer watched his grip on the strap of his bag grow tighter. "Maybe together we can convince them to trust us."

Both Ongel and Eland looked ignorantly optimistic.

"You'll do fine," Eland said with certainty. "Now that everyone else is with us, there's no way they won't believe you."

Sweat prickled at the back of Archer's neck. "Exactly. We'll be fine."

"We'll be back in a few days," Wick said, slinging his bag over his shoulder.

"Good luck," Ongel said. He gave both of them a firm pat on the back and sent them on their way.

Archer didn't like the sick feeling he got from lying to Ongel's face.

Two days later, Wick and Archer were hurrying through the dark forest with the unfillable bag in their hands, heading for the leshy museum. No one seemed to be on guard.

Five minutes after that, they had slipped through the empty doorway and into the museum, where the lights were low and no one was anywhere to be seen. The Oak Leaf waited on the candlelit shelf, exactly where it was supposed to be.

Ten minutes later, they sprinted out of the village with the Oak Leaf, and still, no one had seen them. Wick handed the Oak Leaf to Archer to put in his unfillable bag.

Three hours after that, they were leaving leshy territory, only three days after they had started.

Two sunrises later, they walked back into Tor with the Oak Leaf in their possession and no one the wiser that it had been stolen.

"They gave it to you!" Eland exclaimed when they walked into the Rep House with the Oak Leaf in Archer's open hand. The room they met in had been moved into a downstairs dining room, because while the sitting room had been full before, with their added numbers it was now out of the question.

"They did," Wick said, and maybe Archer only saw the funny look in his eyes because he expected it. "But they didn't want to send any representatives. We understood."

Ongel gave them a reassuring smile. "What matters is that we have it. Now we have all eight of the stones. All that's left to do now is to get them to the cavern in the valley and cast the spell there."

"Those creatures are looking for these," Wick said. "We'll have to be careful."

Archer tilted his head. "If we need to get them all there, why didn't we bring them all to the valley in the first place?"

"Because remember, you still have a few enemies there," Ongel reminded him. "Tinor is not happy with what we're doing here, and there's a select group who agree with him."

Tinor could shove it, in Archer's opinion. After everything Tinor had said when Archer came to get the centaur stone, Archer had no respect to offer him.

"And besides, this was where you wanted to set up your base of operations. I wanted to let you make your own plans at that time," Ongel added. "This was what you chose."

"What's our plan to get the pieces safely there without the creatures realizing what we're doing?" Wick asked.

"Dragonkin," Archer said.

Wick corrected himself. "The dragonkin."

"How would they even know we had them, let alone where we were going with them?" Hirim asked, leaning his elbows on the dining table. "It doesn't seem like they know much about us."

"I agree," Ongel said. "But if they saw a lot of us, with such a group as we have, all headed in the same direction, it would seem significant even if we weren't doing anything at all."

"We could go in small groups, or pairs or something," Archer offered. "Would attract less attention."

"But if the dragonkin caught on, small groups would leave everyone more exposed," Eland pointed out. "If we lose even one stone, we can't cast the spell."

"We'll come up with something," Wick said. "In the meantime, everyone pack what you need. We're leaving for the valley as soon as we can. We don't know when the dragonkin will get here, but currently the odds don't look good, so we're leaving as soon as possible."

As the representatives dispersed to get what supplies they needed for the trip, Archer leaned over to Wick and muttered, "You're telling me it isn't looking good. Did you see the trees on the way here?"

"I did," Wick murmured.

On the walk to the Rep House, Archer had happened to look up at the trees in passing. Almost every tree had greying leaves, and on every other trunk, red lines stretched up the tree bark, like a disease from the roots.

Wick crossed the room. "Ongel, I had an idea about the stones that I wanted to discuss with you. Fowl thought of it. . ."

SOMEONE GOT the bright idea to send Archer down as a marker for the meeting spot. For thirty minutes he stood at the base of the tree with his bag over his shoulder, telling the representatives that they would be leaving any minute once everyone arrived. A manghar and one of the satyrs nearly got into an argument, but Archer got the manghar to speak to one of the nixie soldiers instead, and the conversation changed directions.

With that potentially life-threatening situation over, Archer backed up to the edge of the crowd, where hopefully none of the other manghar would see him. He couldn't shake the idea that maybe the manghar were assassins sent to kill him. Caihu's note about them hadn't helped his paranoia.

He'd rather stay alive if he could help it, thank you.

Wick and Ongel arrived with the final representatives, and Ongel told all the representatives that their stones had been secured away in the wooden case that Ongel himself was carrying.

The plan, they said, was to leave Tor immediately and travel quickly until they reached the valley. As far as they knew, there was no time to lose, so they would immediately go to the cavern and cast the barrier spell to drive away the dragonkin.

"And what about the creatures that are already inside our borders?" Otho's son asked. "You said there were some already here."

"With any luck, the spell will recognize them and they'll be thrown out of Aro," Ongel said, "but we aren't sure about anything. If the worst happens—"

"Our people will eradicate them!" one of the manghar roared. The other manghar cheered. Archer edged further away. Maybe they were assassins after all.

"Eradication won't be necessary yet," Ongel said. "That remains to be seen. But your people will be called upon if it becomes necessary."

The eyes of the manghar representatives gleamed murderously.

Ongel looked around. "Well then. If we have everyone, we can make a start!"

"Stop!" a voice bellowed.

Archer instantly recognized the odd, flat sound of a telepathic voice. And from the thunderstruck expression on Wick's face, so did he.

Archer turned around to see how many leshy had come for them.

"Is there a problem?" an ignorant Ongel asked the six leshy that were striding down the street toward them. A distant part of Archer's mind wondered if Wick knew any of them. Two of them seemed to be armed with some sharp sticks, and metal plating covered their chests. Was that supposed to be armor?

"There is a problem," one of the armed leshy said bluntly. "These two," here he pointed his stick weapon at first Wick, then Archer, "broke into our museum and stole the Oak Leaf from us not three nights ago."

Archer winced. Why had he thought this would go smoothly, again?

"That's not—" Eland said, but his father shot him a warning look.

"I'm sure there's some kind of misunderstanding," Hirim said smoothly. "We were told that the leshy had agreed to lend the Oak Leaf to our cause. We'll be more than happy to return it to you immediately after we're done with it."

"You will get it back soon, I promise you," Ongel added.

"No," the armed leshy said flatly. "It was stolen, and by a banished member of our race, no less. We won't leave here without the Oak Leaf in our possession."

"Banished?" Ongel asked. There was a hidden question in his tone.

"Yes. Wick is forbidden from returning to our territory unless the royal family lifts his banishment," one of the other leshy said. "But he crossed our borders again, which is another offense, and he brought another thief with him. They stole our people's most prized possession. We want it back."

Archer glanced back, and he could see the indecision behind Ongel's eyes. "I'm sure we can come to some kind of compromise," Ongel said at last.

The pair of armored leshy shouldered their way into the crowd of representatives, and no one stopped them. "No compromises," one of them said. He held out a woody hand, palm up. "The Oak Leaf, please."

Ongel opened his mouth, then closed it again. A new resolve came over his face. He opened the wooden case in his hands. Inside, nestled on mounds of black velvet, were all the pieces of the Heather Stone. The leshy took the Oak Leaf out of the case and handed it to his companion, who slid it into a pouch around his neck.

"Thank you," the first leshy said. Then he and his friends turned back and walked away.

Archer didn't know how to stop them. He turned back toward Wick and saw the agony on his face. Being banished was one thing, but it was another thing to be openly humiliated in front of their new allies. At least Archer had nothing left to lose. Wick, despite all he had already lost, still had further to fall.

The manghar were the first to react. "I will not stand for this dishonorable conduct," the outspoken one declared. "The manghar are not thieves and tolerate none. There is no truce."

One of the other manghar snatched the manghar stone out of the case. "We renounce your cause."

The third wheeled on Archer with teeth and claws bared. Archer backed up a step, and the manghar pressed closer. "If our paths cross again, thief, you will regret ever knowing me."

"I know," Archer said. He kept his face utterly empty, the way Fowl did. "If we see each other again, I think you'll regret knowing me, too."

The manghar snarled in his face, and as Archer was starting to think maybe they wouldn't need their paths to cross again, the three manghar took off and soared East.

They hadn't even disappeared over the trees before Kanri, the female satyr, said, "We'll also need to reconsider." She reached out and removed the satyr stone from the case. "Frost and I will remain in the city until we can make a decision, but this hasn't gone unnoticed."

The tension behind Ongel's eyes increased slightly, but he nodded to the two satyrs as they left the group and returned to the house.

"We'll give the rest of you time to consider the best course of action," Ongel said to the other representatives. His voice was strained, but he held his head up like a statue of a conqueror. "We can reconvene later today to discuss what happened, and explanations will be offered then."

"Understood," Othos' son said. "I'm sure everything can be explained."

Ongel nodded to him. "Thank you."

When all the representatives had returned to the house, Wick and Archer were left alone with the centaurs. Eland didn't look like he knew what to say.

Ongel's mouth hovered open, for a moment, before at last he said, "Boys."

Wick looked away. Ongel's gaze turned to Archer.

"What?" Archer held up his hands. "What do you want me to say? We messed up, okay? It was my idea, if that's what you're asking. I suggested it. As usual, something was good and I made a mess out of it. We didn't know how to make them help us, so we took their stupid rock. I don't know what else there is to say."

"If you had spoken to me," Ongel said gently, "I'm sure we could have found another way."

"We didn't have *time*," Archer shouted. "We still

don't! Can you think of a single way this could have gone better? Because I can't. We're all going to die, and I can't think of another *stupid* way we could have done better. We messed up, yeah, I messed up most of all, yeah, but this is what *I* could do. This is what *I'm* good at."

Ongel looked like he wanted to speak, but he didn't. Archer couldn't stand the look on his face.

"Just. . . never mind." Archer waved a hand at him and turned away. "We can *reconvene* later, if that's what you want. Maybe I'll have something to say by then. Maybe I'll come up with one of those lines that all of you use to say something you don't mean. I don't know. I'll be back."

He marched down the road and made the round and round journey up the stairs to his own house.

His father met him inside the door. His expression was not a kind one.

"I guess you heard, then," Archer said.

"Actually, I saw," his father answered icily. "I thought you were through with stealing things to get your way."

"Oh, so it's me trying to 'get my way' when I'm trying to help everyone?" Archer demanded. "What would you have had me do?"

"There are ways other than stealing."

"Not that I can see." Archer made a big deal of shrugging, such a small motion, but his whole body seemed to be full of fire. "Either I took the stone or nothing happened."

"This is not the way we raised you," his father growled.

"*Did* you raise me?" Archer met his father's gaze with just as much steel. "Pretty sure I was on my own for most of my childhood. You wonder why I left."

"I know why you left. Because you never wanted any of the things we wanted for you."

"You bet I didn't. I didn't want a part in anything that you do. You want to put yourself on a higher and higher pedestal. You've never done anything just because it was right. Well, congratulations, now I do the same thing. Does it look familiar?"

Ochre's eyes hardened. "Don't speak to your father that way."

"I don't get what you want from me," Archer said, shaking his head. When his father didn't answer, he shouted. *"What do you want from me?"*

"A quieter tone, to start."

"No," Archer said. "Quiet around here means convenient. Convenient means ignored. I'll stay loud, thanks."

Fowl appeared in the hallway, a book tucked under his arm. "What's going on?"

"Your brother thinks we put too much pressure on him to behave," Ochre answered coldly. "Give him some time, he's being unreasonable."

"I'll be unreasonable all I like," Archer snapped. "If you wanted a perfect son, there he is." He jabbed a finger in Fowl's direction. "Don't expect me to be him. If you think the only expectations you ever put on me were to behave, you're wrong. Since forever you've wanted me to sell my soul to your agenda. Since I was born you had this perfect picture of me in your mind, you had my whole personality picked out, and then you were disappointed when I turned out nothing like it. It's not my responsibility to be the way you picture me, okay? I'll figure out who I am on my own."

"Well. If you can do it on your own," Ochre said, drawing himself up, "then you're welcome to do it on your own. Leave my house."

Behind Ochre, Fowl turned to his father in surprise, but Ochre's expression never wavered as he stared down at Archer. "The door is behind you."

Archer blinked once, then caught up his bag off the floor. "I was ready to go, anyway. See ya." He paused, then added with venom, "or maybe I won't. Who knows."

He left the house without another glance and walked across town, looking for a place to hide. He didn't want to see Ongel, he didn't want to see Annalise, and he didn't want to see Wick. His anger was more than enough company to fill the silence. Finally, he found some abandoned gazebo. A few of the posts were crumbling, and dead leaves covered the floor, but it was enough shelter for now. Archer threw his bag into the depths of the gazebo and sank down at the base of the entryway.

In one day, it had all fallen apart again.

He didn't know if he ever wanted to see his family again.

The anger lasted him long enough to throw a few chunks of wood, send them hurtling into the forest, and then the hollowness set in. He curled up in a ball under one of the gazebo's benches and tried to sleep off the pain the way he always did. Though he would never admit it, he may have shed a few tears.

When sleep did come, the emptiness and darkness were a welcome distraction.

CHAPTER TWENTY-ONE:

A List of Things That Went Wrong

IT WAS MID-AFTERNOON before Wick got up the courage to face anyone again. He sat in the back sitting room the host had kindly shown him, hiding in the quiet and trying to think of what he would say to the others.

To be honest, he still didn't know what to say. The facts were just as they appeared to be, and he couldn't bend them into a shape that seemed heroic or even decent. He and Archer had agreed together to revert to their old ways because his people didn't want to see him, let alone listen to him. And now the worst had happened.

No. The worst was still on its way.

He stared at the back of his hand as the skin's tone fluctuated between light brown and ashy grey, and he almost wanted to laugh. No wonder Archer was always worried. It seemed so inhuman, and it looked so drastic. But it really did appear on the outside the way he felt inside. Maybe that was why it was frightening.

Finally, he got up the courage to go talk to Ongel and the others. Maybe together they could come up with a solution. When he ventured out of the back sitting room, he found all the centaurs standing in the front hall, speaking in low voices.

"What's the damage?" Wick asked, approaching hesitantly.

Their heads turned toward him, and he noticed with relief that their expressions were more tired than hostile.

"The manghar have left for good," Hirim said. "The nixies are reconsidering their allegiance, as are the satyrs. And you saw the leshy. The others are waiting until our meeting in an hour to decide, but at this point, everything is hanging in the balance."

"What a mess," Wick murmured.

"It is a mess," Ongel agreed, nodding. His eyes slid over to Wick. "Can you offer any kind of explanation?"

Anxiety spiked through Wick's veins, but he did his best to fight it back. "It's like Archer said, unfortunately. We couldn't see any way around it, so we stole the leshy piece. They never agreed to give it to us. But I'm still certain that if we had asked, they would have said no, or worse, they might have tried to hunt us down. They told the truth about my banishment from my home territory. I'm not allowed back."

Some of their eyes became pitying.

"It's not that either of us thought it was right," Wick said. "We just thought it was necessary. We were running out of time. I couldn't see another option."

"Wick." Ongel approached Wick and placed his hands on Wick's heavy shoulders. "You should have asked me for help. You could have asked any of us for our help; that's why we came. If you had told me you were so desperate, we could have helped you come up with a plan that worked."

Wick couldn't respond.

"Did you know that the same day you and Archer left to speak to the leshy—well, I know now that it was to take the leshy stone—I had planned to get letters of personal testimony from all of the representatives and send them to the leshy? I know that your people are often disconnected from the rest of Aro, but I thought if nothing else could convince the royal family, the word of the other races could. But you never gave me that chance."

Wick's shame only deepened. "I didn't know. And I didn't ask. I should have. But we were both scared that the time would come and we would be defenseless. It was foolish to act on our own, but it's too late to take it back, so I expect we'll have to make do with the consequences."

"I see," Ongel said. He was silent for a long moment. "That's what we'll tell the others, then. They'll most likely want to hear it from you, not any of us. And Archer as well, I would suspect. Where is Archer?"

Wick shrugged helplessly. "He disappeared."

"I asked at the Hessen house," Eland said. "His father said he left a few hours ago, and they haven't seen him since."

"I have no clue where he would be," Wick murmured. "This is his city. And according to his brother, he has hiding places all over. He could be in any number of places. We could search the city top to bottom and probably never find him."

No sooner had the words left his mouth than the door swung open.

*

"HEY," ARCHER SAID.

Wick looked tired and anxious, but his brow wrinkled. "What happened to you?"

Archer took a good look at himself in the mirror across the hall. Streaks of dirt ran down his face and clothes, and a few leaves stuck out of his hair. Red imprints marked the side of his face where it had rested on the floor of the gazebo. Only his bag appeared to be clean.

"Nothing much," Archer said, dropping his bag by the door and walking over to stand beside Wick. "I just watched my life fall apart for the second time since we started this whole thing, and now I'm not allowed to go home, either. We're in the same boat again, you and me." He paused. "And then Fowl came and found me because he's rotten like that, and we got in a fight. He hit me."

"Did you hit him first?" Wick asked.

"Maybe. Probably. I don't know." Archer shrugged. "What are we doing?"

"We have to decide how we're going to offer an explanation to the remaining representatives," Hirim said, and the others nodded.

Archer chewed his lip and then asked, "What would you suggest?"

"Well, how would you explain yourself?" Ongel asked. Archer looked at him in surprise, realizing no one had ever asked him to explain. They always accused, assumed, and moved on. He had never realized how nice it would be for someone to ask.

"There's not much to say," Archer admitted. "I thought our only option was to steal the Oak Leaf, and I thought there was no other way. I know it was a bad idea, and it looks bad since all the representatives trusted us when they didn't have to. But it's too late to change it now. I guess they'll have to live with it."

The side of Wick's mouth quirked. "Up until the end, you almost had something there."

"And what would *you* say, oh special one?" Archer asked. The group looked at Wick.

"You said almost everything there is to say," Wick responded. "It was like that, and I agreed with you. We did it together, and we're both to blame."

"Then that's what you'll say to the representatives," Ongel said. "I'll call them together." With that, he left them and climbed back up the stairs with the other centaurs in his wake.

"Archer," Wick said. "We have to fix this."

"You think I don't know that?" Archer kicked at imaginary dirt on the floor. "It's worse than that, too. I tried to read through Caihu's journal with Ongel, and we found some cryptic notes he left behind about all of this. It wasn't very helpful, but he did tell us we needed all the stones to succeed. And I think if we need the stones, we need the people too. We need all the people behind us if we're going to do this."

"I agree," Wick said. "It makes me wary, but I know we need them. What we need to do, we can't do on our own. Our biggest leaps and bounds have been with the help of others. We can't do this without them."

Archer knew Wick was right. He had been making almost no headway before Ongel arrived to help, and they had made more progress as a result of visiting his friends in human territory than they had anywhere else. Even Annalise and her ringing endorsement to Otho had been a huge help in the fair folk assembly. Everyone they had met in the last few weeks had improved their chances I some way. The manghar and their willingness only a few hours ago to hunt down the dragonkin now looked so different in Archer's mind. For only a little bit of time, they had created an alliance with the manghar, something they had originally thought would be impossible.

He looked at Wick. "We have to get them back. I don't know how we're going to do it, but we have to get everyone back together if we're going to do this."

"I'll go to the leshy," Wick said. "If I'm going to part ways with my people, I'll do it on good terms. And I want to see my friend Twill. Other than my family, she's the only one I can't do without. I want her on my side."

"Hmm, but that leaves me with the manghar," Archer said. "I'm banned, remember?"

"So am I. I'm banned from my own territory, and thanks to you, I've promised never to go back into manghar territory. And do you really think you'd do any better in leshy territory?"

Archer sighed. "No. But if I come back in a box, I'm blaming you."

"If you come back in a box, I'm blaming *you*," Wick said. "Are you going to patch things up with your family before you go?"

Archer avoided Wick's eyes. "There's nothing to patch. They'll be fine."

"All right," Wick said at last. "Well, let's go upstairs and explain ourselves. Then we'll leave right after."

Explanations to the representatives went about as well as expected.

"I think your apology is genuine," said the satyr Kanri. "And I want to believe you, but how do we know that you won't do anything like this again?"

Both Archer and Wick were at a loss for words. "I. . . guess you can't," Archer said. "Our word won't mean anything. But stranger things have happened. The nixies used to be enemies with the manghar, and now they've been allies with the manghar for a long time."

"A hundred years," Wick murmured.

The nixies strangely looked interested. Kanri's expression didn't change, but at least Archer could assure himself that he hadn't made anything worse.

"I know," Wick began slowly, "that there isn't much of a foundation to believe on, especially with how things have gone recently, but the best I can offer is that we're learning from our mistakes and trying to do better. Once we're through talking to you, we're leaving to work things out with the manghar and the leshy if we can. We're doing our best."

"I will say this," Otho's son said, getting up from his seat on the arm of a plush chair. "I hardly know either of you, but I'm drawn to believe you. If you were only after the Heather Stones for your own gain, there would be no point in trying to regain all our trust like this. You had all the stones a few hours ago, and I think that if you were going to do something ill with them, you would have done it while you had the opportunity."

None of the other representatives argued with him.

"We should go so we can get to the territories and back," Wick said, "but we'll let you think about it while we're gone. We'll be back in about six days or so."

With their explanations made and their bags still packed from that morning, Wick and Archer split up their separate directions.

"Good luck," Archer said.

"You never need it," Wick said. "Why would I?"

Archer adjusted the unfillable bag on his shoulder. "I don't know, I might take the luck this time. The manghar might still want me dead."

Under normal circumstances, Wick probably would have laughed, but this time he just forced a smile.

They looked like such an odd pair. As if Wick didn't normally look odd enough, he was now carrying the Door in the Wall, which the centaurs had retrieved from the valley for them on their last visit. He said he planned to use it to skip over hills and through larger obstacles so he could travel more quickly and make a quick escape if necessary. Archer, as always, was a seraph that never flew and had an unfillable bag that he kept all manner of things in, including the horse that he planned to ride halfway to manghar territory once he was out of the forest. If he had to make a quick escape of his own, he would probably do it the way he normally did: by running for dear life.

They wished one another good luck again and went in opposite directions.

CHAPTER TWENTY-TWO:
Archer Versus the Manghar, Once Again

THE MOMENT MANGHAR territory came into view, Archer's heart began beating a mile a minute. He had already put Sasha back into the bag and had it back over his shoulder with his knuckles turning white on the strap. If the manghar took the bag from him, he didn't know what he would do.

When the border came into view through the trees, he could see that the number of guards had gone back to normal, but there was still no way he would get through without one of them noticing. He hadn't expected to sneak through, but he still didn't like the alternative. "Uh, hi," he called through the trees as he approached. "I'm here to—"

Claws grabbed him from above and scooped him up into the air. The talons dug directly into the burns from the dragonkin. Archer went thrashing the whole way, yelling for them to "Watch the arms, watch the arms!" For a terrible moment, he thought they would take him straight into the pit of spikes. But then he realized they were instead flying toward the part of the palace where the throne room was.

Archer was going to have yet another trial. The manghar had to be sick of holding trials for him by now. To be honest, he was sick of attending them himself.

He wondered if the manghar still wanted to kill him.

Then he wondered if the manghar guards he had made into enemies over the years still wanted him dead.

Then he wondered if the other manghar would spare him even if the Crowned Head did. It wouldn't take long to find out.

The manghar carrying him dove through an open window and threw him across the throne room floor. Archer hit the floor on his shoulder and went rolling. His bag thumped across his ribs. Finally, he came to a stop in the middle of the room.

"Ouch. Thanks a lot."

The up-close view of the flagstone floor was getting familiar by now. Slowly he sat up, his burned arms throbbing, trying to both avoid further abuse and get his bearings.

"You've come back," a voice said.

Archer's nerves electrified. That voice was too close. His eyes leaped up. Across from him, only steps away, loomed the Crowned Head.

"Are you here to steal something else?" the Crowned Head asked, tightening his grip on the arms of his throne. It looked even bigger and more ornate than when Archer had seen it last. It also appeared to be bolted to the floor. Apparently they hadn't forgotten how easily Archer had stolen the throne on his last visit to this room.

"Actually, no?" Archer got up, wincing when a

bruised calf had to take his weight again. "I'm here to apologize."

The manghar in the throne room laughed. Archer sighed and waited for them to stop.

The Crowned Head stopped laughing with a snap of his jaw and lurched forward on the throne. Archer fought the urge to jump away. The Crowned Head stared him down through fiery eyes. "I am in no mood to accept any apologies."

Archer hesitated, then decided to go ahead with it. "Well, too bad. I have one anyway, and you're getting it whether you want it or not."

The Crowned Head tilted his chin, his face an empty mask.

"I don't know if you read any of the letters I sent you," Archer said, "but I did send you a couple. I think I said that Wick and I saw the error of our ways and wanted to do better. That's why I'm here, because we're trying to do better. Stealing things again was all my idea and it was wrong."

"And that is why we don't want your apologies," the Crowned Head said. He leaned back on his throne again. "The tree messenger I could forgive. I was disappointed in him, but he's too careful and discerning to make such a mistake on his own. It's your influence that ruined him."

Archer's temper flared. "I didn't ruin him." He forced his tone to be even. "He's struggling, but he knows more now than he ever did. He's a fuller person now, all because of me."

"You did ruin him," the Crowned Head said. "He's just another Archer now."

"He's not," Archer repeatí. "He's someone else, and he's going to be someone else still. He's still changing.

And I know that some of the parts of him that changed looked an awful lot like the worst parts of me. I didn't like seeing that happen any more than you did. I didn't like watching him act erratic and violent and careless. But he's not done reinventing himself yet, I can tell. He's still working on it. Someday soon he's going to be a force of nature all by himself, you wait and see, and if we're lucky enough, you and I might be around to see it. Just wait for him."

The Crowned Head said nothing for a moment, seeming to study Archer. "You seem to care about the messenger a great deal. I agree with you, he could turn out for the better. But what can you say to prove that *currently*, you are honorable enough for us to join your cause again?"

Archer tried to come up with a good reason. But everything Wick told him to say before he left Tor turned to vapor in his mind. None of it sounded like what the Crowned Head probably wanted to hear. "I. . . don't know."

"As I thought," the Crowned Head said dismissively. "No, we won't join you again."

"Hey!" Archer instantly leaped to his own defense as the guards started moving in. "I know we messed up, but you were completely on board a few days ago! You can't give us another chance?"

The Crowned Head waved the guards back to their positions by the doors and windows. His fingers tapped against the arm of his throne for a moment. "You may not know this, seraph, but the manghar are not a well-trusted race. We are perhaps the most disliked race in all of Aro, and that is greatly deserved. We don't like most of the other races, either. They're weak and won't protect themselves when their lands need defending. We are allies with the nixies, and the nixies like us well enough, but the others only tolerate us. You're right when you say that you made a critical mistake in stealing the leshy piece of the heather stone, but it wasn't the only reason my representatives withdrew from your cause."

Archer's brow furrowed. He hadn't heard anything about this before now.

"Yes, my representatives were invited to your territory and given a place to stay alongside the other representatives, but they did not feel welcome. The other representatives wanted nothing to do with them, and everyone seemed to shy away from them when they approached. They did not feel welcome or important. But for your sake, and the sake of their people, they stayed. And while it's true that they left because they felt they couldn't trust you, they were also more than happy to return to a place where they felt valued."

Watch over the manghar; they need your help even more than you need theirs.

It hadn't been a threat after all.

"I—" Archer didn't even know where to start. He had dashed in and out of manghar territory so many times over the years, crossed paths with them so often, but he had never thought that they had emotions other than rage and violence. And he had certainly never considered that maybe they felt. . . lonely in seraph territory. Like outsiders.

For the first time in his life, he found that he knew what to say.

"Here's the thing," Archer said. He hesitated, then took a few steps closer to the throne. He was only a few feet from the Crowned Head now. If the bat king stood up, they could have reached out and touched each other. "I didn't know that they felt unwelcome, and if they did, I'm sorry. Like I said, I didn't know. But I can understand that feeling." He didn't normally like sharing anything about himself because it left him feeling too exposed, but to get the trust of the Crowned Head back, he would. "I've never been on good terms with my family or any of the seraphs, and to be honest, I've never felt very welcome in their territory, either. I always leave as quickly as I can. I don't like it there."

The Crowned Head said nothing. Archer wasn't sure if the bat was getting anything he said. But Archer kept talking.

"But I've been there, using it as my base of operations for a month and a half now. I don't like it with my family any more now than I did before, but I've found some good people there. It's not all bad." He cringed a little bit. "And this doesn't sound like me—normally I wouldn't say something like this—but if there are good people in Tor, I think we can assume that there are good people scattered all over the place, in every territory. Even among the reps. Everywhere."

The Crowned Head's chin had tilted a few degrees. There was a look in his eyes that gave Archer a bit of hope.

"I'm not much of an advocate that everyone is good. I think a lot of people are awful and that's the truth of it. But there are more good people in this country than I thought, and if there's any reason I'm doing this other than because Wick said so, it's because I want to see what all those people do with their lives. I wouldn't have cared about all that a while ago, but I've seen Wick do so much, and his friends, and even people I don't know. I want to see where all of them are going. They're worth the effort it takes, even if that's a lot of effort, and it is. It's worth it." Suddenly Archer realized he hadn't inhaled in far too long, and he took a deep breath. His lungs thanked him for it. He looked to the Crowned Head for his reaction. "That's all I have to say."

The Crowned Head said nothing at first. Then he shifted. He planted both palms on his armrests and got up out of his throne. Now he and Archer faced one another, the bat man towering over Archer with his superior height and breadth. "Is that the only reason?" he asked.

Archer's heart sank a little. "It's the only one I can think of."

"Good," the Crowned Head said. "If you had any other reason, I would have considered it less worthy. I think the tree has made you like him, just as you made him like you. Another Wick."

"Nah," Archer said. "Only the good parts of him."

"That may be," the Crowned Head replied with a nod. "Well then, seraph, you made a good case. You've convinced me."

Archer blinked. "I have?" Then he remembered himself and boldly stuck out his hand to shake. "Then are we allies again?"

"We are. I think I'll accompany you myself, this time, and if those fiery creatures of yours think they can cross us, let us see what happens to them!" With a bright gleam in his eyes, the Crowned Head caught up Archer's hand and shook it with a grip like a vise.

Archer thought his hand might break, but he couldn't get the smile off his face.

CHAPTER TWENTY-THREE:

Trees Hold Grudges

"PLEASE, LISTEN to me!" Wick begged, but the leshy royals would have none of it. One of them called the guards to remove him from the palace. Knowing they would throw him out of the territory, Wick ran. Once again, he managed to shake them off and hid in the bare bushes of someone's garden until the heat died down.

When the guards were gone at last, he looked around and realized he was on his own street. He slipped out of the garden to dash down the road and into his house.

"Wick!" his sister's voice exclaimed. She stood up from her chair. "What are you doing back? They'll catch you, and you have another trial now that they want you for."

"I know," Wick said. "I was just in it. It wasn't pretty."

"Your face really is different," his sister said, trying for humor but ending up with something that sounded too much like criticism.

"Yeah," Wick said, dragging a hand down the side of

his face. "Where are our parents?"

"Work and visiting a friend on the other side of the village," his sister said. "Why? You didn't want to see me?" She sounded hurt.

"No, no," Wick said, wrapping his arms around her shoulders and squeezing her tight. "I just wanted to tell them something. But it's good to see you, too. How has everything been?"

"I found a job," she said, letting him go and sitting back. "I'm going to be an artist, like Twill. I'll be doing paintings and glassblowing to sell to the royal family and the other territories, too."

"That sounds good."

"Oh. And I'm not going by Lif anymore," she added, referring to her childhood nickname. "Everyone started calling me Reesa again at school, and I like it."

"It sounds so grown-up," Wick said, but his mind was on something else. Twill. Even if he couldn't be on good terms with the rest of his people, he wanted to reconcile himself to Twill. "Is Twill home today?"

"I think so," his sister said.

Wick took another look out the door. No one appeared to be on the road. "Then come on." Together they ran out the door and down the street further to Twill's dwelling, where she lived alone. She said she preferred the quiet over living with anyone else, even her family, though she visited them often.

They raced through the door and Wick got away from the windows as quickly as he could. "Twill!" he called down the hall.

"Wick?" Twill's head appeared from a doorway.

"It's me," Wick said.

Twill stepped fully into the hall, her arms full of

paintbrushes and paper. "What do you want?"

The accusation in her tone cut like a knife. Wick braced himself. "I came to speak to the royal family again, and I wanted to see anyone else I could while I was here. Neither of my parents are home, so I came to see you."

"And you brought Reesa," Twill said, her eyes flickering toward Wick's sister.

"Yes. I don't have a lot of time, so I'm keeping her with me until I leave." Wick looped an arm around Reesa's shoulders and squeezed once, all while trying his best to look Twill in the eye. "Twill, I wanted to say I'm sorry. I know this wasn't how you wanted this to turn out for me."

"You think that's why I'm angry?" Twill demanded. She released the art supplies. Brushes and papers clattered and splattered all over the floor of the dwelling. Wick jumped back.

"I'm not angry because you got in trouble; I'm angry because you didn't take me with you!" Twill shouted. "I know, you were on this great important mission, and you weren't supposed to tell anyone, but you knew how much I would have wanted to know! Actually, no. I wouldn't have cared if you told me what your oh-so-important mission was, but I would have cared to know that you weren't a traitor. I know you weren't just following orders. You were doing something big, something I don't even understand, and I didn't get to be a part of it. I'm one of your only real friends in the whole world, and you didn't tell me a thing! I would have gladly cheered you on or slapped some sense into you, but what did you say? Nothing!"

"Twill, please let me apologize," Wick said.

Twill fished through a cupboard and slapped a piece of paper in Wick's hand. It was a carefully, beautifully drawn map of Aro, marked with arching lines and little zigzags across the country. "I can't even tell you how hard it was to find out where you'd been. I questioned everyone I saw. And after all that, what did I find but that you must have passed by us three times or more, and you never came to even tell me what was going on." Twill's eyes burned bright and hot. Wick had never seen her this worked up.

"I'm not angry about what you did, I'm angry because I didn't know what it was," Twill snapped. "And when I saw you had come back again, but not to see me, it made it even worse. I didn't want to even see you anymore then. It took me a week to stop being angry, and then I was just hurt. Now, if you have an explanation, it had better be good. And you had better get talking, before someone comes looking for you here." With that, Twill snatched the map back and slapped it back in the cupboard. Then she faced Wick and crossed her arms, silent.

"Really, I'm sorry," Wick said. "I don't know how I managed to pass by so many times without telling you anything. I did want to see you when I came back through before. But that visit didn't go the way I planned." He paused. "It didn't go well at all, actually. If you can stand the sight of me any longer, I'll tell you everything that happened."

The three of them sat on the floor as Wick rehashed everything that had happened across the last few months, everything he and Archer had discovered, and how it had resulted. Some of it Twill already knew from rumors and hearsay, but most of it was a surprise both to her and Reesa.

"And this is the form you chose," Twill mused. She looked Wick up and down. "It's interesting, that's for sure."

"I had to choose details on the spur of the moment," Wick admitted. "I didn't have a lot of time to think things through. I think that's why I ended up with these." He pointed to his yellowish eyes. "I didn't pick a color."

"I still wouldn't have changed," Twill said, leaning back against the wall. "I like myself the way I am."

"And I like myself the way I am now," Wick said. "Even if it isn't strictly what I planned on. Besides, the change is permanent, so what other choice do I have?"

Twill tilted her head at him. "Now there's an answer I wouldn't have heard before. You've changed. You're more sure of yourself. I like it."

"Thank you."

"What now? You don't have the Oak Leaf, you didn't get the royal family to believe you. What are you going to do now?"

"Well, to be honest," Wick said, "we never lost the Oak Leaf."

"Excuse me?"

"We didn't," Wick said. "Most of the stones were distributed to the representatives for safekeeping, and we planted fake stones in the case to fool the dragonkin if they stole it. Only a few of the races were confident enough to leave their stone in the case. Since I was our only leshy, I had ours in my pocket the whole time. When the other leshy showed up to take it back. . . I don't know. I was still so afraid of failure that I didn't tell them that the one they were taking was only a replica. I know it was probably wrong."

"I don't think you did a thing wrong." Twill's eyes narrowed. "But where did you get all those replicas?"

"Archer's brother rounded them up for us. I don't know who he gets to make them, but they were ready in one morning."

"Impressive," Twill said. She thought for a moment. "Well then, if you still have the Oak Leaf, I suppose all you need is a leshy representative. Will I do?"

Wick's heart leaped. "You want to?"

"Of course I want to. You need someone from this territory on your side. And just because I didn't want to be a messenger like you doesn't mean that I hate traveling. Yes, I want to come."

"Can I come, too?" Reesa blurted. "Please?"

"I wish you could," Wick said. He turned to his sister. "Really I do. But if I took you with me there might be all kinds of upheaval. The last thing either of us needs is people thinking you were kidnapped. Stay here and take care of our parents for me. Try to convince them that I'm not a traitor."

Reesa looked more than a little disappointed, but she reluctantly agreed.

"Well, come on, Wick, let's move," Twill said, getting up. "If you're in as big of a rush as all that, we'd better start running."

*

ARCHER SPOTTED WICK coming down the street before Wick ever saw him. "Tree!" he shouted, waving an arm above his head.

Wick looked up and waved back. By his side was some tall, slender leshy that Archer didn't recognize. Wick said something to her.

They met in the middle of the street.

"Good job!" Archer said, bounding to Wick's side. "What did you say to get your royals back on your side?"

"A lot of things. None of them worked," Wick said, a little dismally. "But we still have the Oak Leaf, and Twill is willing to be our leshy representative. I think I've met yours," he added with a raise of his eyebrows.

At first, Wick's friend Twill looked a little intimidated by the sight of the Crowned Head, but before Archer's eyes, she squared her shoulders and erased the fear from her eyes. "*I* don't know who he is."

It took all of Archer's will to squelch a laugh as Wick's spine tensed. Clearly, Wick made friends with a lot of outspoken people.

Archer took charge of the introductions himself. "This," he said, gesturing to the Crowned Head, "Is Crowned Head Theodore. You know, the ruler of the manghar people."

Twill looked the manghar up and down. "Interesting."

Her attitude filled Archer with glee. This Twill was a kindred spirit and a challenger.

Together he and Wick brought Twill, the Crowned Head, and the Crowned Head's three personal guards to the Rep House and told them where to find their rooms. With the others gone, they both collapsed onto the couches in the house's little back sitting room.

Wick had hardly sat down before Archer said, "You got someone on your side after all."

"So did you," Wick said. He laughed a little. "How did you get the Crowned Head himself to come all the way here?"

Archer shrugged his shoulders, mystified. "I still don't know how I didn't get murdered the minute I stepped over their border."

"I don't understand it either," Wick said. "By rights, they should have killed you on sight. All the same, we're running out of time. We'd better get everyone together so we can leave."

Ah. Archer felt a little flutter of unease in his chest as he held up a finger to interrupt. "About that."

"What now?"

"You don't need me to come with you to the valley." Archer picked at a loose thread on the sleeve of his shirt. "I'll stay here. If the dragonkin army is as close as we think, then they could burn up anything they like between now and when you arrive in the valley. I'm going to stay here and protect my grandfather's house. Some of the others can stay as well if they want to. The manghar would probably want to protect something."

"You don't want to come?" Wick asked, visibly baffled.

"My grandfather's house is the closest thing I ever had to a home," Archer said. "It was more home for me than my house ever was. I don't want anything bad to happen to it."

Wick was silent for a moment. "I understand," he said at last. "I'm happy to leave you here so that you can do that. But please be careful."

"Be careful yourself," Archer said, relieved that Wick hadn't tried to talk him out of it. "I'm not the one who'll have a target on my back. By the way, Caihu's notes said something about you. He said to keep an eye out overhead while you're returning the stones to the cavern. Something is going to come from above you."

Wick nodded. "I'll keep an eye on the sky." He started to get up.

"It's funny," Archer said. "Most people don't even speak their people's old languages anymore, not since we all banded up and decided to make the centaur language our common language. But my parents made me learn the old seraph language anyway."

Wick waited for him to get to the point.

"I've forgotten most of it by now," Archer went on, staring at the blue sky from the window across from his seat, "but there was this one word that I liked because we don't have anything like it in the common language. It's *skorffv*. It's the moment between flying and falling, when you aren't rising anymore but gravity hasn't yet taken hold. It's a moment where disaster is imminent but nothing is impossible. That's where we're at right now, you and me, and all of them, too. Failure is staring us in the face, but here we are trying anyway because we know that right now there's nothing that can stop us."

"That sounds right," Wick said. Then he smiled. "Even if we are destined to fail, we've come too far to give up now."

"Agreed." Archer got up too. "Well, you'd better go get everyone."

As Wick left the room, Archer tried not to think about how if all of this went wrong, he might not see his closest friend ever again.

In the end, the manghar were hired by the Hessen family to guard their house and surrounding street. The rest of the city was split up into sections, each guarded by a different group of volunteer seraphs. There wasn't much for Archer to do, so he saw Wick and the others off and walked to Eri alone. When he arrived a few hours later, he found that it was much hotter than he would have normally expected from autumn. The air felt strangely steamy hot.

He met his grandfather's caretaker at the door of the house. "They're on their way to cast the spell right now," he told the caretaker, "but I don't know if they'll get there before the dragonkin army arrives. I'm going to protect the house. Are you with me?"

"The house won't come to harm on my watch," the caretaker said grimly.

They both broke hefty branches off the trees and slung them over their shoulders to wait for the first of the dragonkin.

CHAPTER TWENTY-FOUR:

Soldiers With Sticks

WITH THE HELP of the horses, they traveled much faster than Wick expected, but was it fast enough? If the dragonkin arrived before they could reach the valley, he didn't know if they would make it there at all. The dragonkin were so large and so fast. They could catch and kill their whole party in minutes.

Ongel ran beside Wick's horse. "Can we push it any faster?" Wick asked him.

"I'm worried we'll wear the horses out," Ongel said. "I'm already getting tired myself. But then, I'm not as young as I used to be. We'll just have to maintain this speed and hope it's enough."

Wick glanced over his shoulder at the sky. Despite it being midday, a strange orange glow lit the western part of the sky.

He didn't like it.

*

THE AIR GREW HOTTER. If Archer squinted into

the distance, he could see shimmers of heat rising from the ground. As much as he hated shoes, he couldn't help but think that shoes would help the burning soles of his feet.

So far, even though he was keeping an eye out in every direction, nothing had appeared. But every breaking twig in the forest made him jump.

He thought back on the last conversation he had with his father before leaving Tor.

"You're not going with them?" Ochre had demanded. "Why not?"

"Because I'm going to look after the house in Eri. You might not want it, but I do, and I'm going to protect it."

Ochre towered over Archer. "This was your opportunity to make a name for yourself! You could have gone with them, you could have taken back a slice of the glory. Your name would have gone down in the history books and been remembered by every person in this country for hundreds of years!"

Archer lifted his chin. "That's why I'm not going. That right there, what you just described, that's what you would do. I don't want anything to do with what you would do."

"Is it so awful to want to be remembered and revered?" his father hissed.

"Yes," Archer said. "If it costs all that it cost this family, it's not worth it. And I'm doing everything I can to avoid following your example. So I'm doing this."

"You are going with them," his father growled.

"No." Archer looked at his father with a practiced empty expression. "I'm going to Eri to protect your father's house, like it or not, because that's what I would do. I'm not asking permission. I just wanted to tell you where I was going." As he stepped out of his father's study, his mother met him at the door.

"Please be careful, whatever you do," she said, embracing him.

"I will. But you be careful, too." Archer cast a look over his shoulder. *"I don't think he would put you or Fowl in harm's way, but you never know. Keep an eye on the sky. Big things are coming."*

His mother nodded and her hands glided down his arms to clasp his hands. "I love you, my son."

Archer paused a moment. "I love you, too. Bye." Then he darted for the door.

Archer shifted his stance as the ground under his feet grew even hotter.

His conversation with Fowl had gone no better.

"I don't see why you want to protect an empty house when you could be protecting the very stones that ensure our survival," Fowl said when Archer met him at the base of the tree.

"Those things that want the stones are bigger and scarier than you think," Archer responded. "If they attack everyone that's traveling to the valley, I wouldn't make much of a difference. I can't even fly. I wouldn't be useful to them. So I'm going to be useful somewhere else."

Fowl shook his head. "Do what you like." He hefted a heavy mace over his shoulder and faced the street.

Fowl had been put in charge of the manghar and the others protecting the Hessen house and the rest of the street. Archer was certain he would be fine on his own.

And if he wasn't, nothing could save him then.

*

THE SUN STARTED to slide down the other side of the sky when they reached the valley. By now the air was hot and dry and the clouds writhed in grey masses above them. Occasionally a flash of orange would appear in the clouds, then disappear again. As he watched the sky, Wick started to worry that something out there was only playing with them. Already they had seen something large dart through the forest a hundred yards from them. That had made them increase their speed.

As they reached the peak of the mountains and started down the other side, the first of the dragonkin lunged from the trees.

With a roar, their only manghar removed his crown and took up his sword.

*

THE TREETOPS BURST into flames.

Archer leaped to his feet as something rocketed from the sky, heading straight for him. He raised his branch club and swung at it, hitting the dragonkin in the side of the head. The thing roared, its neck bent sideways. It shot back up toward the sky and disappeared into the clouds. Two more came in its place.

After two whole days of nothing, dragons dropped on the city like fiery rain.

As he waited for the next attack, Archer realized that this was not the army he had been promised. He had expected the creatures to come in droves, but the dragonkin were only appearing in small groups. They weren't nearly as big as he remembered, either. Were these just the forerunners?

He could only guess. But judging from the hotness of the air, more were still to come.

Archer snatched up his stick again as another dragon

plunged from the clouds. As he fended it away, another plowed into him from the side, knocking him off his feet. Claws dug into his shoulders as heat from the dragonkin's mouth rolled over Archer's face. His stick flew out of his hands, landing out of reach behind his head.

One of the other seraphs who had volunteered to protect the house attacked the dragonkin from the side, bringing his weapon down full force on the dragon's neck.

The creature shrieked and pulled back. It snapped at the other seraph, but Archer grabbed his own stick and jabbed at it from the other side. Now thoroughly overwhelmed and disoriented, the dragonkin disappeared.

Immediately, another three flew down. They were relentless. Archer didn't know how they could fight them all with only sticks and fists.

He raised his makeshift club to catch a dragonkin between the teeth as it came after him with jaws open.

Then he caught a glimpse of something glowing orange off in the distance, brighter than anything else in the sky. His arms struggled to keep the dragonkin at bay while his eyes searched for whatever was shining so brightly and so ominously. When he made sense of what he was seeing, his grip on the wood tightened.

It was a group of at least thirty dragonkin flying straight over Eri, headed for Tor.

That was why he had seen so few dragonkin. Eri wasn't their target. They were really aiming for Tor. Archer cursed his own stupidity. The scout dragon, Ryga, had seen Wick and Archer come and go from Tor, and might have seen the representatives arriving one by one, too. It might even have known they were keeping the stones there not too long ago.

And he had left Fowl there to defend their house by

himself.

Archer was in the wrong city.

Ducking the grabbing jaws of the creature in front of him, he punched it in the side of the head, kicked it in the leg, and looked around for his grandfather's caretaker.

On the other side of the house, almost out of view, stood the caretaker, with a dragonkin dropping on him from above.

Archer threw his stick, catching the descending dragonkin on the jaw and at last drawing blood. A bright, hot liquid poured from the creature's cheek as it screamed its rage. The dragonkin hadn't fled. Weaponless, Archer made a quick decision. He charged the dragonkin with the scream of a lunatic.

The dragonkin scrambled backward with fear in its eyes and took off into the sky. With it gone, Archer grabbed the caretaker by the shoulders. Both of them were covered in dirt, soot, and the smell of fear.

"I've got to go back to Tor. I need to make sure my family is okay. Can you and your friends look after the house on your own?"

The caretaker shook his head with a look of fear in his eyes. "We're barely handling it as it is. We'll be overwhelmed soon."

"Then forget about it," Archer said. "There are other people in Eri who probably need your help. Take care of them. And if the house burns—" He looked up at his grandfather's house and blew out a little sigh— "then let it go."

The distress in the caretaker's face was the same that Archer felt squeezing in his chest, but other things mattered more right now. The caretaker nodded.

The two of them raced in their separate directions.

Archer found a space between some tree roots and opened the flap of his unfillable bag to let Sasha out. Sasha's eyes widened in alarm as she took in the fire and the fighting around her, but she didn't bolt.

Archer grabbed her bridle and looked back at the house. Two dragonkin slithered headfirst down the sides. Flames reflected in the glass windows.

Archer's heart ached. The child inside of him didn't want to let go. Couldn't. In that house he had been welcomed, and given kisses for his fresh scrapes, and laughed the pain away, and eaten the best apple pies, and helped with his schoolwork, and had his clothes mended and his nightmares soothed and given the hugs and care and affection that his father couldn't muster and his mother didn't understand he needed. He didn't want to let it go.

But as sparks rained down around him and his horse, it finally sank in: the reason he had felt loved in that house was already gone.

"I'm sorry I couldn't do better for you," he told the house. "I'm sorry I was too late to say goodbye. But if I don't get to Fowl, I'm just going to do this all over again."

The dragonkin crawling down the house turned toward him, and Archer lunged back behind the tree. "Come on, girl, we have to get to Tor as fast as we can." He swung up onto Sasha's back. "Let's go!"

As a pair they took off through the city, heading for Tor.

*

THEY WERE DOWN by several members of their party by now. The Crowned Head had long since left to draw a group of dragonkin away from the others, and all the nixies were off fighting dragonkin across the valley. The two satyrs and anyone else with a weapon hovered at the edges of their group, fending off dragonkin as they came.

Wick didn't have a weapon, but he wished he did. A club would be useful. He ducked the biting jaw of another dragonkin, and Kanri knocked the lizard out of the sky with her axe.

The entrance to the cavern wasn't far. Wick hadn't seen it since their release from prison, and he only now realized repairs were still going on. Supports held the roof of the tunnel where Archer had collapsed most of it a few weeks ago.

The thought gave him part of an idea.

"We need to knock the entrance in again," he shouted to Ongel as the sounds of clashing weapons around them increased. "If we don't, they'll just come in after us."

"I agree," Ongel yelled.

Just before they reached the entrance, three massive dragonkin dropped down between them and the cavern, blocking their path. Necks long, flaming wings stretching, eyes glowing bright, they seemed to dare any of the party to move closer.

Then the Crowned Head, who Wick had thought was still busy on the other side of the valley, leaped over the party with his wings outstretched and a war cry bellowing from his open mouth. He landed square on top of one of the dragonkin. All three were disoriented as they tried to grab hold of the new projectile. The one whose back the manghar had landed on writhed its spine, trying to throw him. But the Crowned Head hung on with both hands, digging his claws into the dragonkin's back. The creature snapped its head back and forth, trying to reach far enough back to bite the bat clinging to its back. The king would allow no such thing.

One of the others reached its head over to snap at the Crowned Head and help its companion, but the king raised his weapon at the last moment, stabbing the second dragonkin in the eye. The second one lurched backward, screeching and clawing at its eye.

Without meaning to, the creatures lurched apart, creating a gap that wouldn't last long.

"Come on!" Wick hissed, and they all dashed toward the gap. Only some of them made it. Before the last five or so of their guards could make it through, the dragons suddenly realized what they had done and slithered over to block the gap. One of them thrust its head inside the tunnel to snap after the people that had escaped.

"Keep going!" Kanri called, stopping in her tracks with Frost right behind her. "We'll stay here and collapse the entrance."

"I'll stay as well," said Otho's son.

Wick, Ongel, and Eland raced down the tunnel together. Wick spotted the tension in Eland's brow as they ran. They had lost track of Hirim ages ago as they were making their way through the middle of the valley. He had grabbed the neck of a persistent dragonkin and dragged it away from the group, and they hadn't seen him since.

"Your father will be all right," Wick said. "He's a smart man; he won't be caught."

"I hope you're right."

Down the tunnel they raced, then across the raised bridge of stone to the chamber where the rest of the Heather Stone was. Already everything was different than the last time Wick had been inside the chamber. The biggest piece of Heather Stone, taking up most of the floor of the chamber, glowed green and yellow from within, and beneath his feet, it seemed to be somehow vibrating.

The stones were active.

"Quickly," Ongel urged them, opening the case of stones. "We don't have much time left."

Wick had seen the bright orange glow in the distance as they entered the valley. These were only the first of the dragonkin. The bulk of the army was still to come. And if they couldn't put the spell in place before the rest of the army arrived, Aro would be lost.

Everything he had ever loved, every place he had ever been, *everything* would burn.

Wick couldn't fail everyone that way.

He and Eland each scooped up some stones and split up across the chamber.

Wick slid the centaur piece onto the first golden stand with trembling fingers. He almost dropped one of the other stones. His hands were shaking too much. Dust fell onto his shoes from above.

Wick frowned and looked up.

Emerging from a passage he hadn't seen in the ceiling, another dragonkin slid free and snapped at his face.

"Caihu said something is going to come from above you."

Already Wick had forgotten.

"Look out!" he shouted to Ongel and Eland as the dragonkin turned on them.

A split-second decision happened in Ongel's eyes. He threw the bag of stones to Eland and reached over his shoulder for the large fighting staff strapped to his back. Wick remembered that staff always hanging over the shelves in Ongel's study. It was as thick as one of Wick's arms and as long as Ongel was tall. In one effortless motion, Ongel swept the staff out of the straps holding it to his back and swung it around his head, striking the dragonkin across the face.

"Over here, you!" As Ongel jumped back to avoid the snapping jaws that followed him, Ongel caught Wick's eye. He jerked his head toward the far side of the chamber and the remaining empty stands.

Even as his heart beat out of his chest, Wick understood. He grabbed Eland's arm and rifled through the bag for the final stones. "We have to fill all the stands while it's still distracted."

Eland nodded, and they split up to attack opposite sides of the chamber. The dragonkin's tail swung as it fought with Ongel, and it hit Wick in the chest. He struggled to keep the stones in his fists from touching the floor of the chamber. Even the smaller pieces of the Heather Stone caused an explosive reaction when they touched one another. If they came into contact with the floor of the chamber, which was made of nothing but Heather Stone, who knew what would happen?

Once he got his breath back, Wick scrambled up from the floor and deposited the nixie stone in its place. The filled stands around the cavern vibrated in reaction with one another. The rattling filled the chamber, intensifying each time they placed a new stone.

A wing swiped over Wick's head. He ducked. His hands clutching the last stone shook.

I can't mess this up.

If I mess this up, the Scorch will win, and all I'll be is a—

In his mind, Archer's voice interrupted. *Who cares, Tree?*

Just get it done.

How was Eland doing? He glanced across the cavern and saw Eland plastered against the rocky wall, blocked in by the body of the dragonkin. He seemed to be stuck there, but as he caught Wick's eye he held up his hands. They were empty.

The stone in Wick's hands was the last one. His heart beat a mile a minute as his eyes darted around for the last empty stand. It was only a few steps away, the only stand that wasn't shaking.

Failure or no, I'm the only one holding this stone.
I can finish this.

He darted toward the empty stand with the stone in his grip.

The dragonkin's gaze snapped toward Wick, and out of nowhere, its tail swung toward him, ramming into his legs and knocking him flat on his stomach. Ongel raced toward him, but another swing of the tail slammed Ongel into the wall of the chamber. Wick pulled himself up on his elbows, his eyes still fastened on the last golden stand. He had to get the stone into the stand.

Then the dragonkin's clawed foot crashed down on the stand. The metal screamed. When the creature pulled away, all that remained of the stand was a pile of twisted metal.

The last Heather Stone gleamed between Wick's fingers. The other stones in the stands still vibrated, more violently than ever. He had barely managed to keep the last stone from touching the floor again, but now what could he do? There was nowhere to put the stone.

He couldn't fail on the very last stone, not again. Aro depended on this. On him.

The flaming face of the dragonkin drew nearer, reflected in the shine of the Heather Stone floor. The dragonkin would kill him, then Ongel and Eland, and then the stones would be taken by the Scorch.

What do I do?

"Wait," he murmured. The shining floor beneath his hands glowed, brightest below his fingers as they clutched the final piece of the Heather Stone. He remembered Archer clapping the stones together and blasting both of them across the water, and across the length of the valley. Maybe that was what they needed. It would be enough to blow the dragonkin away.

Or maybe. . .

Maybe they didn't need the stands after all.

Maybe they just needed enough precision.

As the dragonkin closed in, Wick gently lowered the final Heather Stone down to brush the floor of the chamber.

Wick felt a *thud* deep in his chest. The stones blazed. For half a second, silence.

Then a wave of green shot out from the green floor of the Heather Stone chamber, slamming into the dragonkin and crumpling it back through the hole in the ceiling. It screamed and clawed at the rock, but with added vigor, the spell forced it up the hole and out of sight.

With loud screeches of war, a swarm of dragonkin shot across the cavern toward them. As if in response, the Heather Stones rattled. The cavern exploded with light.

CHAPTER TWENTY-FIVE:

Flying Too Close To the Sun

NO DRAGONS HAD NOTICED them as they ran through the forest, but now that they had entered Tor, enemies appeared on every side. Archer punched a dragonkin in the face as it tried to descend on them, and Sasha made a loud and terrified noise.

"I'm sorry Sasha. I'm sorry," Archer said over and over, clinging to her neck. "We're almost there, I promise, and then you can go back in the bag. Just get me to the house."

They hurtled down the street, dodging small flames and seraphs that swooped after the dragonkin like hawks trying to fend off eagles. Every so often a flaming branch dropped from the treetops, almost landing on Sasha's mane or Archer's shoulders. Wherever they fell, Archer smacked them away so they couldn't scare the horse. A few of them singed his fingers.

They reached the street at last, and Archer squinted

through the smoke and falling sparks for even a glimpse of the house. Through the smoke, he caught a faint glimpse of someone wildly fighting a dragonkin at the base of the tree.

Fowl.

Where his parents were, he had no idea. Maybe they were still inside the house, or maybe they were elsewhere in the city.

Archer pulled Sasha to a stop. "Well done, girl. Come on, I'll get you back in the bag." He slid the bag off his shoulder and tugged the top of it down over Sasha's head. In a moment, she disappeared into the safety of the bag. Passing the stream, Archer threw the bag under the bridge, where it would be damp and safe.

He pelted toward the Hessen house.

But he didn't run fast enough. Fowl's dragonkin drew back its head and snapped, faster than a cobra, at Fowl's torso. Fowl dropped his mace and clutched at his midsection.

A scream tore from Archer's mouth. He snatched up a burning branch from the ground. *"Get away from my brother!"*

Swinging at the beast, he clubbed the dragonkin over the head with the burning branch, then flipped his grip on the branch and stabbed it in the neck. *When you need to take down the dragonkin, stab them under the chin.* The dragonkin crawled away, weakening as it bled.

Fowl was somehow still standing, but doubled over with pain, blood dripping between his fingers as he clutched his hands to his stomach. "Too slow again," Fowl grunted, the muscles of his face trembling as he grimaced.

"Is that a comment about you or me?" Archer asked. He glanced down at Fowl's injury, and his stomach turned.

The blood spread quickly across Fowl's shirt, and through the rip in the fabric Archer could see a little more torn up flesh than he cared for. "Never mind. Get back in the house. If you think you can fly, then fly, or if you have to walk, just get up to the house and get somewhere where you'll be safe. I'll take care of things out here."

"You can't protect yourself without wings," Fowl grunted.

"Never seems to stop anyone else," Archer said sharply. "Get inside the house, I'll deal with it." He picked up Fowl's mace off the ground and slung it upright in his grip. Where was Wick with those stones? He had no way of knowing if they had even reached the valley safely, or at all.

But he did know that if they didn't cast the spell soon, all of Aro would go up in flames.

Fowl was halfway up the stairs now. If he could make it to the top and inside the house without collapsing, he would be safe enough.

Through the trees, the huge wave of orange he had seen from Eri grew steadily brighter and closer. The bulk of the army would be here any minute.

Archer hefted the mace again and faced toward the fire in the sky. When they arrived, he would be ready.

A new horde of dragonkin spotted him and swooped down from the air.

Then a gust of cold wind raced past Archer's ears, bringing with it a bright green glow that swept over the trees. It knocked the nearest dragonkin back and hit Archer like a shove from behind, making him stumble.

The spell. They cast the spell.

He turned to yell to Fowl that they had won, then suddenly realized. . .

The dragonkin were off balance now, but they weren't gone. The horde in the sky only grew closer. The trees crackled as another blast of green wind came billowing through, stronger than the last but still not strong enough. The dragonkin dug their claws into the dirt roads to brace against it with their blazing crests streaming backward.

Archer understood in a flash. The spell was cast, but it was still warming up. It wouldn't be fast enough to save the city. The dragonkin army dove into the trees. The branches broke and blazed.

He had to take cover.

Archer raced for the nearest tree. He leaped into a hollow between two tree roots and covered his head as Tor was swallowed up in flames.

CHAPTER TWENTY-SIX:
When It's All Over, the Bag Will Still Be Unfillable

ARCHER LEANED THE SIDE of his head against the wall and closed his eyes. His bandaged arm hurt.

The tree roots hadn't been nearly enough to protect him. According to Wick, when he was found he had been both unconscious and decently crisped down his right side.

"If it scars," he had said when he saw the damage to his shoulder, leg, and side, "at least it's only on the right side. I've already got a broken wing on that side, some scars won't make any difference. I'll still be beautiful from the left."

Wick hadn't looked at all impressed at Archer's vanity.

His burns felt crackling and prickly, on the outside and from the inside. The doctors said he was lucky not to have been more burned.

Fowl on the other hand. . .

Archer opened his eyes again so he wouldn't fall asleep. He was tired enough to fall asleep on the spot, but he couldn't drift off yet. He wanted to wait for Fowl. He widened his eyes to fight back the weight resting on them.

Across from him, Fowl lay in one of the makeshift hospital beds put together by volunteers. Granted, it was on the floor, which Fowl undoubtedly wouldn't like, but it was made of mostly blankets and soft enough that he wouldn't be uncomfortable.

Fowl had still been on the stairs when the first wave of the dragonkin army arrived, and he had taken worse damage than Archer. He was burned down most of his back and across his arms, not to mention the injuries he had already sustained from where the dragonkin bit him. And then there was the damage from falling off the stairs afterward. The little chain railing had held about as well as butter. He was lucky to be alive.

Their parents had yet to be found. But they were just two out of hundreds of missing people. In time, he would hear news.

Archer just wasn't sure if he'd want to hear the news when the time came.

Archer scrubbed at an eye with his good fist. All he needed to focus on was Fowl, for now. He needed Fowl to wake up.

As though he had somehow heard, Fowl stirred, and his eyes opened a crack.

"Awake yet?" Archer ventured.

"Unfortunately." Fowl's voice rasped. He cleared his throat, then screwed up his face as he swallowed. "Somehow I thought by this part, we'd both be dead."

"And Wick says *I'm* dramatic," Archer said, but honestly he had considered the same thing.

"How bad is it?" Already Fowl looked exhausted.

"You got yourself burned all over. That's what you

get for not walking fast enough," Archer said, making a scolding gesture with his injured arm, something that Fowl caught and understood with a grimace. "And you still have other injuries from the dragonkin. It'll be a while before you can get out of bed, so get comfortable."

"What about you?"

"I only have some injuries. I hid pretty quick when I saw the squadron coming."

Fowl spotted the window behind Archer's head and craned his neck to look out. "What about the city?"

"Don't look out there." Archer got up to block the window with his body. He turned and used his good arm to shut the curtains. "Not yet, anyway."

"Why?" Fowl's brow creased for a moment, then he winced when the burns on his forehead wrinkled as well. He closed his eyes for a moment. "I thought us being alive meant your friend put the spell up in time."

"They did put the spell up. Wick said it seemed like the spell burned them or something; at any rate, a lot of people said the dragons were screaming. Then that green wind came through and pulled them away for good, blew them out over the water somewhere. Ongel said they kept the spell up for a few days, to be safe, and they took it down about two days ago. The Heather Stones couldn't keep going without recharging or I would have told them to keep the spell up forever." Archer adjusted his footing. "Anyway. The dragonkin shouldn't be back for a long time."

"Archer, tell me what's wrong with the city." Fowl's voice was sterner this time.

Archer floundered for a way to avoid the subject. "I—"

"*Archer.*"

"They knew our base was in Tor, so they sent dragons here. A lot of dragons." Archer squeezed his eyes shut. "Everything's on fire out there."

SEVERAL WEEKS PASSED before Archer and Fowl were allowed to walk around the room, let alone leave the Rep House, which was now a makeshift hospital. By that time, Wick reported that the fires had been put out and people were starting to clear away the wreckage to rebuild. Archer dared to be hopeful when they were finally released and allowed to take a visit to the great outdoors. He asked Fowl if he was excited to stretch his wings again, but Fowl stayed quiet. He hadn't said much in days, not since the corpse of their father had been found mauled in a street somewhere. Their mother was yet to be found.

As Archer reached the bottom of the stairs, Wick appeared out of nowhere with a candied apple on a stick. "A gift to congratulate you on your recovery," he said cheerfully. "I can't even tell you how hard it was to find."

"I believe it," Archer said, taking the apple in his good hand. "We only have oatmeal and dry bread at the hospital. There doesn't seem to be a lot left in way of food." As Fowl reached the bottom of the stairs behind him, Archer surveyed the street. "It's worse than I thought it would be."

Only a quarter of the entire street remained intact. Many of the houses had been knocked out of the treetops, and the ones that remained were either damaged or burned, many with entire portions of floors missing or burned away. Wreckage had been piled in splintery drifts on either side of the street. Between everything, the grass was burned down to chalky stumps. Seraphs in gloves and aprons dug through the wreckage for anything salvageable, as they had been doing for weeks and would for weeks to come.

"It isn't good," Wick admitted. "Whole streets will have to be replanted and built again. People are being relocated to places where the trees are already tall enough to build on. A lot of things are gone. But believe me when I say it looks better than it did."

"What about Eri?" Archer asked.

"It wasn't as much of a target as Tor, but there are still casualties," Wick said. "Your grandfather's house is ashes now. I'm sorry."

Archer took a deep gnaw off his candied apple so that he couldn't think about the house too much.

"But your grandfather's caretaker survived," Wick added quickly, "and so did the other seraphs protecting the street with him. Apparently they were quite the set of warriors."

Archer nodded, looking back at Fowl. Fowl still wouldn't meet his eyes. Instead, he gazed down the street toward where their house used to be. His hair was tied back today, gathered at the base of his neck in a way that reminded Archer altogether too much of their father.

"The rest of the country is about the same, I hear." Wick looked out at the city himself. "There are plenty of deaths and plenty of injuries, but on the whole, most people survived and all the territories are making plans to rebuild immediately. For the most part, I'd say we did well."

"Good," Archer said. The sweetness of the candied apple was sticking in his teeth.

Further down the street, a seraph hovered in the air for a moment between two trees, then her head turned in their direction. She swooped down to land in front of them.

From the hair tied back and tall, thick boots still covered in ashes, Archer guessed she worked with the group excavating resources and belongings out of houses.

"I have news for Archer and Fowler," she said, her ash-covered face grim. "Your mother's body was discovered in the wreckage of the house."

Archer froze. In his ringing head, only one thought remained.

Both of my parents are dead.

Then, slowly, one more thought drifted in behind it.

I never made up with either of them.

"I'm so sorry," the seraph girl said, looking at Archer.

Archer's hands went numb. His mother and father were dead. For certain. He wouldn't have to wonder anymore; they were dead.

"Don't be sorry," Fowl said bitterly. "I'm sure you have better things to do. Don't worry about us." Suddenly starting forward, he pushed past the girl and strode out into the filthy street.

Archer's single remaining family member was walking away from him.

His mind came alive again. Archer raced after Fowl. "Fowl! Come back!"

Behind him, he heard Wick say, "Thank you for telling them. They appreciate it, I'm sure."

The girl probably said something, but Archer was too busy chasing Fowl's retreating back into the street. Fowl picked up the pace and spread his wings. His beautiful, whole, grey wings.

Archer poured on more speed. He grabbed one of Fowl's arms in both hands and dragged him back down to the ground. "Don't you dare."

Fowl wheeled on him, fast enough to knock Archer's

hand off his arm. "What for? Hmm?"

The problem was that Archer didn't know exactly what for. He floundered for words.

Wick's voice cried, "Look out!"

Both Fowl and Archer's eyes snapped up. Through what remained of the treetops, the sky was boiling orange. A swarm of flaming creatures erupted from the clouds, diving toward the city.

Archer's heart thundered.

They had driven the dragonkin away. They were gone.

They had to be gone.

But as the treetops broke and a dozen flaming creatures burst through, Archer knew he had been wrong.

With an angry shout at the sky, he grabbed Fowl's shoulder and raced for cover as the flames descended upon Aro.

The heat scorched on his skin.

ENDE.

Turn the page for more!

- Glossary

- Author's Notes

- Excerpts from the series conclusion

Author's Note

I was nervous about writing this book from the very beginning. After all, it's a trilogy's second book. Have you ever read any middle book of a trilogy that didn't drag? As excited as I was to write about Archer's family drama and to see my two boys temporarily trade places as the fighter and the organizer(both ideas that had existed since I drafted *Robbing Centaurs*), I didn't even know how the story ended. To add to my anxiety, I hadn't written a sequel in ages, and *Robbing Centaurs* came out so well that I wasn't sure I could write anything like it, let alone do it justice with a sequel.

Therefore, I chose this solution: I told myself that if I didn't make *World Saving* into the best book in the series, it would be the worst book in the series. That way, the book had to turn out at least above mediocrity.

I still say that working toward that goal helped, but when you're sorting out the fifth boring political scene or you discover your main characters had the same emotionally charged conversation in three different places, you start to doubt yourself as a creator. Oftentimes it was just the need to finish that got me through.

That never meant I gave up on quality, though. I want to learn to craft good stories more than anything in the world, so I made a lot of fixes. I organized the three conversations into a trilogy of connected scenes. I made the frutelken parts readable. I focused the political scenes more on Archer. I found out who Fowler was and made him an interesting character, seemingly even a favorite of some of my beta readers. Bless y'all for liking him.

In the end, is it the best book of the series, like I planned? I'm not sure. But I am sure that I made it the best I could. I'm also sure that I love it and I'm excited to finish the third book and finally complete Wick and Archer's story.

See you there?

The Scorch: Book 3

Coming soon!

Archer got up, suddenly realizing he needed a long walk, right now. Away from everyone else. "I'll be back," he said to no one in particular, and stepped off into the darkness.

Walking across the side of the mountains, he could see peeks of the valley flashing between the trees. On a clear night it was like a small city, or a puddle full of stars. The torchlight in the buildings flickered warmly across the faint shapes of the people sleeping outside. The moonlight glinted cool off the lake, outlining the dark outline of the fallen statue.

Somebody really should fix that statue.

Archer glanced up at the sky. Funny how the stars hadn't changed. They looked the same as they had the day he had started traveling by himself years ago. Despite how fast the world had changed because of the Scorch, they still hadn't budged.

Maybe they should have.

Something dark darted overhead, momentarily blocking out the stars. With it came the smell of ash.

Fear shot through Archer's veins. One of the dragonkin was here. Too close to the valley, and much too close to him.

He hid under the shelter of a tree. He knew from years of practice evading the manghar that if he had enough branches in between him and whatever was flying, it would never see him.

This time, it didn't work. Something collided with the top of the tree, shaking even the trunk. Despite the fear still buzzing in his veins, Archer didn't move, hoping that the dragonkin hadn't seen him. Then the tree started shaking again, differently this time. Something was crawling down.

It was too late for staying still. The fear in Archer's veins told him to run. He bolted. A great crashing sound came from the tree as the dragonkin he hadn't seen took off once again, flying after him.

He had to lose it. If he couldn't, it would catch him, and then who knew what would happen. Well, he did know.

He could still hear the snap of wings behind him; he hadn't lost it yet.

He spotted a place where the trees were thicker and closer together and dove for it.

–

The exciting conclusion is coming soon!

ABOUT THE AUTHOR

Bethany Meyer grew up in Maryland and finds it odd to write about oneself in the third person. She discovered a love of writing when she was eleven and has been creating stories ever since. When she isn't writing, she enjoys reading, drawing, or consuming a large number of animated movies.

FIND HER ON

Instagram: @scribbledfiction
Twitter: @ScribbldFiction
Website: https://rb.gy/mkz0e5
YouTube: https://rb.gy/ld4bsq

ACKNOWLEDGMENTS

Hello, friends. Here we are again at the end of another book, and yet again I have ever so many people to thank.

As always, my first thanks goes to my Lord and savior. If He didn't build the house, or rather this book, I would surely have worked in vain. I owe Him everything.

Secondly, thank you to my fabulous family. Never stop being cool. Thanks for being so cool about my book rambles and my nerves and being in videos and picking up coffees for me. So many coffees. You're the best.

Thanks to my editor, Angela! Thanks for all the work you do and all the confidence you give me about my books.

Thanks as well to other friends who make the writing journey that much better. Thanks to the friends through the screen, Lauren Fulter (I love how you call it "The Archer Book"), Ariana Tosado, Patricia, Harmony, Danni, and Penny, and thanks to the in-person friends as well: to Naomi for the hype and the questions and the art, to Mike for thinking I'm cool.

And thanks to you, for reading this! Not just the acknowledgments (because do people even read these?) but for reading the book. You're what keeps me going. Thank you, thank you, thank you.

THANKS FOR READING! PLEASE ADD A SHORT REVIEW ON AMAZON

AND LET ME KNOW WHAT YOU THOUGHT!

YOU CAN ALSO JOIN MY MAILING LIST AT

MEBETHANYDANNI.WIXSITE.COM/BETHANYMEYER-1

TO KEEP UP WITH THE NEWS ABOUT FUTURE BOOKS!

CPSIA information can be obtained
at www.ICGtesting.com
Printed in the USA
BVHW032027251122
652771BV00028B/338